"We shouldn't be doing this," Ashley whispered as Erin's lips trailed a path along her neck. "You promised you'd send me away."

Terrified that Ashley would change her mind, Erin kissed her again. As the kiss deepened, any thoughts of turning back vanished.

Ashley allowed Erin to lead her into the small bedroom but hesitated when she saw the bed.

"It's impossible. There can't be anything between us," Ashley said.

"Give me this one night," Erin begged. She held her breath as Ashley struggled with her inner demons. Only after Ashley began to unbutton Erin's shirt did Erin finally breathe.

No further words were spoken as they slowly undressed each other. Erin even forgot about her limited experience in the art of lovemaking as she pulled Ashley down onto the bed and began to kiss her. Her body shook with desire, but she forced herself to move slowly and take her time. She wanted to savor every touch, scent and taste. If this was to be the only night they would ever have together, she intended to remember every single moment of it. Precious minutes slipped rapidly by as they kissed, and Erin tried to memorize every curve and contour of Ashley's body.

Visit

Bella Books

at

BellaBooks.com

or call our toll-free number

1-800-729-4992

VOICES OF THE HEART

FRANKIE J. JONES

Bella
BOOKS

2006

Bella Books, Inc.
P.O. Box 10543
Tallahassee, FL 32302

Printed in the United States of America on acid-free paper
First Edition

Editor: Christi Cassidy
Cover designer: Stephanie Solomon-Lopez

ISBN 1-59493-068-6

For Martha—My rock

Acknowledgments

I'd like to thank Martha Cabrera, Peggy J. Herring and Carol Poynor for reading the manuscript and providing invaluable feedback.

Skip—the drill sergeant is just for you!

Christi Cassidy—Thanks for all your hard work. I'll try to stop *surprising* you with all those *surprises*.

About the Author

Frankie J. Jones is the author of *Rhythm Tide, Whispers in the Wind, Captive Heart, Room for Love, Midas Touch, Survival of Love* and *For Every Season*. She enjoys fishing, traveling, outdoor photography and rummaging through flea markets in search of whimsical salt and pepper shakers.

Authors love to hear from their readers. You may contact Frankie by e-mail at FrankieJJones@aol.com.

CHAPTER ONE

Erin Fox's heart pounded as she stared at the screen filled with customer accounts and codes. How had she allowed the situation to reach this point? When had she lost control of her life? She was the sort of woman people called level-headed, dependable and honest. Only she knew she was no longer any of those things. At least she wouldn't be after tonight. It was time to stop kidding herself. She couldn't continue living with the secret she had been clinging to for the past three months. Tonight, one way or the other, she would put her demons to rest.

It all began simply enough at a Christmas party. Erin hadn't been invited directly. Her friend and coworker Mary Vaughn and her partner of nearly thirty years, Alice Raye, invited her to go with them. They assured her that the women hosting the annual event wouldn't mind. Erin didn't really want to go, but Mary kept nagging her. "How are you ever going to meet someone if you never go anywhere except work?" Mary persisted. So Erin went and now it seemed like the biggest mistake of her life.

Mary and Alice picked her up a little after eight. The party was located in San Antonio's prestigious Dominion. When they drove across the stone bridge leading into the estates Erin was grateful she had ridden with her friends. She felt certain the stern-looking security guard wouldn't have allowed her old truck to enter the gates.

"How did you two get invited to this shindig?" Erin asked after the guard had checked them off the guest list and waved them through.

"Sue had a thing for Mary years ago," Alice answered. "Personally, I don't think she ever got over it."

"Please," Mary said, exasperated. "She does this every year." Mary nodded toward Alice.

"Is it true?" Erin teased. Although there was almost a twenty-five-year difference in their ages, Erin considered these women to be her best friends. She and Mary had worked together at South Texas Communications for eight years. She loved their dependability and undying sense of fun. It was her dream to someday have a relationship as strong and loving as these two shared.

"Yes and no," Mary replied. "I went out with Sue a couple of times but things never really clicked between us. Then I met Angie and we started dating."

"Now wait a minute," Erin interrupted. "You and Mary have been together almost thirty years. Now I'm hearing about someone named Sue and then Angie. How old were you when you started dating women?"

"Four," Alice chimed in.

"Oh, stop it," Mary chided. "I was eighteen the first time I kissed a woman."

"Yeah, but she enjoyed it so much she couldn't stop," Alice said. "After that she kissed as many women as she possibly could."

"I stopped all of that the minute I saw you," Mary said.

"That's not the way I remember it," Alice said coyly. "As I recall you did quite a bit of kissing after that."

"Now, Alice, you know you shouldn't talk like that in front of Erin."

Despite Mary's protest, Erin could hear the smile in her voice.

"Here we are," Mary said as a valet waved for them to stop.

"We'll park the car," the young woman replied as she opened the door for Mary. "You ladies enjoy your evening."

Erin and Alice stepped out of the car and waited for Mary to deal with the valet.

Erin studied the brilliantly lit stone-fronted mansion before glancing down at her slacks and jacket. "Are you sure I'm dressed okay?" she whispered to Alice.

Alice placed a hand on her arm. "Trust me, you're fine. For all their hoity-toity ways, Sue and Linda like to pretend they're just regular folk." She shook her head as she looked at the house. "Never mind that their monthly utility bills are probably more than a family on minimum wage earns."

"You don't sound like you care for them very much."

"She's just jealous," Mary interjected as she joined them.

As they reached the door, it opened before they could ring the doorbell. Erin tried not to stare at the woman dressed in a traditional maid's uniform or at the swirl of people she suddenly found herself surrounded by. From the back of the house a state-of-the-art stereo system pumped out a pulsating rock beat.

Erin blinked in surprise as a woman dressed in jeans starched to the point of cement-like texture and a yellow silk western shirt grabbed Mary and kissed her soundly on the mouth.

"I'm so glad you could come tonight," she gushed when she finally released Mary. "And Alice dear, you're looking wonderful." The kiss she gave Alice was much less enthusiastic. "Who is this enchanting creature?" she bubbled when she released Alice.

Erin glanced behind her to see who she was referring to.

"Oh, isn't she adorable." She took ahold of Erin's arms. "I'm talking about you, gorgeous."

Before Erin could recover, she found herself in a lip lock with the stranger. The strong aroma of bourbon stung her nostrils, warning her that the woman was probably more than a little tipsy. Shocked by the woman's boldness, Erin stood with her arms hanging awkwardly at her sides as the woman kissed her. When the kiss continued long beyond a friendly glad-to-know-you peck, a warm glow began to build in Erin's stomach. Her arms came to life and slipped around the woman's waist, pulling her closer.

In a less than gentle movement, Alice separated them. "Erin, this is Sue Bradley. Erin is the friend we mentioned we'd be bringing."

"Well, I'm so glad you did," Sue continued to stare at her and, flustered, Erin could only nod.

"Mary, Alice, I'm so glad you could make it tonight." A tall, wide-shouldered woman dressed in a man's gray suit complete with tie and cigar grabbed Mary's hand.

Erin's jaw nearly dropped when Mary introduced her as Linda Koonz, Sue's partner. Erin managed to nod and suffered through a bone-crushing handshake as Linda pumped her arm. Had Linda seen Sue kissing her? She held her breath as Sue slid into Linda's arm as smoothly as a well-oiled cog in a wheel.

A new group of women came in.

"You two know where everything is," Linda said, already moving toward the new arrivals. "Have a good time. If you need anything just give a holler and somebody will find it for you."

"Crap," Erin mumbled as they made their way out of the entrance hall. "Why didn't you two warn me?"

"And miss that little episode," Mary chuckled. "For a minute there, I wasn't sure you two were ever planning on coming up for air."

"Stop it," she whispered, embarrassed.

As they made their way from room to room, Erin quickly realized she didn't know anyone there other than Mary and Alice. When they entered a large room filled with people seated around a dozen card tables, Mary turned to her. "Okay, kid. It's time for you to go mingle with the younger folks."

"Why? What are you two going to do?"

"We're going to be playing Mexican Train and as you can see it's a roomful of old fogies, so go mingle with the younger women."

Erin tried to mingle, but it wasn't something she was very good at. She had once read that the best way to break the ice with strangers was to ask them questions about themselves, but it seemed rude to her. Besides, most questions sounded like tired pickup lines.

As she slipped through the crowd looking for someone she might start a conversation with, she noticed that everyone at the party seemed to already know one another. Everywhere she looked, groups of women were laughing and talking as if they were lifelong friends. Across the room, she spied six young women who appeared to be in their late twenties. Since the gathering was small and they were near her own age, she slowly drifted over to them. They were discussing a camping trip they had all recently returned from.

"Hi," she said as their conversation lulled. She swallowed convulsively to ease the dryness that suddenly enveloped her throat. Her hands felt like ten-pound hammers hanging from her dangling arms. She stuffed her hands into her pockets, but the room was so crowded she ended up elbowing the woman behind her. "Sorry," she mumbled over her shoulder as she snatched her hands out of her pockets and crossed her arms. But that wouldn't do. She had recently read somewhere that folding your arms across your chest made you appear closed off. She let her arms fall to her sides and berated herself for ever accepting Mary's invitation. *I should have gotten myself a beer.*

A couple of the women spoke but most of them simply looked at her.

"Nice party," Erin croaked and almost dropped dead of embarrassment when one of the women turned to another of the group and rolled her eyes. As a glaring blush raced up her neck, she mumbled an awkward good-bye and slipped away. *I'm such an idiot. They probably think I'm some kind of weirdo.*

She allowed herself to be pushed back against a wall and surveyed the crowd. Most of the group seemed to be couples.

"Great," she muttered. *There's nothing more unwanted than a single woman in a room filled with lesbian couples.* She gave up trying to join in and fled to the patio, hoping the colder than usual night air would provide her with the solitude she sought. As she reached the French doors she could see dozens of people sitting on the patio around an outdoor fireplace. With a discouraged sigh she turned back to the room of partiers. In a house this big there had to be someplace she could hide out for a while. She spied the bar across the room and considered going for a beer, but the crowd of people packed six deep around it convinced her that she wasn't that thirsty. Instead, she eased her way through the crowd, going from room to room until she spied another set of doors leading outside. A quick glance through the glass revealed a much smaller side patio. After several moments of watching and not seeing anyone, she casually slipped outside, hoping no one would follow her. She prayed the patio would be empty. If it wasn't, she made up her mind to go back inside and superglue herself to Mary's side.

The only light on the patio came from the dim glare of a few Christmas bulbs strung over two large potted corn-like plants that were sitting on either side of the door. Erin squinted, trying to peer into the darkness. There didn't appear to be anyone around. The only sounds came from the party within. Exhaling a loud sigh of relief, she made her way to the canopied lawn swing that faced toward the backyard. When she came around the end of the swing a woman jumped up suddenly.

Taken aback by the unexpected movement, Erin stepped back. "I'm sorry if I startled you," she said.

"That's okay. I didn't hear you," the woman said. "I guess I was daydreaming." In the dim glow of the Christmas lights Erin could see the woman's extended hand. "I'm Ashley Wade."

Despite the chill of the night air ,the woman's hand felt warm as Erin shook it. "Erin Fox," she replied. "I didn't mean to disturb you. I stepped out for some fresh air. I'll go back inside." She tried to hide her disappointment.

"You don't have to leave. There's plenty of fresh air here for both of us."

Erin heard the touch of teasing in the words and relaxed slightly. "I'm not much of a social butterfly."

"If you don't mind the company we can share the swing."

Erin sat down. "Thanks."

After Ashley sat down, an awkward silence fell between them. Erin found herself wishing she had remained inside. At least there she could get lost in the crowd. To make matters worse, the swing was enclosed on three sides. That and the fact they were sitting in the dark gave the situation an intimate feel that Erin found disturbing.

"So, how do you know Sue and Linda?" Ashley asked as her fingers tapped nervously against the seat of the swing.

"Who?" Erin asked without thinking. "Oh, you mean the women throwing the party," she sputtered as she gave herself a swift mental kick. *She probably thinks I'm a moron.* "I don't know them at all," she admitted. She was thankful for the darkness when she recalled Sue's kiss. She knew her face was beet red. "I came with a couple of friends."

"I see," Ashley murmured as she gave the swing a slight push with her foot.

Erin struggled to think of something interesting to talk about, but as usual when she found herself in these situations her brain went on vacation. "How about you?" she asked. *God, Erin you're such a dweeb.*

Ashley took a deep breath before answering. To Erin it almost sounded like a sigh. Whether it was from sadness or the lameness of the question she couldn't be certain. "Linda used to work for the San Antonio Police Department. At least she did before her father died a couple of years ago and left her a small fortune. She and Jess"—she hesitated for a moment—"my partner, were police officers. Jess still is. I've known them for three or four years. They have a lot of parties that we're invited to."

"Oh." Erin wondered if it was a good idea for her to be sitting out here in the darkness with the partner of a cop, but the thought of going back inside was worse than the prospect of ruffling a few feathers of a jealous woman. If Linda didn't object to Sue kissing all their guests, then maybe Jess wouldn't be concerned about Ashley being out here with her. "Are you a cop also?" she asked, surprising herself with her ability to keep asking questions.

"No. I'm an accounts manager for an insurance company," Ashley replied as she brushed her hair back from her face. "What do you do?"

"I'm a data entry clerk for South Texas Communications. It's nothing fancy, but I like working there." Erin cringed at the defensive sound of her voice. It embarrassed her that she hadn't gone to college. Even though she'd always been a voracious reader, she had never been very good in school, especially math and science. The concepts of algebra seemed to always be just out of her reach. No matter how hard she studied, she couldn't quite grasp it. Eventually, she gave up and accepted the fact that her life would have to proceed without the benefits of higher math. The problem didn't overly concern her. After all, it wasn't as though her checking account would ever have to be factored to the nth degree.

"That's more than most people can say," Ashley replied.

"Don't you like your job?" Again, Erin wondered where she was finding the courage to ask so many questions. Her eyes were adjusting to the darkness and she could see a vague outline of the woman next to her. She seemed to be very thin with long hair. Erin found herself wondering what color it was and what color her eyes were. She pushed the thoughts away and tried to concentrate on what Ashley was saying.

"I used to like my job." She leaned forward and braced her arms against the seat. "I don't know. I guess I still do. It's just that sometimes I feel like I'm stuck in a rut and can't seem to get out of it." She stopped suddenly. "I'm sorry. I didn't mean to sound so whiny. I have a good job and should be grateful." Ashley moved around on the seat as if trying to get comfortable.

Her fidgeting made Erin wonder if she was more nervous than she sounded.

A sharp breeze swept over the patio causing them both to

8

shiver. "There's a small firepit over there." Ashley pointed to Erin's right. "There's wood beside it."

"Would you like me to light it?" Erin asked.

Ashley hesitated. "It might encourage others to join us."

As Erin recalled the large crowd on the back patio she tried to interpret Ashley's statement. Did she want others to join them or was she saying she didn't want the fire because others might join them?

Ashley suddenly jumped up. "I'll be right back."

As Ashley disappeared into the darkness, Erin considered using the time to escape back into the house, but instead she sat staring into the darkness where Ashley had gone, until a ripple of laughter floated from the back patio. She wondered where Ashley's girlfriend, Jess, was and why Ashley wasn't inside with people she knew. Erin tucked her hands under her arms to warm them. Her jacket wasn't warm enough for the night air. The smart thing to do would be to go back into the house. Even though she knew they weren't doing anything wrong, it might not look too cool to be caught sitting in the dark with someone else's girlfriend.

A small metallic clink echoed from the direction in which Ashley had vanished. It took Erin a moment to recognize the sound of a gate closing. Ashley had left by a side gate. A small pinprick of disappointment struck her. Ashley had left. *Why did I ask her all those asinine questions? She must have been bored silly.* Ashley was probably already inside telling her girlfriend about the dork she'd met on the side patio. Erin considered slipping back inside to let Mary and Alice know she was leaving. She would take the bus home. Then she realized that there weren't going to be buses running way out here, and cab fare back to her apartment would be more than she could afford. With nothing else to do she waited, not daring to hope that Ashley would come back. Her ears strained, listening for the sound of the creaking gate. As time slipped away, she stood to leave and again Ashley suddenly materialized from the darkness, surprising her.

"I didn't mean to startle you," Ashley said as she took her original spot on the swing. "Here, sit back down. We can share this." She unfolded a blanket.

Erin was suddenly glad for the darkness. She didn't want Ashley to see the silly grin on her face. "I thought you had left," she admitted as she sat down.

"I told you I'd be back. Put this over your shoulders."

Erin realized Ashley was wrapping the blanket around them. "Isn't your girlfriend going to be a little upset if she comes out and finds us sitting under a blanket together?" she asked uncertainly.

Ashley gave an odd chuckle. "She thinks I'm lying down. I told her I had a headache. She won't come looking for me and even if she did, we aren't doing anything wrong. I just don't want to light the fire and encourage a crowd."

Despite her better judgment Erin pulled the blanket up under her chin. They soon discovered that they both loved hiking and nature. They had been talking for over two hours when Erin heard Mary calling her name. "It sounds like my ride is ready to leave," she said with regret. She had enjoyed talking to Ashley.

"You came with Mary and Alice?"

"Yeah. Do you know them?"

It seemed to Erin that Ashley hesitated a moment too long before answering, "I don't really know them, just by sight."

"I'd better go."

Ashley remained seated as Erin stood to leave. "It was nice meeting you, Erin. I enjoyed talking to you."

Erin smiled as she slipped her hands into her pockets. "To be honest, I wasn't looking forward to the party tonight," she said. "I'm glad I came."

"I'm glad you did too." Ashley stood and extended her hand. As she did, the illumination from the Christmas lights revealed her features.

Erin saw Ashley clearly for the first time and her breath caught. It was at that moment that Erin Fox fell head-over-heels in love for the first time in her life.

CHAPTER TWO

"Hey."

Erin's head snapped up.

"Girl, if you don't stop daydreaming you're going to get yourself written up," Mary warned. "Come on. It's lunchtime."

Erin quickly logged off and followed Mary out of the room and over to the elevators. Half the team went to breaks and lunch on the same schedule, so there were fifteen or twenty other people milling around waiting for an elevator.

"Let's take the stairs. I'm starving," Mary said.

Erin nodded and followed her down the two flights to the ground-floor cafeteria. Erin bought a soda and a bag of chips from the vending machine and waited until Mary had gone through the line to pay for her tea and salad. She knew something was up when Mary walked on past the table of women they usually ate lunch with.

"Let's go outside. It's too nice of a day to stay in here," Mary said as she waved to the group on her way out to the large patio.

The sun was warm and for a change the wind wasn't whipping around the building. Mary chose a table off to the side, away from the other diners.

"Erin, what's going on? Sonia came by my desk this morning asking me if you were okay. She said your production has dropped and your keying errors are up."

A flash of anger shot through Erin. What right did their supervisor have talking to Mary about her? "Sonia needs to mind her own damn business."

"Whoa. Your job is her business. She only came to me because she's worried about you and knows we're good friends. She said she tried to talk to you, but you blew her off." Mary took a bite of her salad and peered at her.

"Nothing's wrong," Erin said with a shrug. From the look of doubt on Mary's face, she knew she would have to do better. "I've just been a little restless. Maybe I have spring fever or something."

"Or something," Mary murmured doubtfully. "Do I know this Ms. Spring Fever? And please tell me you aren't thinking about Sue Bradley and that kiss. Believe me, kid, when she's had a few too many, she'd kiss a horse's backside."

A shot of panic hit Erin. She hadn't told anyone about her feelings for Ashley Wade or the fact they were seeing more and more of each other. She sipped her soda. The week after the Christmas party, Erin had gone to the bookstore to use the gift card her mother had sent her. The store's selection of lesbian fiction was always poor, but they would special-order books for her. She had ordered in advance, knowing the annual gift card would be arriving in the mail two days before Christmas as it had for the past six years. As she was leaving the store, Ashley Wade was coming in.

"Hi," Ashley said with a brilliant smile that nearly melted Erin's sneakers off her feet.

"Hi." Erin's response sounded more like a croak.

They stood in awkward silence. "I'm off this week and thought I'd buy a couple of *good* books," Ashley said as she bounced slightly on her toes.

Erin smiled and held up her bag. "Yeah, me too."

"Oh, good. That means they've got some new ones."

"Not really. I ordered these last week."

Ashley frowned in disappointment. "Why didn't I think about that? I should have ordered some books. Sometimes I'm so stupid." She slapped herself sharply on the forehead.

"Hey," Erin reached out to take her arm. "There's no need to be so upset. I've got four. You can borrow a couple of them if you'd like."

"No. I couldn't do that."

"Sure you could. Here, take whichever two you want." She held the bag out to Ashley.

Ashley relaxed and smiled. "Thank you. That's so sweet of you." She took the bag and selected two. "Are you sure this is okay? I mean, I could buy something else."

"Sure it's okay." Erin didn't even mind that Ashley had chosen the book she had been waiting to read. If Ashley would smile at her again, she'd give her the whole bag.

"Do you drink coffee?" Ashley asked suddenly.

Erin nodded even though it wasn't her favorite drink. She would have preferred fruit juice. The way Ashley was fidgeting she probably drank a lot of coffee.

"If you're not in a hurry, let me buy you a cup." Ashley gestured to the Starbucks located in the store. "We'll call it a thank-you gift for loaning me the books."

"You don't have to do that."

Ashley cocked her head as she looked at Erin and smiled. "I know I don't, but I want to."

A wave of fluttering butterflies tickled Erin's stomach. "Okay."

Ten minutes later, they were seated at a table with their coffee and a large slice of chocolate pound cake.

"I really enjoyed talking with you the other night," Ashley said as she removed the lid from the frothy concoction she had ordered.

Erin stirred a second packet of sweetener into her plain cup of coffee. "Me too." She took a sip and tried not to grimace before stirring in another packet.

"You don't drink coffee, do you?" Ashley said with a chuckle.

Erin took a deep breath. "Is it that obvious?"

"Let me get you something else." Ashley started to stand.

"No. Really. This is fine. Please, don't leave." Erin cringed as the intensity of her words seemed to echo around the room.

"Are you sure?"

Erin nodded.

Ashley shrugged and sat back down before glancing at her watch. "Are you on your lunch hour or something?"

"No. I'm on vacation also. I was going to go home for Christmas but things didn't work out."

"Where's home?"

"I was born here in San Antonio but my parents moved to Austin a couple of years ago after Dad retired. He was a plumber."

"Why Austin?"

"My youngest brother, Andy, and his wife live there. After their daughter was born, Mom and Dad wanted to be closer to their granddaughter."

"It's good that they're not so very far away," Ashley said before sipping her coffee.

"No. They're close enough for us to visit occasionally, but my parents and Andy decided to spend Christmas with my older brother Tom in Chicago, so I didn't go."

"Was it the trip, or don't you get along with your brother?"

"Yeah, he's fine. It's his wife, Edith, who I have a problem with." Erin hesitated. "I guess I should say she has a problem with me."

"Let me guess. She doesn't approve of your lifestyle?"

Erin was struck by a touch of playfulness. "I didn't know you knew my sister-in-law."

"Know her," Ashley teased back. "I think we have the same sister-in-law."

"Lord, I hope not. That would make us family." Erin's face flamed with embarrassment. Would Ashley think the remark was disparaging or that she was hitting on her? "I . . . ah, I didn't mean that to . . . to sound . . . you know."

Ashley sipped her drink.

Mesmerized, Erin watched as the tip of Ashley's tongue slowly licked the thin line of froth from her lips. Erin's throat seemed to turn to dust when she glanced up and found Ashley watching her intently. Erin quickly looked away.

"I'm glad we aren't family either," Ashley murmured.

Erin took a quick gulp of coffee and almost cried out as she quickly swallowed the scalding brew. Tears of pain blurred her vision.

"Are you all right?"

Unable to speak, Erin nodded as Ashley sprang out of her chair and rushed to the counter. A moment later she returned with an icy bottle of water.

"Drink this. Maybe it will help."

Feeling like a fool, Erin twisted the cap off the bottle and drank. Her scorched tongue was instantly soothed.

"Is that better?" Ashley asked as she sat down.

Erin nodded.

"I sure hope you don't have a hot date tonight," Ashley said as she leaned toward Erin.

"Why not? I have the hot tongue for it," Erin replied without thinking. The shock of her boldness was forgotten as Ashley began to laugh. Erin had never heard a sound so beautiful.

CHAPTER THREE

"Hello. This is Earth calling Erin. Is there anyone in there?" Mary leaned across the table and tapped Erin's forehead. "Girl, where are you?"

"I was just thinking, that's all."

"I've been talking to you for ten minutes and you haven't heard a word I've said."

"Well, no one wants to listen to a ten-minute speech," Erin replied defensively. When she saw the look of concern on Mary's face, she felt bad. She wanted to tell Mary about Ashley, but if she did Mary might tell her friends Sue and Linda, who might in turn tell Jess. "I'm fine," she added in a softer tone. "I'll stop daydreaming while I'm working. I promise."

Mary continued to watch her. "You'd better, because you know I couldn't stand working in this hellhole if you got fired."

"I'm not going to get fired." Erin glanced at her watch and Mary's half-eaten salad. "Hurry up, or we'll be late."

Erin was suddenly grateful for their short lunch. Thirty minutes barely gave them time for lunch. There wouldn't be time for Mary to question her further or for her to break down and tell Mary what she intended to do tonight. As she picked at her chips her thoughts returned to Ashley.

That day in the bookstore had not ended there. Over the pound cake, they discovered that they were both avid readers and spent three hours chattering about the various books they had read. To Erin it seemed like only minutes had passed when Ashley glanced at her watch.

"Gosh, where has the time gone?"

Erin took that as her cue to leave and stood. "I should let you get on home."

"Are you hungry?" Ashley asked as she leaned forward.

"I'm starving," Erin replied without hesitation.

"Do you like Italian food?"

"I love it."

Ashley jumped up. "Great. There's a wonderful little restaurant just a few blocks over. It's been there for years. The place doesn't look like much from the outside, but the food is fantastic." Her eyes rolled in anticipation.

"With that endorsement, I can hardly wait," Erin replied as she tried to stop staring at Ashley's long chestnut hair and blue eyes.

When they walked to the parking lot they found that their cars were separated by only two parking slots. "Will you look at that," Ashley exclaimed after they had each pointed out their cars. "Erin Fox, I do believe our meeting was destiny."

Erin ducked her head and said, "I'll follow you." But no amount of willpower could wipe the smile from her face. After cranking her trusty old Ford Ranger she turned on the radio and cranked up the volume. As she followed Ashley's new silver Toyota Corolla out of the parking lot, she began to sing and didn't stop until they arrived at the restaurant.

Once inside, they were seated by a short heavy-set man who wore a white towel tucked into the front of his belt. "Your waiter will be right with you," he assured them as he made a great fuss of pulling Ashley's chair out. Erin hopped into her seat before he could help her. When Ashley ordered wine, Erin followed her lead. After taking their wine orders, the waiter left them with menus. They studied the selections in silence, but Erin couldn't help sneaking a peek at Ashley over the top of the menu. She was shocked to find Ashley peeking back at her.

"What looks good?" Ashley asked as she quickly began to scan the menu again.

"Everything," Erin replied, even though the menu was nothing more than a large blur to her. Had she imagined that Ashley was watching her with more than a "what looks good on the menu?" sort of gaze? Erin had only been aware of her true sexual orientation for about six years.

"How long have you been out?" Ashley asked as if reading her thoughts.

Taken aback by the timing of the question, Erin hesitated.

"I'm sorry. If you'd rather not talk about it, I understand."

"No," Erin replied. "The question caught me off guard. That's all."

The waiter appeared with their wine. "Are you ladies ready to order?" he asked.

"I'll have the lasagna," Erin said.

Ashley sighed. "I can't decide between the lasagna and the ravioli." She glanced at Erin. "The three-meat ravioli is wonderful, but so is the lasagna." Her foot began to bounce nervously, causing the table to shake slightly. "Why can't I make up my mind?" She looked at Erin apologetically. "I'm sorry. I don't know which one to order."

"If you like, you could order the ravioli and then we could share. That way you won't have to decide," Erin offered as she sipped her wine. Beer was her alcoholic beverage of choice. She'd never developed much of a taste for wine.

"Are you sure?"

Erin nodded.

Ashley smiled brightly before turning to the waiter. "I'll have the ravioli, then."

The waiter smiled back and took Ashley's menu. "Excellent choice," he said, his eyes never leaving Ashley's face.

Erin knew how he felt. She couldn't keep her eyes off of her either. When Ashley smiled it seemed as though the entire room lit up.

As soon as the waiter disappeared Ashley said, "You were about to tell me all about your love life."

"I was?" Erin squeaked.

"Yes, and I want all the sordid details." Ashley leaned forward with a look of anticipation.

Erin took a deep breath. The only good thing about having practically no experience was that it didn't take long to tell all. "Okay." She tried to gather her thoughts. "I was twenty-two before I realized I was gay."

Ashley's eyebrows shot up.

"You look surprised."

Ashley shrugged. "It's just that you seem so . . . I mean, you look—" She stopped and tilted her head to the side. "What I'm not saying so well is that you're sort of . . ."

"Butch," Erin supplied.

"Yes," Ashley admitted.

Erin traced the checkered pattern of the tablecloth with her fingertip. "Mom says I was a late bloomer."

"So your parents know you're gay?"

Erin nodded. "They knew before I did."

Ashley blinked at her. "What do you mean?"

The waiter reappeared with their soup and a basket of bread. Erin waited until he had left. "When I was growing up, I was a bit of a tomboy."

Ashley gave a look of disbelief. "Really?"

"When I was twenty-two, I fell in love with my best friend. The only problems were that she was straight and married. I didn't realize I was 'in love' with her." She used her fingers to make quotation

19

marks. "I thought we were just really good friends. I mean, we had been friends since junior high. Her name was Gina. Everything sort of imploded when we made plans to go to a concert." She gave a small shake of her head. "Strange. I don't even remember who we were going to see now. Anyway, a couple of days before the concert, her husband comes home from work and tells her he won a weekend trip to the coast and she cancelled our date." She dipped her spoon into her minestrone as the memories came pouring back. She cringed as she recalled that horrible time. "I made a complete fool of myself. I went to her house and picked a horrible fight with her. Her husband finally made me leave. I was devastated and angry that she had broken our date just to go to the coast with him. After I left Gina's house I went home and swiped a bottle of my father's Scotch. I went to my room, where I proceeded to get seriously plastered. My mom found me and in my drunken stupor I told her what had happened. The next evening after Mom came home from work she made me get dressed and go with her. She took me to a coworker's house." She looked at Ashley and smiled. "This woman's son was gay. I remember he took one look at me, rolled his eyes and said something like 'how can there be any doubt?' He and I talked for a long time and he helped make a lot of things about my life clearer."

"Was there anyone after Gina?"

Erin felt her neck getting warm. She made a big show of tasting her soup. When it was obvious that Ashley was still waiting for an answer, she said, "I've dated a few times but nothing very serious." She wasn't about to admit that she had only gone out with two women and both times had proved to be bumbling disasters. "What about you?" she asked, wanting to take the attention from herself.

Before Ashley could reply, the waiter arrived with their entrées. It wasn't until later that night when Erin was lying in bed unable to sleep that she remembered Ashley had never answered her question. In fact, Ashley never talked about herself at all. Erin didn't know anything about her really, except that she had a girlfriend. A flicker of guilt caused her to squirm, but she pushed it away. They had done nothing wrong. *Yet*, a tiny voice buried deep inside her whispered.

As she watched the shadow of a limb outside her bedroom window dance on the wall, Erin thought about how easy it was for her to talk to Ashley. They had talked about everything except Jess. Her name had never once been mentioned. The sense of guilt blossomed when she realized she was on the verge of making the same mistake with Ashley that she had made with Gina. She wondered if there was something about her that propelled her toward unavailable women.

CHAPTER FOUR

Erin retreated from her memories of Ashley as she and Mary gathered up their trash from lunch. She was grateful for Mary's silence. It wasn't until they reached the doorway of the office that Mary spoke.

"Erin, if you change your mind and need to talk, you can call me anytime. Okay?"

Erin again reminded herself of how wonderful a friend Mary was. "Thanks. I appreciate the offer, but for now I'm fine."

Mary nodded. "Then get busy and get those keystrokes up to par. I don't want Sonia bothering me again." She gave Erin's arm a quick tap and walked away.

Erin studied the woman who had become her friend. At fifty-two, Mary was twenty-four years older than her. Mary had grown up in San Antonio and ran a little wild until she met a pretty young college coed, Alice Raye from Midland, Texas. When Alice graduated from college and decided to stay in San Antonio to teach history to high school students, Mary Vaughn moved in with her and their lives became a love story that Erin dreamed of being able to replicate someday. For years, Erin's dream woman was a vague shadowy lover, but recently it was Ashley's face she saw in her dreams. The elevator doors opened and spat out a loud group of Erin's coworkers. She followed them into the work area. When she passed by Sonia Delgado's desk she saw her supervisor eyeing her. Erin tried to look as though she didn't have a care in the world. As she sat down, she pushed all thoughts of Ashley away. She wanted to get her stats back up. The last thing she needed now was to be fired.

Erin spent the next two hours keying data as if her life depended on it. When afternoon break rolled around, she returned to her desk five minutes early and started again. Even though it was Friday, she didn't start shutting her machine down five minutes early as she usually did, but continued to work until five o'clock. It wasn't a strong work ethic that kept her at her machine so much as it was her wanting to avoid giving Mary another chance to talk to her.

"Are you working overtime?" Mary asked on her way out.

"No. I'm leaving as soon as I finish this record. I'll see you Monday. Tell Alice hi."

"If you don't have anything better to do why don't you come by tomorrow and see the house?" Mary and Alice lived in a rambling older home and were constantly working on some home improvement project. The house had once stood alone in a large meadow, but over the years dozens of homes had gone up around it. Erin loved the place but hated the sprawling neighborhood.

"Oh, no, you don't. I'm not falling for that again. The last time I dropped by to see what you two were up to I ended up hanging wallpaper. My arms were sore for a week afterward. What are you doing this time?"

Mary chuckled. "We're tiling the kitchen. It's real easy. It won't take you any time to figure it out."

Erin rolled her eyes. "Yeah, right. I think I just remembered I'm busy all weekend."

"All right, but someday when you have your own house don't

blame me if you don't know how to lay down tile. Have a good weekend." Mary walked away.

"You too." Erin stopped typing and called out, "Hey, call me if you really need help."

Mary just waved.

Erin waited until enough time had passed for Mary to be out of the parking lot before she started shutting down her system. As she did so the nervous jitters returned. She was meeting Ashley later for dinner and a movie. During the past two and a half months, they had spent every Saturday together walking the trails at either Eisenhower or Friedrich Wilderness Park. They'd even met for dinner a few times during the week. Erin never asked what excuses Ashley used for being away from the house or whether Jess was even aware that they were spending so much time together. In the beginning she told herself that she and Ashley were only friends, but recently it was getting harder and harder for her to be around Ashley without touching her. She lost track of the number of times during the week that she picked up the phone to call her. She never did, though, mainly because Ashley wouldn't give her a contact number. The one time Erin asked for it, Ashley had grown very quiet and told her it would be better if Erin didn't call. She knew she should stop seeing Ashley but she couldn't. At first, she tried telling herself that her feelings for Ashley would dim over time, that all of this was nothing more than a crush. As time passed she realized that her feelings were growing stronger rather than diminishing. She was in love with Ashley Wade and no matter how much she pretended otherwise, it wasn't going to go away. Her life felt as if it was coming apart at the seams. It wasn't just her work that was affected. She seemed to walk around in a daze most of the time. Earlier in the week she almost ran a red light. She'd been think-ing about Ashley and never even noticed the signal change until she was right on it. That was when she realized she had to do something. Even as she told herself to walk away from Ashley, she knew she'd never be able to make the break on her own. The only thing left to do was to tell Ashley and then maybe Ashley would leave her as Gina had.

Erin rushed home and showered before dressing in her best jeans. She chose the black western shirt that Ashley liked so much and shined her boots to a high gloss. They were going to La Casa for dinner before the movie. As she dressed, Erin ran through a dozen scenarios on when and how to tell Ashley. In each situation, Ashley would look at her shocked before sending her away. No matter how she worded her feelings, the ending was always the same. By the time she was ready to leave the house to meet Ashley, she had worked herself into such a state of panic that she could barely breathe.

Erin arrived at the restaurant twenty minutes early. She sat in her truck rehearsing what she would say to Ashley. She was well into receiving her tenth imaginary rejection when there was a sharp rap on her window. She couldn't stop the small startled shriek from slipping out. When she turned to find Ashley's face mere inches from her own, her heart felt as though it might explode from the love she felt. Their gazes locked and Erin felt herself being pulled toward Ashley's full red lips until suddenly her face banged against the side window. Embarrassed, she fumbled with the key to activate the window button.

"Are you okay?" Ashley asked as she reached in and rubbed Erin's forehead. "You really whacked your head on the window."

Erin opened her mouth to reassure Ashley she was fine, but what came out of her mouth startled them both into silence. The words hung between them as potent and deadly as a king cobra. When Ashley didn't respond, Erin repeated them. "I love you."

Ashley took a step away from the truck and held up a hand as if to block the words. "You can't love me," she said fervently. "No one can love me."

Watching her turn to leave, Erin leapt out of the truck. "Ashley, please don't go. I know I shouldn't have said anything. I know you're with . . . you're not . . . that anything between us is impossible, but please don't walk away." To her surprise Ashley stopped. They were standing at the back of Erin's pickup. Neither of them spoke. They were still standing there when a family of five went by. Erin saw the man frown as he took in her clothes and short haircut. She glared at him until he looked away. When Ashley continued to stand in silence Erin pressed on. "Could we maybe sit in the truck and talk for a while?"

Silently Ashley walked to the passenger side and climbed inside.

Neither of them spoke for several moments. "I'm sorry," Erin began. "I shouldn't have said anything."

"I'm the one who should be sorry." Ashley's voice was barely more than a whisper. "I shouldn't have continued calling you. I should have realized."

"It's not your fault," Erin countered. "You never pretended our friendship was anything other than exactly that. I'm the one who let my emotions get out of control."

"It's not just you."

Erin stopped breathing. Did she really hear what she thought she'd heard? Did Ashley say—*No.* she told herself. *Don't start imagining things.* She had to remind herself to breathe.

Ashley rubbed a trembling hand over her face. "It's my fault. I like talking to you. It's so easy. You don't judge me or nag me about taking my—" She stopped.

Briefly, Erin wondered what Ashley had been about to say, but Ashley's next statement was such a bombshell that all else was quickly forgotten.

"I think I started falling in love with you at the Christmas party," Ashley said quietly. Suddenly, she grabbed the door handle. "Erin, I'm sorry, but there are so many things you don't know. Please try to forget everything I said. You're a wonderful person, but there can never be anything between us." She clutched Erin's hand so hard that Erin had to bite her tongue to keep from crying out. "You have to be the strong one. If I weaken and call you again, you have to be the one who ends this. You're so much stronger than I am. Please, promise me that you won't see me again. Jess will go berserk if she ever finds out."

Before Erin could respond, Ashley jumped out of the truck and raced across the parking lot. Erin wanted to follow her, but all she could do was stare helplessly after her. She was still sitting in the parking lot when the family of five left the restaurant over an hour later. The man's curious stare barely registered through her tears.

CHAPTER FIVE

Erin believed that everyone should have one safe haven. A place where you can go and not be condemned or judged for your actions, no matter how stupid or wrong you may have been. When she finally pulled out of the La Casa parking lot, she knew she was headed to that place, Mary and Alice's. When Alice answered the door and found her sobbing, she simply pulled her inside and held her until the tears stopped. Afterward, with a cup of hot tea liberally laced with brandy, Erin sat on their couch and let the entire story spill out. When she finished she heard Mary exhale loudly.

"Hell's bells, Erin. You sure know how to open a can of kick-ass."

"Mary," Alice scolded. "Now's not the time."

"Well, excuse me, but would you mind telling me when it is time?" Mary asked, clearly frustrated. "Do you know what Jess Lawler is going to do when she finds out?"

"There's no reason for her to find out," Alice reasoned.

Erin looked up in time to see Mary roll her eyes. "When did anything in this community ever remain a secret?" She waited for an answer. When she didn't receive one, she continued, "I'm amazed they've been able to keep it a secret this long." She turned to Erin. "My advice to you is to keep as far away from Ashley Wade as you can. If Jess hears you've made a play for her woman, she'll rip your head off and spit down your neck."

"Mary Vaughn!" Alice scolded. "You hush this very minute. Erin didn't come to us so we could scare her half to death." She patted Erin's hand. "Don't you listen to anything she says. I believe you when you say nothing has happened between you and Ashley, and so will Jess if she ever hears anything."

Mary made a rude sputtering noise. "Alice, I've never known you to live in such a dream world. You know Jess is half crazy when she's sober and completely crazy when she isn't. And from what I've heard Ashley is as—"

Alice sent a withering glare toward Mary and stopped her in mid-sentence. "A lot of time has passed since you and Jess ran around together. You two rarely see each other. A person can change."

"Yeah, well. You might be right," Mary answered, meekly backpedaling.

"Is Jess Lawler dangerous?" Erin asked as a bubble of fear rose in her throat. "Is Ashley in any danger?"

"Of course not," Alice said, still patting her hand. "There's no reason to believe Jess will hear about any of this. But for the good of everyone involved, it might be best if you and Ashley didn't see each other again until Ashley and Jess have—well, decided what they want."

"You don't have to worry about that," Erin said miserably. "She'll never want to see me again after tonight."

"You'd better pray that's true," Mary mumbled.

"Drink your tea." Alice nodded toward the cup Erin was holding.

Erin downed the tea. "I should be going. I've upset you two enough already."

"Nonsense. You're going to spend the night. We have plenty of room," Alice insisted.

"Yeah," Mary joined in. "It'll work out perfect. You'll be able to see how I measure the floor off for the tile and everything."

Alice shook her head as Erin stood.

"Thanks for listening, but I think I'd better go on home." Erin handed the empty cup to Alice. "Thanks for the tea."

Alice took the cup and gave her a quick hug. "I wish you'd stay. You shouldn't be alone tonight."

"I'll be fine," Erin assured her. "I'm going home and to bed."

Mary took Erin by the arm. "Come on. I'll walk out with you."

Erin said good-bye to Alice and walked out with Mary.

"You're not thinking about doing anything stupid, are you?" Mary asked as soon as they were outside.

"Like what?" Erin asked.

"Like you getting a wild hair up your ass to go looking for Ashley Wade."

"You don't have anything to worry about. Ashley doesn't want to see me, remember?"

"You promise me that you won't go looking for her or try calling her," Mary insisted.

The vehemence in her voice made Erin stop.

"Promise me." Mary squeezed her arm.

"Okay. I promise. What's wrong with you? I've never seen you like this."

Mary stopped and looked sharply at her. "Do you even know Jess Lawler?"

Erin frowned. "No. I know she's a cop. Is that what you're worried about?"

Mary was shaking her head. "Jess and I are about the same age. She's maybe four or five years younger and built like a brick shithouse. Erin, I'm not joking with you now. She's as crazy as a Bessie-bug and if she's been drinking, which is most of the time, then she's even meaner. I've seen her tear up more than one bar and even a few people. You stay as far away from her as you can, and don't you ever forget that she carries a gun twenty-four hours

29

a day, seven days a week. She carried a gun before she became a cop, and if she were pushed far enough I don't think she would hesitate to use it."

"All of this sounds like it happened years ago," Erin said.

Mary shrugged. "Well, yeah. We were a lot younger then. Truth is, after Alice and I got together I sort of drifted away from that crowd. Jess and I used to run into each other occasionally, but I haven't seen her in three or four years." She tugged her earlobe. "Maybe even longer," she added thoughtfully. "I guess she could have changed. But if I were you, I wouldn't bet on it." She shook her finger at Erin.

"I don't understand how a woman can abuse another woman. Someone she's supposed to love."

"Abuse? Now, wait a minute. I never said Jess ever abused her girlfriends. I just meant she has been known to bust up a bar if she got too drunk and someone pissed her off. She liked to fight, but I've never heard of her beating up her girlfriends."

Erin slipped her hands into her pocket and realized the things she was telling Mary only served to make Mary more worried about Jess. "I think Ashley is afraid to leave." Erin said. "I think she's afraid of what Jess would do to her, or maybe she's afraid for me."

"Did she say so?"

"No, but something is wrong. I can feel it."

Mary exhaled slowly. "Dang, I can't believe that. I mean, I know Jess had a temper, but I've never heard of her hitting any of her girlfriends." She stopped and shook her head. "If it's true, then that's all the more reason you should be careful. I wish I could say something that would help you more, kid." Mary squeezed her arm as Alice had earlier. "You promise me, you'll stay away from her."

Mary seemed worried about her. She felt bad that she had barged in with her troubles and worried them. She tried to lighten the mood as she bumped her shoulder against Mary's. "You know me. I'm the biggest chicken in the state. I'm certainly not crazy enough to piss off some maniac with a gun."

Mary peered at her. "Under normal circumstances maybe, but once you stop thinking with your head, things have a way of changing."

Erin opened the truck's door and held up her hand. "Don't worry. I promise I won't do anything that might bring the wrath of Jess Lawler down on my head."

Mary didn't look convinced, but she kept any further comments to herself. "You call me if you need anything," she said as Erin got into her truck.

As Erin drove home she couldn't help but wonder what sort of woman Jess Lawler was. It was obvious that Ashley wasn't happy at home or she wouldn't have been spending so much time with Erin. Mary wasn't the sort of woman who scared easily. If she was that worried about Jess then it would probably be a smart idea for Erin to avoid her. Which shouldn't be hard, she reminded herself. After all, she and Jess didn't exactly run in the same circles. She thought back to the Christmas party where she had first met Ashley and wondered if she had actually seen Jess that night. There had been a lot of women there and she couldn't recall meeting anyone named Jess. It struck her that Mary had said she hadn't seen Jess in years; apparently they hadn't crossed paths at the party. She shrugged it off. There had been so many people there it would have been easy to miss someone. Besides, Mary and Alice had been playing cards in a side room.

As Mary's warnings faded, Erin's pain in losing Ashley began to surface again, but she refused to let it take life. If she was going to get over Ashley, she had to go cold turkey. No more Ashley Wade in her life or thoughts. From now on, she'd make it a point to not even talk to a woman who was in a relationship.

When Erin arrived at her apartment, the light on the answering machine was blinking. Her resolution to avoid antagonizing Jess Lawler was forgotten as soon as she heard Ashley's voice.

CHAPTER SIX

As soon as Ashley's message ended, Erin hit the replay button and listened to it again.

"Erin, it's me. I'm sorry about the way I left you at the restaurant. I . . . I wanted you to know that I meant what I said. My feelings for you, I mean. It's just that . . . well, things are complicated. This was a mistake. I shouldn't have called you. I'm sorry. Please, you have to be the strong one."

She replayed the message several more times before searching through the call list on the phone. As usual Ashley's ID was logged in as a private caller. Dejected, she poured a glass of juice before going into the living room and turning on the television. She couldn't concentrate on the show but at least the noise helped to drive away some of her loneliness. She flipped through the channels, wondering if Ashley would call back again. She went to check the time the call had come in. The log showed seven twenty-two. That would have been shortly after Ashley left the restaurant parking lot. She must have called on her cell phone. For the first time in her life, Erin wished she owned a cell phone. They had always seemed like an extravagant nuisance, but if she'd had a cell, Ashley would have called her on it and she would have been able to speak to her again. There were so many things she wanted to say, things she wanted to ask.

She wandered back into the living room and stretched out on the sofa. Why hadn't she ever asked Ashley about Jess? *Because you were already feeling guilty about your feelings for Ashley*, her conscience answered. She pushed the thought away and closed her eyes.

When the phone woke her it was almost midnight. She dashed across the room and grabbed it.

"Hi. Did I wake you?"

Erin closed her eyes and smiled as she heard Ashley's voice. "No. I was watching television."

"I wanted to talk to you. I know I shouldn't have called."

"Yes, you should have. I wanted to talk to you, too." Erin remembered Ashley imploring her to be strong and end their relationship but she couldn't.

"About tonight you mean?" Ashley asked.

"I mean about tonight, tomorrow, next year, the rest of my life."

"Please, don't do that."

"What?"

"Don't make it any harder than it already is," Ashley whispered.

"If it's so hard why do you keep pushing me away?"

Ashley took a deep breath. "There are things you don't know about."

"I know Jess has a bad temper and that she drinks a lot."

"Who told you that? What else did they tell you?" She rushed on before Erin had a chance to respond. "Never mind. I don't want to know."

"Where are you?" Erin asked. She wondered if Ashley had been drinking.

"I'm at home."

"Where's Jess?"

"It's Friday night. Every Friday night she and some of the guys she works with go to a bar downtown."

"That's why you were able to get away to see me for dinner and a movie," Erin said.

"Yes."

"What about all those Saturdays? How did you manage that?"

Ashley was quiet for a moment. "She drinks enough Friday night that she sleeps all day Saturday."

"Have you ever mentioned me to her?"

"No! Jess is not the type who would want to hear me talking about other women."

"If she's so bad why do you stay with her?" Erin was puzzled that a woman who seemed as independent as Ashley would let anyone rule her life.

Ashley laughed abruptly. "You don't know Jess. She's a hard woman to say no to."

"Have you ever tried to leave her?"

There was a long silence before Ashley finally spoke. "I don't want to talk about Jess. I don't even want to think about her."

"Okay. What do you want?"

"I want to see you. I can't stay long. I'll have to be home when Jess gets in around three."

The blood raced to Erin's head so quickly she had to sit down. "I'd like to see you too," she managed to say. "Where do you want me to meet you?" She wanted to ask Ashley if she had been drinking but thought better of it.

"I was wondering if it would all right if I came to your apartment."

Despite Mary's warning ringing in her ears, Erin gave Ashley the address.

After hanging up, Erin dashed madly about the already tidy one-bedroom apartment, making sure everything was tidy. The place was so small and neat that the inspection took practically no time at all.

Barely twenty minutes had passed before her doorbell rang. The Ashley standing at Erin's doorway was a very different woman from the one she normally saw. Tonight the usually bright smile was missing and her laughing, teasing eyes looked tired and bloodshot from crying. Ashley stepped into the apartment and stood by the door as Erin closed it. When Erin turned to her, the haunted look in Ashley's eyes was more than she could bear. Without a word, she pulled Ashley into her arms and kissed her.

"We shouldn't be doing this," Ashley whispered as Erin's lips trailed a path along her neck. "You promised you'd send me away."

Terrified that Ashley would change her mind, Erin kissed her again. As the kiss deepened, any thoughts of turning back vanished.

Ashley allowed Erin to lead her into the small bedroom but hesitated when she saw the bed.

"It's impossible. There can't be anything between us," Ashley said.

"Give me this one night," Erin begged. She held her breath as Ashley struggled with her inner demons. Only after Ashley began to unbutton Erin's shirt did Erin finally breathe.

No further words were spoken as they slowly undressed each other. Erin even forgot about her limited experience in the art of lovemaking as she pulled Ashley down onto the bed and began to kiss her. Her body shook with desire, but she forced herself to move slowly and take her time. She wanted to savor every touch, scent and taste. If this was to be the only night they would ever have together, she intended to remember every single moment of it. Precious minutes slipped rapidly by as they kissed, and Erin tried to memorize every curve and contour of Ashley's body.

Her resolve nearly left her when Ashley pulled her down on top of her and wrapped her legs around her. *Slow down*, she admonished herself. The next few moments might have to last a lifetime. It was useless to try and hold back any longer. As soon as Ashley began to rock against her, Erin knew she was lost. She slipped her hand between them and let her fingers carry Ashley over the edge.

As Ashley's cries of pleasure grew, Erin let herself go and soon their cries blended into one.

A short time later, Ashley brushed the damp hair from Erin's forehead. "As much as I'd like to, I can't stay," she said as she glanced nervously at the clock on the bedside table.

Erin was shocked to see it was almost two a.m. "Why not? She won't know where to find you."

Ashley pulled away. "Don't start clinging. I told you I have to leave. You knew it would be this way."

"Please, don't leave yet," Erin replied, stung by Ashley's sharp tone.

"I have to. The bars will be closing soon. If I'm not there when she gets home, Jess will be angry and she'll . . ." Ashley let the unfinished sentence hang in the space between them.

They got up and began to get dressed.

"Will you be okay?" Erin asked as they walked to the door. "Maybe I should follow you home and wait close by."

"No." She took Erin's face between her hands and stared into her eyes. "Swear to me that you'll never do that."

The look of intensity in Ashley's eyes disturbed Erin. "Okay, I won't. I'm just worried about you. That's all."

Ashley released her abruptly. "There's nothing to worry about. I'll be home, pretending to be fast asleep when she comes in."

"When can I see you again?" Erin pushed.

Ashley stopped and again looked into her eyes. "If you were smart you'd be running away from me as quickly as you can."

Erin shrugged. "I've never been accused of being too smart." She tried to make it sound like a joke, but the frown on Ashley's face only deepened.

"I'm not sure you understand what you're getting yourself into."

Erin kissed her softly. "Don't worry about me. I can take care of myself. Can I see you tomorrow?"

Ashley hugged her tightly. "I don't know. I'll call you when I can," she promised as she pulled away.

"I'll walk you down to your car."

"No. I'd rather you didn't."

Erin started to protest, but something in Ashley's face made her stop. "Okay," she agreed. "Will you call me and let me know you got home safely?"

Ashley nodded. "If I can, but if you don't hear from me, don't worry. It just means I didn't have time." She left before Erin could say anything else.

Erin stood in the opened doorway and watched as Ashley rushed down the hallway and disappeared into the stairwell. After locking up, she sat by the phone until it rang twenty minutes later.

"I'm home safe and sound," Ashley said, her voice little more than a whisper. She sounded like she had been running.

"Is she there?"

"No, but she will be soon. I'll talk to you as soon as I can. 'Bye."

Erin held the dead phone for several seconds after Ashley disconnected. As she hung up she noticed a number glowing on the call log. Ashley had apparently forgotten to block her number. With a small sense of guilt, Erin reached for a paper and pencil and copied the number. She knew she was taking advantage of Ashley's carelessness, but in less than ten minutes she had signed onto the Internet and, by cross-referencing the phone number, managed to locate a home address for Jessica M. Lawler. She added the address to the scrap of paper. Ashley lived less than ten miles away. After staring at the address for a long moment, she carefully folded the paper and tucked it into her wallet.

CHAPTER SEVEN

The following morning Erin stood in her kitchen whistling as she waited for the toast to pop up. In her heart she knew Ashley would call her today and she intended to sit next to the phone until she did. The phone rang just as the toast was done. She snatched up the receiver on the second ring.

"How are you doing this morning?" Mary asked. "Alice was worried about you. I tried to tell her you were fine, but she insisted I call and check on you."

Despite her disappointment that it wasn't Ashley calling, she smiled. She knew Mary was probably just as worried about her as Alice was. "Tell her I'm fine. In fact, I'm better than fine. I had a great night's sleep." She realized she was probably going over-board.

"You little dumbass," Mary exploded. "You went ahead and did it. Didn't you?"

Erin cringed. She could hear Alice in the background asking what was going on. "I can explain," she began.

"Explain! What is there to explain? You're involved with Ashley Wade. I hope to God your life insurance is paid up."

"Come on, Mary. It's not that bad."

"Not that bad!" Mary echoed. "Well, do me a big favor and make me your beneficiary. Then I'll be able to retire next week."

"Mary Vaughn," Alice's voice floated through the phone. "You stop talking like that. What's going on? Is Erin all right?"

"Here, see if you can talk some sense into her. She obviously hasn't listened to a damn thing I've had to say."

"Erin, it's Alice. Sweetie, what's going on? Why is Mary so angry?"

Erin leaned her head against the wall and sighed. "She told me to stay away from Ashley. Mary thinks Jess is some kind of lunatic or something."

"From Mary's reaction, I'm guessing you didn't heed her advice."

"No. Ashley called me last night and . . . well, you know. One thing led to another."

"I see. Does Jess know anything?"

"I don't think so. She was out at some bar. Ashley said she never comes home before closing time."

"You be careful. For what it's worth, we've known Jess for a long time and I have to agree with Mary that the woman is trouble. I never understood what Ashley saw in her, but then I was surprised that Jess got involved with Ashley."

"Why?"

Alice hesitated. "They didn't seem very compatible to me."

Erin started to ask for more details, but Alice was faster.

"I'd better go find Mary," Alice said. "You know how she has to be working at something when she's upset. By now she's probably dug up half the backyard."

"Tell her I'm sorry I upset her," Erin said.

"I will. Call us if you need anything."

After hanging up, Erin pitched the slice of toast into the trash. She no longer felt like eating. Instead she poured herself a glass of apple juice and settled into the old blue floral, overstuffed chair that once sat in her parents' den. She eyed the three books she had gotten from the library earlier in the week. Her gaze drifted from the books to the battered coffee table where they rested. She had purchased the cheap pressboard table at a thrift store six years ago after moving into the apartment. The table was supposed to have been temporary. Something she could use until she could do better. She glanced around the apartment. From where she sat in the small living room she was able to see most of the living space. Only a short wall topped by a bar separated the living room from the combination kitchen and dining room. To her right was the cramped bedroom with its tiny closet and bathroom. Erin appreciated the apartment for its location. She was only fifteen minutes from work, and the drive to Mary and Alice's house took only about twenty minutes. She didn't like the fact that she had no room for guests. Whenever her parents drove in for an overnight visit, she slept on the couch and let them have the bed, or else they stayed in a hotel. She wished she could afford a slightly larger place with an extra bedroom.

"Wishin' ain't gettin'," she said, quoting her maternal grandmother Devers. Her grandparents had owned a small farm south of San Antonio. They raised a few cows and chickens, and twice a year they would plant an enormous garden. They referred to them as their spring and fall gardens. Whenever Erin and her family visited them or her grandparents ventured into San Antonio, the Foxes' refrigerator would be filled with fresh vegetables and farm eggs. They were both dead now.

Pushing away the memories, Erin chose one of the books on the table and opened it to the first chapter. The harder she tried to read, the more evasive the words became. Nothing made sense this morning. She finally set the book aside and went to her bedroom closet to retrieve the box that held the pieces to the antique lap desk she had been restoring for her mother. She had found the piece at a garage sale and had intended to give it to her mother for Christmas, but with all the overtime she had been doing, there hadn't been enough time. Now she hoped to have it ready by her mother's birthday in May.

It needed a lot of work. Thankfully the leather blotter on top was still in good condition, but the wooden bottom had split. Erin had already taken the piece apart and repaired the bottom. She was currently working at stripping away the numerous layers of paint that had accumulated over the years. The gel stripper could only be used in a well-ventilated area, and she normally took one piece at a time and sat at one of the picnic tables outside to work. Since she didn't want to get too far away from the phone, she chose a piece that she had already stripped and after spreading several sheets of newspaper on the kitchen floor to catch the dust, she began the delicate work of sanding the finely detailed scrollwork that trimmed the sides of the piece. As she worked, her thoughts returned to Ashley. Would she call back? A small voice somewhere deep within warned her that she should probably end this thing with Ashley before it got completely out of hand. What would she do if Jess were to ever catch them together? She shook her head to chase away the thought and realized she was sanding against the grain of the wood. Disgusted with her carelessness, she put the project away and cleaned up the scattered newspapers. With nothing else to do, she began to pace the short stretch from her living room to the kitchen counter.

No matter how hard she tried to concentrate on something else, her thoughts always returned to Ashley. It occurred to her that maybe she should have listened to Mary. After all, Jess Lawler didn't sound like someone you wanted to piss off. "I can take care of myself," she muttered. She had grown up rough-housing with her two brothers. Tom was two years older and Andrew was eighteen months younger. She had managed to hold her own with them. Besides, Mary had probably exaggerated. Women weren't prone to actual physical violence. Were they? She stopped pacing and tried to remember if she had ever seen two women fighting, other than on television. She couldn't remember witnessing a single incident. Women fought verbally. Either way, a confrontation with Jess was easy enough to avoid. She simply wouldn't put herself in a position to be around her and if she called, Erin could always hang up the phone. Just as she was starting to address

Mary's warning that Jess carried a gun, the phone rang. She grabbed it and smiled brightly when she heard Ashley's voice

"I can't believe how badly I missed you," Ashley whispered.

"I was afraid you wouldn't call," Erin admitted. "I can't stop thinking about you. Can you get away today?"

"I don't think so. For some reason Jess didn't drink as much last night. She's still asleep but I don't think she'll sleep all day."

"What about an hour or two?"

Ashley hesitated. "I don't want her to start wondering where I am. I'll try calling you later if I'm able to get away."

Erin swallowed her disappointment. "I'll be here if—" A loud metallic crash from the hallway interrupted her.

"What was that noise?" Ashley asked. "Is there someone else with you?"

"Of course not. It sounded like someone dropped something in the hallway. The apartment across from me has been empty for a while. I guess someone's moving in." The contractors had taken advantage of every square foot of land when they designed the complex. At either end of the main building was a small extension that was large enough for two one-bedroom apartments on each of the four floors. Erin appreciated the additional sense of privacy it offered.

After Ashley hung up, Erin looked around her apartment, searching for something that would keep her occupied. There was laundry that needed to be done, but the laundry room was on the ground floor and she was afraid she might miss another call from Ashley. She stood by the window that overlooked the back parking area and let the warm mid-March sunlight soak into her body. She and Ashley had been hiking almost every Saturday since they'd met. As she stood staring out the window, she made up her mind to get a cell phone on Monday after work. She went to the computer and logged onto the Internet. It took her a while, but she finally found a service plan and phone that would serve her needs and an estimate of the costs involved. Then she went to work on her carefully planned budget. Somehow she had to find a way to squeeze out enough for the cell phone. After working the numbers for an hour, she realized that in order to afford the new phone, she would have to put in at least six more hours of overtime each month. Luckily, it wouldn't be hard to get the overtime. Sonia was always begging them to put in extra hours. Erin grimaced as she looked at the figures. She still owed four hundred dollars on the credit card she only used for emergencies. The transmission on her truck had gone out just before Thanksgiving. Prior to meeting Ashley, she had been working overtime on Saturdays to pay off the charges. If she spent money on the cell phone it would take even longer. Disgusted, she went to the kitchen to fix herself a bowl of cereal. As she passed through the living room, she heard another noise in the hallway.

"Great," she mumbled. "Noisy neighbors. That's all I need."

Erin tried to read, but couldn't sit still. It was only a little after ten in the morning. She turned on the television and flipped aimlessly through the channels. After going through the entire lineup three times, she turned it off and tossed the remote on the table. It was now ten minutes after ten. She went into the bathroom and pulled out her cleaning supplies. Even though it didn't need it, she began to clean the bathroom. From there she moved on to the bedroom before working her way through the living room and kitchen. When she finally put the mop away, she glanced around and realized the apartment didn't really look any different than it had before she started. She groaned aloud when she looked at the clock and saw it wasn't yet noon.

"Okay, this isn't going to work," she said as she stared out the window. "I'll go nuts if I stay in here all weekend." She was startled by the phone. It was Ashley.

"Can you meet me at Friedrich Wilderness Park?" Ashley asked. "I can be there in thirty minutes."

"I'll see you there," Erin said. After hanging up, she raced to the shower, grumbling as she went. She had wasted all that time cleaning everything but herself. After taking the fastest shower of her life, she yanked on a pair of shorts and her favorite Spurs T-shirt. She grabbed a pair of socks and her sneakers and headed for the door. She'd put them on at stop light on the way.

As she raced into the hallway, she noticed the door to the apartment across from hers was open. She could see two women inside struggling with a large chair. With her shoes in hand, she rushed to her car, smiling. Maybe the new neighbors wouldn't be so bad after all.

Several vehicles sat in the parking lot when Erin arrived. She spotted Ashley's silver Corolla near the trailhead. After parking as close to her as possible, she quickly tied her shoes before getting out of her truck.

"I was starting to wonder if you'd changed your mind," Ashley said as Erin arrived.

"Traffic was a little heavier than I had anticipated," Erin said, trying not to notice Ashley's gorgeous legs as they emerged from the car.

"It's such a pretty day," Ashley said. "I thought we could have a picnic. I brought us a fabulous feast." She opened the back car door and leaned inside. As she did so, her shorts stretched and molded to her shapely bottom, leaving little to Erin's imagination.

The force of her body's reaction jolted her. She jammed her hands into her pockets and forced her attention elsewhere to keep from reaching out and touching Ashley. Her efforts were helped when a van filled with shouting teenagers parked across from them.

"I hope they're taking a different trail than we are," Ashley murmured as she slipped a backpack over her shoulders.

"We'll make it a point not to follow them." Erin was still trying to get her raging hormones under control.

Ashley ran a hand over Erin's hair. "Your hair is wet. You should have taken time to dry it."

Erin tried to ignore the flurry of sensations Ashley's touch caused. *It's not just my hair that's wet*, she thought as she shifted uncomfortably. "You sound like my mother," she said, trying to find something else to focus on. "Can wet hair really give you a cold? I thought colds were caused by a bacteria, or virus."

"I think you're right, but going outside when you're so wet is still uncomfortable. Isn't it?" Ashley gave her a wicked smile before turning and jogging up the trail.

CHAPTER EIGHT

Erin and Ashley left the trail and climbed until they found themselves in a small glade. Erin noticed that clouds were beginning to build up in the east.

"This spot is perfect," Ashley said as she removed the backpack. From it she pulled out a blanket and spread it over the ground. "Sit by me," she said, kicking off her hiking boots and sitting down.

Erin quickly removed her sneakers and complied. As Ashley continued to pull things out of the backpack, Erin glanced around to see if they would be visible to anyone casually passing by.

"Don't worry," Ashley said as if reading her thoughts. "There's no way anyone on the trail can see us, and I doubt very many of the hikers who come here ever leave the trails anyway."

"I was just looking at the scenery," Erin said, not wanting Ashley to think she was paranoid or anything. She was feeling a little guilty about leaving the trail since hikers were asked not to do so. "This park has a lot of golden-cheek warblers. Have you ever heard one sing? They have a beautiful song." She realized she was rambling and stopped.

Ashley smiled at her and handed her a glass. "Wait until you see what I bought for us." She pulled out a bottle of Champagne and handed it to Erin. "Open this."

Erin took the bottle and studied the wire wrapped around the top. It took her a moment, but she managed to get it off without embarrassing herself. Not much of a drinker, she had never opened a bottle of Champagne before. She had seen them being opened and tried to replicate the maneuvers she could remember. The stopper was a lot harder to uncork than she had anticipated. She finally held it between her knees and used both hands. Suddenly, the stopper exploded out of the bottle and Champagne spewed all over her. Ashley burst into hysterical laughter. Erin tried to smile and hide her distaste for the smelly brew.

"Here, use this." Ashley handed her a snowy white linen napkin.

"I don't want to get this dirty," Erin said holding the napkin by one corner.

Ashley sighed loudly before grabbing the napkin from her and roughly wiping Erin's arms and legs off. "Now, did the world come to an end?"

"No. I just didn't want to—"

"Stop worrying. Pour us some Champagne."

Erin poured a glass for Ashley before carefully propping the bottle against a rock.

"Look at what else I brought," Ashley said as she took the glass and pushed a small jar into Erin's hand. "That's Beluga caviar."

Erin's eyes grew large as she saw the price stamped on the bottom of the jar. "Is this correct?" she blurted. "Did this little jar really cost one hundred and forty-seven dollars?"

Ashley ignored her as she continued to pull things out of the bag. Erin picked up a small can labeled Duck Foie Gras. She had no idea what it was, but it was marked thirty dollars. How could Ashley afford such expensive food? Just those two items amounted to the bulk of Erin's monthly grocery bill.

Ashley tossed her a plastic bag. "French black summer truffles," she said with a moan of appreciation.

Erin held the bag up to look at it. The contents didn't look like something she wanted to eat. "Aren't you supposed to cook these or something?" she asked, uncomfortable with all the unknown things sitting around her. As she turned the bag over to examine the contents more closely, she suddenly threw it down. "Ashley, that bag cost over five hundred dollars?"

Ashley's eyes snapped with anger. "Did anyone ask you to pay for it?"

"Well, no, but still that's a lot of money."

Ashley's anger disappeared and tears filled her eyes. "I wanted to have a special day with you. Why are you yelling at me?"

Erin felt like a heel. "I'm sorry. I wasn't yelling at you. I was just shocked by the amount." She reached for Ashley's hand. "Please don't cry. I'll eat it." She got on her knees and tried to hug Ashley, but Ashley pulled away.

"You don't have to eat it." She shoved the food away.

"Don't do that," Erin pleaded. "Let's try some of this." She picked up a large package that read Gorgonzola Dolce. She knew Gorgonzola was a type of cheese. As she picked it up, she couldn't help but notice the label that indicated it weighed three pounds. Before she could dwell on why anyone would bring so much cheese along on a picnic for two, Ashley grabbed the cheese and threw it into the woods.

Erin sat quietly, not sure how to handle the situation.

After what seemed like an eternity, Ashley finally broke the silence. "Here," she said, pulling a bottle of water from the bag. "I knew you'd want this."

Feeling even worse, Erin took the water. "I'm really sorry."

Ashley waved it off and stretched out on the blanket.

Erin fiddled with the bottle and tried to think of something to say that wouldn't upset her more. She finally decided that maybe saying nothing at all would be the best option. After a while she began to wonder how Ashley had gotten out of the house with all that food and how long she could stay.

"What's wrong?" Ashley smiled at her like nothing had happened.

Erin shrugged. "Nothing really. How long can you stay?"

The smile on Ashley's face faded as she sat up. "I need to be back by five. Jess went to mow her mom's yard."

The image of the Jess she had been hearing so much about recently and the woman going to help her mom seemed like a complete contradiction. "Does she really carry a gun all the time?" Erin blurted.

Ashley stared at her and for a moment Erin thought she was going to get up. Finally, she gave a long sigh. "I've been trying to avoid talking about Jess, but if we're going to keep . . . seeing each other, I guess you have a right to know what to expect."

A cloud rolled in front of the sun, causing a chill to rush over Erin. "We don't have to talk about her," she said quickly. "I don't want to ruin your day. Let's talk about something else."

Ashley placed a hand on Erin's arm. "Are you scared of Jess?"

"No!" Erin squeaked defensively.

A tiny smile touched Ashley's lips. "It's all right if you are. You should be. Jess is . . ." She stopped and shook her head slightly. "I don't know how to explain her. She can be as gentle as a kitten. She's thirteen years older than me. When we met six years ago, she had already retired from the Army and was just starting out at the police academy. She'd been an MP in the military and she seemed so capable. I felt as though she could protect me from anything. She did well at the academy. We didn't move in together until after she had graduated and was on the force." She picked up a twig and slowly broke it into several small pieces. "She works out of the north substation. When she first started she loved patrol but like most cops, I guess, she dreamed of working homicide, but for some reason she gave up trying." She stopped long enough to take a drink of her Champagne. "Are you sure you want to hear this?" she asked.

Erin nodded and Ashley continued.

"For as long as I've known her, Jess has been a heavy drinker but she used to control it better. She started going out for happy hour after work. It got to the point where she would be out three or four times a week. When I started complaining she became angry. One night, she came home drunker than usual and she reeked of perfume." She glanced at Erin. "I know I should have left, but she promised to never do it again."

"You mean she cheated on you?"

Ashley lowered her head. "That was part of it." She took a deep breath. "We got into a horrible argument. She hit me with a kitchen chair and cracked two ribs."

Erin was so stunned she couldn't speak. She suddenly felt very stupid and naïve. That was what Mary had been trying to warn her about. She had heard plenty about domestic abuse and read that it occurred in lesbian relationships, but never in her wildest nightmares did it occur to her that she would actually know someone who suffered from it. A thousand thoughts ran through her mind. The prevailing one was why someone as smart and capable as Ashley would remain in such a relationship. A sick feeling developed in the pit of her stomach. There was obviously only one reason. "Do you still love her?"

Ashley gazed at her for a long moment. "Yes and no. I love the memory of the woman I fell in love with but I finally had to admit that she no longer exists."

"So why don't you leave her?"

Ashley picked up another stick. "You make it sound so simple."

From Erin's point of view it was simple, but she couldn't help wondering if she'd be as brave if it was her ass Jess was kicking.

"Erin, I know you think I'm pathetic, but the truth is, I'm afraid of her. I honestly don't know what she would do if I told her I was leaving."

"Does she hit you often?"

"No. Just that one time, but sometimes she follows me."

Erin's heart skipped a beat and she glanced around anxiously.

"Sometimes, when she's drinking, she'll sit on the bed with the gun. She has never directly threatened me with it. It's just the way she holds it and watches me."

"Ashley you have to get out of there."

"And go where? Jess is a cop. Where could I go? Do you really think I could hide from her for very long?"

"She has no jurisdiction outside of San Antonio," Erin argued. "Can't you just report her? File harassment charges or something? A restraining order," she added excitedly. "Even cops can't get away with violating a restraining order."

"Restraining orders aren't worth the paper they're written on. If I could prove she's a batterer then she would lose her job, but I don't see how getting her kicked off the force would help matters. Even if they sent her to jail, which they won't, because cops stick together, the sentence wouldn't amount to anything."

"Yeah, I guess that would just piss her off more." They sat in silence for a long moment. "So, what are you going to do?"

"I don't know. Until recently, my fear of what she would do if I tried to leave was greater than my desire to leave, but now . . ." She let the sentence trail off and reached for Erin's hand. "I came to see you today because I wanted to explain that I can't see you again."

Erin felt certain that Ashley was still upset about the picnic. She opened her mouth to protest, but Ashley stopped her.

"Please listen to me and try to understand. I care too much for you to risk putting you in the way of Jess. This is something that I have to do alone. I can't let you be pulled into this. I have to try and figure out what my real feelings for Jess are. I think I know, but I have to try one last time."

"What if she doesn't or can't change?"

Ashley glanced away. "Then I'll have to find a way to leave her."

"What if she won't let you walk away?" A cold fear settled in Erin's chest. Ashley was leaving her. "Let me help you," she pleaded.

"You can't. Don't you see? I have to do this on my own. If Jess won't change, then I have to be strong enough to leave her on my own."

"That's ridiculous," Erin snapped. "What about your family or those domestic abuse centers? Aren't they there to help women in situations like this? If you won't let me help, can't you go to one of the shelters?"

"Please don't yell at me," Ashley said quietly.

Erin forced herself to take a deep breath and tried to hide her anger. Ashley certainly didn't seem to have any trouble telling her to be quiet, so why couldn't she tell Jess to take a hike?

"We should go. It's getting late."

Erin glanced at her watch. "It's only a little after two. You said you didn't have to be back until five."

"What good does it do to drag this out? It'll only make it harder."

"Don't leave yet, please." Hearing the desperation in her own voice, Erin forced herself to calm down. "Stay for a while. We don't have to talk about Jess anymore. Just sit with me."

Ashley put her shoes back on, picked up the backpack and stood. "I can't."

"Why not?"

Ashley stared down at her. "If I don't go now, I might never leave."

Before Erin could respond, Ashley raced on into the trees. Erin thought about following her, but what point was there in doing so? Ashley was going home to Jess.

CHAPTER NINE

Erin continued to sit in the glade until the rapidly sinking sun lost its warmth. Not wanting to leave, she pulled the blanket that Ashley had left behind around her. It still held the faint scent of Ashley's perfume. She buried her nose into the warm softness and breathed in the scent. Would she ever see Ashley again? Could Ashley find the courage to leave Jess and if so, what would Jess's reaction be?

She suddenly remembered that the park would close at sunset. If she didn't hurry, they would lock the entrance gate and she wouldn't be able to leave. After putting her shoes back on, she dumped out the Champagne before gathering all the food, including the cheese that Ashley had thrown into the woods. She carefully bundled the glasses, empty bottle and food into the protective folds of the blanket. As she started back down the hill, she couldn't help thinking that the items in the blanket had cost more than her monthly rent and Ashley had just walked off and left them. When

Erin came out onto the trail she began to jog. It felt good to be moving. When she reached the parking lot, her truck was the only remaining vehicle. For a moment she feared she was too late, but as she grew nearer she could see the gate was still open. After getting into her truck, she placed the blanket full of food on the passenger's seat. Maybe she could use it as an excuse to see Ashley one more time. As she drove out of the parking lot, she thought about going to see Mary and Alice. Maybe they could help. She quickly rejected the idea, since they had already warned her to stay away from Ashley and Jess.

As she flipped her turn signal on to merge into the heavy traffic of IH-10, she remembered it was Saturday night. Everyone was headed into the city for a night of fun and all she had to look forward to was an empty apartment. She was debating whether she felt like going to a movie when a reflection ripped across her rearview mirror. Her heart climbed into her throat when she saw the police cruiser behind her with its lights flashing. She glanced down at the speedometer. She had only been going sixty-two and the speed limit was seventy. Why was she being pulled over? Suddenly she recalled Ashley saying that Jess would sometimes follow her. Had she followed her today? Was that Jess in the car? Her pulse raced as she tried to remember if she was within the San Antonio city limits. She couldn't recall.

Afraid that Jess had somehow found her, she considered waiting until she reached a business before she stopped, but the nearest store was still several miles down the road. There was nothing to do but pull over. As she eased the truck onto the shoulder of the road, she tried to remember if a car had followed her onto the interstate. After putting the truck in park and killing the engine, she pulled her wallet out of her pocket and waited. She knew from watching cop shows on television that the officer would run her license plates before approaching the car. As the seconds stretched into a minute, she told herself to stay calm. There could be a dozen reasons why she was being pulled over. The car's bright lights prevented her from determining whether the marked car belonged to a city cop or a state trooper.

When the door to the police cruiser finally opened and the officer stepped out, Erin almost peed her pants. Even with the blinding lights she could tell that the cop was a woman and she was tall. She fought the ball of fear that was pushing up from her stomach and wished she had possessed enough foresight to ask Mary what the hell Jess Lawler looked like. In the side mirror, she watched her approach the truck with her hand hovering near her weapon. Erin was on the verge of hyperventilating and nearly jumped out of her skin when the officer rapped on the window.

Erin fumbled with the buttons to roll the window down, but it wouldn't work. She finally gave up and opened the door.

"Stay in the vehicle," the policewoman ordered.

Erin quickly slammed the door. After a long second she realized the woman was standing beside the truck waiting for her to open the window. She hit the window button again before realizing that she had turned the engine off. With a deep breath and a warning to herself to calm down, she turned the key enough for the windows to operate and lowered it.

"I'll need to see your driver's license and insurance card," the woman demanded.

Erin opened her wallet to remove her license but it was stuck. As she fumbled with it the policewoman stepped closer to the door. "Are you okay?" she asked as she sniffed. "Is that alcohol I smell?"

"No. I mean yes that's what you smell, but I've not been drinking. I don't drink," she added as she continued to struggle with the stubborn license. "Well, maybe a beer now and then, but nothing today." She glanced at the officer. "I swear it. I opened a bottle of Champagne and it spewed all over me."

The officer removed something from her pocket as Erin continued to struggle with removing her license from her wallet.

"Would you mind looking up?"

Erin glanced up.

"I'm going to shine a small light into your eyes. I want you to let your eyes follow the light, without moving your head. Do you understand?"

Erin nodded. "Sorry, I didn't mean to move." She cringed when she realized she was nodding. She stopped and took a deep breath. "Yes," she replied, remaining as still as she could.

"Just relax and follow the light."

Erin tried not to blink when the light hit her eyes. As the officer slowly moved the penlight horizontally across her eyes, Erin let her eyes track the light's path.

"Thank you." The officer flipped the light off.

Erin went back to trying to remove her license, but the light in her eyes had only made matters worse.

"Are you having a problem?" The cop nodded toward the wallet.

"Yeah. It's stuck." *I'm just scared shitless*, she added to herself as the stubborn card finally came out. After locating her insurance card, she handed both items out the window without turning her head. She sat terrified as she tried to summon up enough courage to look at the officer's nametag.

"I stopped you because your left taillight isn't working."

Erin looked at her in disbelief. "Taillight?"

"Yes, ma'am. It's probably just a blown bulb, but you need to get it fixed."

Erin's eyes finally strayed to the nametag. "O'Conner," she blurted. "Your name is O'Conner." For the first time she noticed the large patch on the woman's sleeve identifying her as a county sheriff. She couldn't stop a small giddy giggle.

The officer frowned and nodded. "That's right."

Erin practically floated out of the truck on a cloud of relief. She tried to control her voice. "I'm sorry I'm acting so weird. It's just that . . ." She hesitated. She couldn't tell this woman that she thought she was the crazy cop partner of her lover. Hell, it didn't even make sense. "I've never been stopped before," she said truthfully. "I guess it sort of shook me up."

O'Conner smiled. "I see. Well, I suppose it can be a little intimidating the first time." She handed the insurance card and license back to Erin. "I'm not going to give you a ticket this time, but you'd better get that light fixed tonight. It would be a shame for you to get stopped twice in one night. You have a good evening." She smiled and was gone before Erin could respond.

When Erin was finally able to pull back onto the road she realized her shirt was drenched in sweat. She left the window down to allow the cool evening breeze in. Suddenly she understood how condescending her attitude toward Ashley had been. The sheer possibility of running into Jess Lawler had scared Erin half to death. She could only imagine how much worse it must be for Ashley.

It was several miles before she was able to make her legs stop shaking. When she finally saw a Wal-Mart sign glowing against the night sky, she pulled in and, with the help of a mechanic, managed to get the bulb replaced. As she was leaving Wal-Mart, she realized she was starving. After one last stop at her favorite fried-chicken place, she headed home with a bag of serious comfort food.

CHAPTER TEN

By the time Erin reached her apartment, she was aching with emotional exhaustion. As she climbed the stairs to the second floor, her stomach emitted a loud growl as the fragrant aroma of fried chicken filled the stairwell. The food from the picnic that she had wrapped in the blanket was tucked under her arm. As she thought about Ashley, a tiny trickle of doubt began to worm its way into her thoughts. Something about Ashley's sudden bouts of anger didn't seem quite right. What if Jess wasn't the problem? What if she was an excuse Ashley used to break off her affairs whenever she grew tired of them? She tried to remember exactly what it was that Mary had said about Jess. Something about her drinking a lot and liking to fight. *A much younger Jess*, she reminded herself. Maybe Jess was a little crazy, as Mary said, but that didn't mean she abused Ashley. Had Ashley had other affairs? What if this was something Jess knew about and they were at home right this minute having a good laugh at her expense and fucking their brains out? Suddenly furious, she yanked the stairwell door open. They were playing her for a sucker. She remembered that she had Jess's home address in her wallet. Would Jess be home now? Didn't Ashley tell her that Jess usually went out with friends on Saturday night also? As she came around the corner she found one of her new neighbors in the hallway struggling with a large box.

"Do you need some help with that?" she asked impulsively. She regretted the offer as soon as it was out of her mouth. She didn't feel up to dealing with small talk now.

"Yes, please," the woman squeaked, straining under the weight of the box.

Erin set her things down in the hallway and grabbed one side of the box. It was heavier than it looked, but together they finally managed to get it inside.

"Over there." The woman nodded toward the far wall. As soon as they set the box down the woman begin to rub her arms. "Thank you. I overpacked the box. I don't think I would have made it inside if you hadn't come along." She held out her hand. "I'm Diana Garza."

Erin shook her hand and introduced herself as she glanced around the apartment. Its layout was a mirror image of her place.

"I'm sorry about all the noise this morning," Diana said. "I never realized there was such an art to packing. Apparently cramming as much as possible into a box isn't the correct way."

"I take it you haven't moved many times." Erin covertly studied her new neighbor, who appeared to be around her age. She was a little shorter, with short glossy black hair and dark eyes. Erin's gaydar was blipping loudly.

Diana shook her head. "No. My moving experience has been limited to dragging my stuff to a college dorm and from the dorm to . . ." She faltered.

Erin's stomach growled a reminder that her dinner was sitting in the hallway. "Do you need help with anything else?"

"No, thanks. That was the last of it. All I need to do now is put it away, and there'll be plenty of time for that."

"Welcome to the building. I'm across the hall if you need anything." Erin started to leave but stopped. She wasn't looking forward to spending a long evening alone. "Have you eaten yet?"

Diana rubbed her lower back. "I've been so busy I haven't even thought about food."

"I'm about to have some fried chicken if you'd like to join me." Erin wondered where the other woman she had seen that morning was.

"Thank you, but I couldn't. I've bothered you enough already."

"It's no bother. You'd actually be doing me a favor. I wasn't looking forward to eating alone."

They stood in silence for a long moment. "That's one of the hardest times, isn't it? Sitting down at the dinner table alone, I mean," Diana said.

"It sounds like it's still a new experience for you," Erin said.

"I should be getting used to it." Diana glanced at her. "Shelly and I split up over three months ago. I've been staying with my sister, Rosa. I kept thinking that if I didn't make that final break of getting my own place, that maybe Shelly would change her mind." She took a deep breath and slowly released it. "I've finally accepted the fact that it's time for me to move on."

Erin thought about Ashley and knew she should be following Diana's example, but she wasn't ready to move on. She didn't know yet exactly how she was going to do so, but she intended to try and keep seeing Ashley. If anyone was moving on, as far as Erin was concerned, it would be Jess. "Come on over," she urged. "I'll make a salad to go with the chicken. I may even have a couple of beers we can cry over later."

"I don't want to be any trouble."

"It's no trouble. The salad is in a bag. All I have to do is open it and dump it in a bowl."

Diana laughed. "I'd like that. If you're sure you don't mind."

"It'll be fun."

"All right. Give me time to change and I'll be over."

After retrieving the things from the hallway, Erin rushed to her apartment to check for messages. Maybe Ashley had already changed her mind. In her haste to open the door, she kept dropping her keys and then tried to use the key to her parents' house that she had never removed from the keyring. When she finally stepped into the apartment, she gave a small leap of joy when she saw the blinking red light glowing in the darkness. She didn't take time to turn on a light as she rushed over to the machine and punched the play button. The metallic voice informed her that she had one unheard message. She held her breath as the machine prepared to play the message. Her elation slowly vanished as she listened to the prerecorded voice of a sales promotion promising her that she may have won either a trip to Disney World or a new Chevy Tahoe. She set the bag of food on the counter and slowly hit the erase button.

"Not the call you wanted, huh?"

Embarrassed, Erin cleared her throat. She hadn't heard Diana enter the room. "Come on in." She flipped on the kitchen light. "Make yourself comfortable while I wash up a bit. Grab yourself something to drink from the refrigerator if you'd like." Without waiting for a response, she rushed into the bedroom. She felt like a complete idiot. Ashley had told her it was over, so why couldn't she accept it and move on with her life? It wasn't as though she and Ashley had been long-term lovers and she was used to having Ashley beside her each day. So why was she so danged lonesome all the time now? She should be used to eating alone, going to bed alone and waking up by herself. Why did her life suddenly feel so empty?

She heard Diana moving around in the kitchen and regretted having invited her over. Her appetite had vanished. All she wanted to do now was climb into bed, pull the covers over her head and stay there until all memories of Ashley Wade were gone. She made up her mind to feed Diana as quickly as was politely possible, then develop a sudden headache and bring the evening to a close. With a plan in mind, she splashed her face with cold water and tried to ignore all thoughts of Ashley.

61

When Erin returned to the kitchen she found the table already set and a large bowl of salad on the counter. Her new neighbor was in the process of opening a bottle of wine.

Diana looked up. "I made myself at home. I hope you don't mind." She easily maneuvered the complicated-looking gadget she was using on the wine bottle. "No matter how angry I get at her, this is the one thing I'll always be grateful to Shelly for." She held up the bottle. "She turned me on to fine wines." She gave a small mocking smile. "That's why I felt justified in taking half of our collection from the wine cellar when I left. I hope you don't mind my bringing it over."

"No, but I'm not much of wine drinker. Besides, a bottle of Ripple is about all my budget can handle," Erin said. Embarrassed by her candid admission, she quickly picked up the blanket that held the picnic foods and carried it to the pantry. She remembered the Gorgonzola and took it out. "I didn't know anyone had wine cellars in Texas," she said as she put the cheese in the refrigerator.

Diana shook her head. "I'm from here originally, but I met Shelly while we were attending UT Austin. She thought she wanted to be a pharmacist. I later discovered she just wanted to get away from her girlfriend. Her family owns a vineyard in Healdsburg, California." She crinkled her nose. "Their wine wasn't that great, but they certainly knew what wine was supposed to taste like. Shelly and I moved back there after I graduated. She decided she was bored with college and wanted to move back home. Luckily, I can teach anywhere." She glanced at Erin. "I teach second grade at Thousand Oaks Elementary. Anyway, we moved to Healdsburg and lived in the house that Shelly's great-grandfather built. The house had a wine cellar. Winemaking is little more than an expensive hobby for them now. Her father is a stock analyst and according to him, he doubled the family fortune. Now he hires people to do all the work at the vineyard." She stopped suddenly. "Sorry, I tend to ramble sometimes. It drove Shelly nuts when I did that."

"It doesn't bother me. If you don't mind my asking, how long were you two together?"

"Almost eight years."

Erin tried to hide her surprise. "That's a long time. What happened?"

Diana poured wine into two jelly glasses she had taken from the cabinet. "I guess we just moved off in different directions." She paused. "That's not true. Shelly moved on. She started working as a pharmaceutical sales rep and became involved with a doctor"—her voice became mocking—"who was more financially capable of providing her with the lifestyle to which she was accustomed." Diana shot her an apologetic smile. "Okay, so I may still be a little bitter. Here, try this." She handed her a glass of wine.

"I see you found my fancy glassware." She sipped the wine and forced herself not to grimace.

Diana began to laugh. "Okay, now I know why your refrigerator is stocked with water and juice."

"I've never had much of a taste for alcohol," Erin admitted. "An occasional beer is about all I can handle."

"Don't drink it if you don't like it." A timer dinged. "Oh, that's the chicken. I popped it in the oven to warm it up a little."

"I'm glad you decided to come over tonight," Erin said, surprising herself.

Diana nodded. "Me too." She held up her glass in a toast. "Here's to new beginnings."

CHAPTER ELEVEN

The following week proved to be one disaster after another for Erin. It started on Monday when she approached her manager, Sonia, to request more overtime hours and was told that upper management had released a memo instructing all departments to stop all overtime immediately. Not only would Erin not be able to afford a cell phone, but now she was going to have to cut back somewhere in order to pay her credit card bill. *It's not like I really need a cell phone*, she reasoned, since Ashley was no longer trying to call her. Each day at break and lunch, Erin called home to check messages, and every afternoon she raced home praying that this would be the evening that Ashley would call. She turned down a dinner invitation from Diana on Tuesday night and spent the evening staring at the silent phone. She lost count of the number of times she picked up the receiver to check for a dial tone. Ashley never called.

Her frustration finally boiled over on Thursday afternoon

when she and Mary walked out together and discovered that someone had backed into the front of Erin's truck and busted the
driver's side headlight and reflector. The impact had smashed one
side of the chrome trim around the headlight. The damage was so
extensive that the trim needed to be replaced. The 1984 Ford F-
150 Ranger was one of two material possessions that Erin prized.
Her grandfather had left her the truck when he died six years ago.
She had been with him on the day he had purchased it. She had
been six at the time, but she could still vividly remember sitting
beside her grandfather in the cab of the shiny new truck and feeling as if she owned the world. Despite her constant lack of funds,
she'd strived to keep the truck in top working condition, but now
that it had over 162,000 miles, the signs of age were increasing
much more rapidly. She knew that maintenance costs would eventually force her to retire the old truck. It wasn't a moment she
looked forward to.

Mary leaned over to examine the damage. "You won't be able to
drive after dark and you'll have to use hand signals for left-hand
turns." She straightened up. "Do you know your hand signals?"

"Yeah, I remember them."

"It'll only be for a couple of days. If you like I can help you fix it
Saturday morning," Mary offered. "We can drive out to the Pick
and Pull junkyard and find replacement parts." She patted the
chrome trim. "This shouldn't cost over ten bucks. The reflector
might be a little bit more. You can get the bulbs at Wal-Mart. I
might even have a signal light around the house. I used to have an
old Chevy truck."

Erin kicked a small rock in frustration. She knew all about
buying bulbs at Wal-Mart, and the last thing she needed now was
more debt. "Asshole didn't even leave a note."

Mary shrugged. "Maybe whoever hit you didn't have insurance
and was scared."

"Or maybe they were a friggin' asshole," Erin shouted.

"Whoa," Mary said, holding up her hand. "Take it easy. We can
fix this."

Erin scrubbed her hands over her face. "Sorry. I'm just so sick and tired of never being able to get ahead."

"We could loan you a few bucks, if it'd help."

"Naw, but thanks anyway. I can charge it. I'm just in a pissy mood."

"You haven't been your usual cheerful self all week," Mary said. "It might help to talk about it. You still seeing Ashley Wade?"

Erin shook her head. Mary had been trying to get her to talk about Ashley all week, but she hadn't been able to do so. "You don't have to worry about that anymore. She broke it off." She struggled to keep the frustration out of her voice.

Mary nodded as she watched her. "I know it don't seem like it now, but someday the right woman will come along."

Erin shrugged. "I need to get home. I'll see you in the morning."

Mary slapped her lightly on the shoulder. "Try to get some sleep."

"Yeah, I will. Tell Alice I said hi." Erin got into her truck and drove home.

When Erin pulled into the apartment complex's parking lot, Diana was getting out of her cherry red Jeep Wrangler. Erin parked next to her.

"Isn't it a beautiful day?" Diana asked when Erin stepped out of the truck.

"I guess spring is here to stay," Erin agreed, too tired to enjoy the warmth.

Diana came around the front of her car and stopped short. "What happened to your fender?"

"Someone hit me at work."

"That sucks. Do you have a high insurance deductible?"

"Yeah, it's the only way I can afford the premiums."

"I know a guy who does mechanical work on the side and he's reasonable," Diana said. "He might be able to repair the damage."

"Thanks. I can do it myself. It won't be hard to fix."

"Wow, I'm impressed, a woman who can repair her own car."

A blush stung Erin's face at the unexpected compliment.

"Look at how red you're turning," Diana teased. Erin's face grew warmer, and Diana changed the subject. "Thank God tomorrow is Friday. I am so looking forward to the weekend."

As they made their way into the building and up the stairs, Erin realized with a start that not only was she not looking forward to the weekend, she was actually dreading the long lonely hours. The damage to the truck was actually a mixed blessing. Going to the junkyard to hunt the parts and then the time it would take to repair the truck would burn up most of Saturday morning. At the same time, she couldn't help but worry that if Ashley did change her mind and call, she wouldn't be home.

When they reached their floor, Diana stopped. "Hey, I owe you a dinner," she said. "I put a roast in the Crockpot before I left this morning. It's too big for just me. Why don't you come over for dinner?" When Erin hesitated, she rushed on. "You'd be doing me a favor. I hate to eat leftovers."

Erin opened her mouth to decline but changed her mind at the last moment. The thought of another evening of waiting for the phone to ring was too much.

"Great," Diana said with a bright smile. "Give me about a half an hour and come on over." She waved and disappeared into her apartment.

Erin took her time in unlocking the door. Part of her was absolutely certain that today was the day that Ashley would call, while the rest of her was sure that she would never hear from Ashley again. After unlocking the door, she stepped inside and forced herself not to look toward the answering machine. Instead she walked into her bedroom and changed into her favorite khaki shorts and a royal blue polo shirt. She placed her dirty clothes in the hamper and took her time with brushing her teeth and hair. Only then did she allow herself to check the machine. Tears stung her eyes when she saw there were no messages. She couldn't stop herself from checking the call log. Maybe Ashley had called without leaving a message, but again nothing. She lifted the receiver and listened for a dial tone. The phone was working fine. A mental image of how pathetic she must look made her cringe. In disgust, she turned the answering machine and call log off. "To hell with Ashley Wade," she muttered. "I'm tired of waiting for her to call. I was doing fine before she showed up and I'll do just fine without her." Feeling stronger after her resolution, she turned to the computer to check her e-mail. By the time she had finished replying to the e-mails from her brother Tom and a couple of people she'd met online, it was time to go to Diana's for dinner.

CHAPTER TWELVE

The neat cozy apartment that Erin stepped into was much different from the cluttered one she'd seen five days ago. The boxes were nowhere in sight. In their place was a room that looked like one of those fancy showrooms that Erin had seen in furniture stores.

With something akin to envy she studied the mahogany oval coffee and end tables with their gently curved legs. Her father had instilled in her a love of fine wood furniture. It was one of the few things they shared. Although he had been a plumber by trade, his free time was spent refurbishing furniture. He would arrive home with an old chair or some other piece of wooden furniture that looked as though it had been sitting in someone's backyard and spend hours tediously restoring the piece to its original condition. Erin was ten the first time he allowed her to help. The piece was a small dresser with a tilt mirror. It now sat in her bedroom.

She followed Diana to a cream-colored sofa that graced the

opposite wall. There were matching striped cream and light terra-cotta armchairs sitting slightly to the side at either end of the sofa. Soft gauzy window drapes floated down from ornate brass rods. A tall mahogany entertainment center filled a large portion of the wall opposite the sofa. The soft illumination from a couple of floor lamps made the wood glow with warmth. Erin's feet sank into the luxurious softness of an area rug. Its cranberry background and floral pattern reminded her of Persian rugs she had once seen in a book.

"This sure looks different with the boxes out of here," she replied as they sat down. Afraid to sit on the delicate-looking furniture, Erin perched on the edge of the sofa. Despite the size of the entertainment center, the room conveyed a decidedly feminine atmosphere.

"Relax, it won't break," Diana said as if reading Erin's thoughts. "Would you like something to drink? I know you prefer juice over wine, so I have apple, cranberry and orange. I also got some beer since you mentioned you occasionally enjoy a beer."

Erin eased herself back onto the sofa, flattered that Diana had remembered what she liked to drink. "A beer would be good," she agreed. She didn't really want it, but maybe it would help her relax.

"Do you prefer a glass or the bottle?" Diana called from the kitchen.

She almost said bottle but asked for a glass. Like her own apartment the living room opened onto the kitchen. As she watched Diana move about the kitchen pouring their drinks, Erin wondered why she had asked for a glass. She always drank her beer from the bottle. Diana returned before she could come up with an answer. "I never realized furniture could make so much difference to a room," Erin said as Diana handed her a glass of beer. "We have the same layout, but your place makes mine look like a dump."

"There's nothing wrong with your apartment," Diana assured her before sitting at the opposite end of the sofa and sipping her red wine.

Erin shrugged. "It's okay, but I could never make a room look like this."

"My father works for Perrini's and my mother is an interior decorator," Diana said. "I guess it's sort of in my blood. I grew up playing with fabric swatches."

Erin knew of Perrini's. It was a high-end, fine furniture store that had been in San Antonio for almost as long as the city had been in existence.

"My mom says a home's décor should reflect the character and personality of its owner."

Erin chuckled. "I'm not sure that's a good thing in my case. Almost all of my furniture is either hand-me-downs or flea-market finds."

"Do you like it?"

The question caught her off guard. Erin sipped her beer to give herself a little extra time to answer. "It was okay when I bought it, but I don't want to live like that forever. I mean, I'm twenty-eight—shouldn't I be doing better?"

"I think the answer would depend on what you want out of life. Where do you want to be ten years from now?"

"Whew! You're starting to sound like a teacher." Erin had meant the comment as a joke but the sudden blush on Diana's cheeks told her she had been misunderstood. Before she could clarify what she meant, a timer dinged in the kitchen.

"The bread is ready. Let's eat," Diana said as she walked into the kitchen.

Erin followed her. Pale green linen napkins and placemats graced a small round wooden dining table set for two. Silverware and white china gleamed in the glow of the kitchen light. "Can I help with anything?" she asked.

"No, thanks. I've got it. Have a seat."

Erin chose the chair that would allow her to watch Diana as she moved about the kitchen, transferring the hot rolls from the pan onto a platter. The table was soon filled with wonderful-smelling dishes. As they ate the deafening quiet pounded against Erin's eardrums.

"I'm sorry if I hurt your feelings," Erin said, unable to endure the silence any longer.

"No. I shouldn't have asked such a personal question. We hardly know each other. I get carried away sometimes."

"I tried to make a joke because I don't know what I want," Erin admitted as she pushed her mashed potatoes into a small mound. When Diana didn't reply, Erin continued. "I'm tired of working in a dead-end job and living paycheck to paycheck, but I don't know anything else I can do."

"Have you thought about going to college?" Diana asked.

Erin gave a harsh laugh. "I can barely afford to pay my rent. I can't afford to go to college."

"There are a lot of programs out there for women now. I'm sure you'd qualify for several of them."

"It's not just money. I didn't do too good in school. I'm not smart enough to go to college."

"Bull crap," Diana replied so harshly that Erin flinched. "You might have to take a few intro courses, but so what? If you really want to go to college, you can."

Erin stared at her, wondering if Diana knew what she was talking about or not. "Do you really think so? I mean, I wasn't joking about my grades. They were pretty low."

Diana put her fork down and gave her full attention to Erin. "What do you want to do?" she asked again.

Erin felt her cheeks redden. "I don't know really. I just know I want to do something more than what I'm doing now. I don't want to spend my life worrying about money."

Diana tapped her finger softly against the edge of her plate. "There's no guarantee you'll get rich simply because you go to college."

"I don't need to be *rich*," Erin stressed. "I just don't want to have to watch every penny." She struggled to find a way to express what she wanted. "Look at what you have. I don't think you're rich, but you have nice stuff. You drive a nice vehicle."

"I'm also in debt," Diana said.

"But you have something to show for your debt," Erin said. "I'm in debt and still don't have anything. My truck is the most valuable thing I own and my grandfather left it to me. It's in pretty good shape, but it has over a hundred thousand miles on it. I want to be able to go out sometimes without having to count every penny or having to work overtime to afford it. Just once I'd like to go into a store and buy a new pair of jeans rather than going to Goodwill or some other thrift shop." She stopped suddenly, mortified by the honesty of her outburst. She could feel Diana watching her.

"I could help you," Diana said at last.

"I don't want to borrow your money," Erin said sharply.

"That's good, because I don't have much anyway. I meant I could help you if you really want to go to college."

"Help me how?"

Diana smiled. "Well, I *am* a teacher. I could help you get ready for the SAT and even help you with your homework sometimes."

A trickle of excitement began to scamper through Erin's body. Could she make it with Diana's help? Before the fantasy could fully develop, a dollar sign raised its ugly head. "What about money?"

"There are a lot of grants you could apply for, and if you go to school at night you could continue working where you are now. Does your employer offer any type of tuition assistance?"

Erin shook her head. "I don't know. I've never checked into it because I didn't think I was smart enough to get in."

"Why don't you check with your benefits office on Monday and see if they do? If they don't offer anything, we can look online to see what's available to you from other areas."

Erin smiled. As she dug into her potatoes she realized her appetite had returned.

CHAPTER THIRTEEN

After dinner Erin and Diana returned to the living room with fresh drinks and again sat at opposite ends of the sofa from each other.

"How are things going with your girlfriend?" Diana asked.

Erin glanced up confused. "Girlfriend?"

"The other night when you invited me over, I got the impression you were pretty devastated when you checked your phone messages. I assumed you were disappointed that someone hadn't called."

"It's sort of complicated," Erin replied as she realized guiltily that she hadn't thought about Ashley since arriving at Diana's apartment. When Diana didn't respond, she continued. "The woman I've been seeing is still . . . what I mean is . . . she's—"

"She's still with someone else," Diana said.

"Yeah. That's what I mean." She snuck a peek at Diana, trying to gauge her reaction. "I guess you think that's pretty low, huh?"

"There are two sides to every story," Diana replied noncommittally.

Without really intending to, Erin found herself telling Diana how she had met Ashley and then about how they had bumped into each other at the bookstore. When Diana didn't judge her, Erin told her about how she and Ashley had started seeing each other on Saturdays and then about Jess. When she was finished Diana blew a soft breath.

"For someone who's so quiet, you sure managed to get yourself into a mess."

"I didn't intend for it to happen," Erin defended.

Diana reached over and patted her hand. "I know you didn't. Life has a way of sneaking up on us sometimes though, doesn't it?" She casually sipped her wine. "Aren't you worried that this Jess woman might come looking for you? She sounds dangerous to me."

"There's no reason for Jess to bother me now. I'm not sure she ever would have. Maybe she's all bark and no bite."

"What are you going to do about Ashley?"

"What can I do?" Erin asked, shaking her head. "She doesn't want to see me again. I don't know how to make her change her mind."

"Do you want her too?"

"Of course I do," Erin said emphatically as she watched a small flicker of something that looked like disappointment flit across Diana's face. For some reason she couldn't quite pinpoint, it bothered her that she might have disappointed Diana.

"You don't have any way to get in contact with her?"

Erin thought about the phone number and address in her wallet that she wasn't supposed to have and shook her head. If she didn't admit to having the information then it would be easier not to use it.

"All you can do is wait for her to call you." Diana shook her head. "That would be hard for me to do."

"I know there's no need for me to continue waiting for her to call. I mean, she told me it was over." She looked at Diana. "So, why can't I just put her out of my mind and go on with my life?"

Diana glanced away before answering. "Maybe it's because you still love her."

The ache in Erin's heart told her that Diana's words rang true, but that still didn't solve the problem of Ashley's wanting to work things out with Jess.

Again Diana reached over and patted her hand. "Don't look so devastated. If Ashley has one ounce of sense she'll leave Jess and call you."

"Why would she do that?"

"Why?" Diana echoed. "Because you're a sexy woman and you're sweet. I can't believe women aren't lined up in the hallway."

Erin rolled her eyes as her face flushed. "Now you're making fun of me."

"I am not. I meant every word I said." She peered at Erin. "Listen, if you're not busy Saturday night, my sister is having a party. I think she's celebrating my moving out." She paused. "Anyway, if you're not busy, why don't you go with me? There will be scads of single women there."

"I don't think so. I don't do very well at big parties."

"Oh, come on. It'll be fun and it won't cost anything. Rosa always throws great parties. She's a fabulous cook."

When she saw the look of hope in Diana's face, she wavered slightly. "I don't know."

"If you're worried about not knowing anyone, I promise I won't leave your side for more than two minutes the entire night. Unless you meet someone and want me to disappear, of course." She winked coyly at Erin.

"I seriously doubt I'll be meeting anyone," Erin said as she gave in.

"Great. It'll be fun. We'll leave here around eight."

"What should I wear?"

"Whatever you want. Rosa has a big back patio so it'll be outside, unless it rains. So make sure you'll be comfortable."

They chattered about the party for several more minutes before Erin noticed Diana glancing toward the clock. She looked at her watch and was shocked to see it was already after ten. After thanking Diana for a wonderful meal, Erin said a quick good-bye and hurried back to her apartment. As soon as she was inside, she rushed to check the answering machine, but no one had called.

The following afternoon Erin signed off the system five minutes early and was out of her chair as soon as the clock announced quitting time. She stopped to say a hasty good-bye to Mary.

"I'll call you in the morning before I leave the house to make sure you're awake," Mary said as she waited for her system to shut down. "It shouldn't take us long to fix your truck if we can find a replacement part."

"Don't worry about calling me. I'll be up."

Mary didn't look convinced. "I'll call anyway." She noticed the folder in Erin's hand. "What's that?"

Erin hesitated. She was sort of embarrassed to tell her. "It's information on the company's tuition plan," she said.

Mary's eyebrows shot up. "Are you thinking about going back to school?"

Erin glanced around before nodding slightly.

"Good for you. I always wished I had gone on to college and made something of myself."

"It's not too late." Erin said with a wave, "Listen, I've got to run. We can talk tomorrow." She took off before Mary could say anything more. Rather than wait for an elevator, she ran down the stairs. She wanted to get home as quickly as possible and shower. It was Friday night. During the past three months, Ashley hadn't failed to call her on Friday night. Despite everything that Ashley had said, Erin prayed that tonight wouldn't be any different.

It was slow getting out of the parking lot, but once she hit the interstate she pushed the speed limit and managed to make it home in nearly record time. Diana's Jeep was nowhere in sight when she pulled in. Erin took the stairs two at a time and ran down the hallway to her apartment. The light on the machine wasn't blinking, but she hadn't expected it to be. Ashley never called until after seven. Stripping off clothes as she went, Erin made her way to the shower. Afterwards, she carefully selected her best khaki shorts and a black polo shirt. By a quarter to seven, she was ready and nervously pacing the floor. She picked up her strewn clothes and put them away before resuming her pacing. By seven fifteen, she was getting dizzy from the continuous circle she kept tracing from her bedroom to the kitchen. With each circuit she would check the bedroom clock and then the clock on the kitchen stove. Seconds dragged out to minutes and minutes became hours. She started feeling nauseous and made herself sit down on the couch, but she couldn't sit still and was soon up and moving again. After several more laps, she stopped by the window and gazed out at the parking lot. It was after eight. Why didn't Ashley call? Surely she hadn't actually gone back to Jess. How long did it take to break up with someone anyway? Erin had never been in a relationship long enough to do more than date someone a few times. She'd never actually broken up with anyone. As she stood staring down at the parking lot, Diana's Jeep pulled in. She smiled as she remembered the previous evening. It had been fun. Diana was funny and easy to talk to. Sort of like Ashley had been. Diana got out of the Jeep. Rather than coming inside, she leaned against the Jeep as though she was waiting for someone. For a brief instant Erin wondered if Diana had failed to see Erin's truck and was waiting for her. The warm glow that accompanied the thought surprised her. Before she could analyze it, another car pulled in and Diana began to wave. Erin watched as a blond woman got out of the car. She frowned when Diana slipped her arm through the woman's and they headed toward the building. Erin stepped back quickly; she didn't want Diana to look up and catch her watching. A few moments later, soft laughter echoed down the hallway. When Erin went to her own door she could barely hear the clinking of keys and the click of the lock as it opened. There was another brief flurry of laughter and then the sound of the door closing. Erin's frown deepened when she heard the deadbolt being slammed into place. She was absolutely certain that Diana had not used the dead-bolt last night when Erin had arrived, but she had heard it when she left for the evening. Apparently, Diana was in for the night.

Erin continued to stand by the door for several moments wondering who the blonde was. Had Shelly, Diana's ex, finally come to her senses? As Erin chased one thought after another, the one that kept returning was why was she so concerned about who was spending the night at Diana's apartment.

Tired of pacing, Erin stretched out on the couch and tried to read the tuition information Sonia had gotten for her. Most of it didn't make sense to her. She decided to show it to Diana tomorrow afternoon. Maybe she would be able to understand it. Erin found the remote, switched on the television and settled down to wait for Ashley's call. Hour after hour slipped away and the phone never rang. Every so often, Erin would find herself at the window staring down into the well-lit parking lot. The dark car the blonde had arrived in was still parked by Diana's Jeep. At three a.m. Erin finally accepted that Ashley wasn't going to call and stumbled to bed. As she drifted off to sleep, she was certain she heard the sound of laughter coming from the apartment across the hallway.

CHAPTER FOURTEEN

On some level, Erin knew she was dreaming because of the speed she was able to achieve. She was in a large room filled with what looked like hundreds of desks. On each desk sat a single phone. One of the phones was ringing and she knew if she could only find which phone it was, Ashley would be on the other end. She would listen, trying to pinpoint which phone was ringing. Once she had chosen a phone, she would zip over to it at an astounding speed only to discover that when she picked up the receiver the ringing moved to another part of the room. At some point in the dream she realized that it wasn't a dream, but her own phone ringing. She fumbled for the phone knowing it was Mary calling. They were supposed to go to the junkyard to find the part for her truck this morning and then fix her damaged headlight.

At the sound of Ashley's voice, Erin came fully awake.

"I woke you," Ashley stated.

"That's okay," Erin assured her as she tried to slow her pounding heart.

"I know I shouldn't be calling, but I've missed you so."

"I've missed you too."

"Erin, do you understand how dangerous it is for us to keep seeing each other?" She rushed on without giving Erin time to answer. "Why don't you tell me to go away and leave you alone? You're so much stronger than I am. You could do it."

Erin realized that Ashley was crying. "What's wrong?"

"What's wrong?" Ashley's voice rose. "What's wrong?" she repeated loudly.

"Ashley, don't talk so loud. You'll wake her."

Ashley gave a harsh laugh. "Do you see what I mean? We can't even talk to each other without being scared that she'll hear us."

"I'm not scared of her," Erin snapped. "I'm worried about you."

"Well, aren't you the little diplomat this morning?"

Frustrated, Erin swung her feet off the bed. "Look, if you called to pick a fight with me, I have better things to do." She held her breath, expecting Ashley to slam the phone down in her ear. Instead Ashley began to cry harder. "Please, don't do that," Erin begged. "I'm sorry. Please don't cry."

"I miss you so much." Ashley sniffed. "I've picked the phone up a hundred times this week to call you. I even drove by your apartment Thursday evening while Jess was at her mother's house."

"I wish you would have stopped," Erin said, even as she remembered she wouldn't have been home. She had been at Diana's having dinner.

"Jess went to the coast for the weekend." Ashley's voice was barely more than a whisper.

"When is she coming back?" Erin asked as a small spark of hope began to flare.

"Late Sunday afternoon. Do you have plans for the weekend?"

"No." Erin thought about her truck but quickly blew it off. It would be fine as long as she wasn't driving after dark. She could always fix it next weekend.

"Can I come over?" Ashley asked.

Erin jumped off the bed in her excitement. "Of course you can," she said as she struggled to keep from shouting with joy.

"I thought I'd stay the night, if you don't mind."

Even standing in the shower ten minutes later, Erin still couldn't believe it was true. She and Ashley had an entire weekend together. Silly songs filled her head and she sang them at the top of her lungs. She was getting dressed when Mary called. Mary would no doubt have a conniption fit if she discovered Erin was still seeing Ashley, so Erin quickly decided to take the chickenshit way out and pleaded sickness as an excuse not to repair her truck.

"You sound horrible," Mary said.

The concern in her voice made Erin feel like a heel. "I'm sure it's nothing serious. It's just a headache."

"If you like I could go over to the junkyard, get the part and fix it for you," Mary offered.

Now Erin really felt bad. "Thanks, but it can wait. It'll be fine as long as I don't go out at night."

Mary was quiet for a moment. "Listen, Erin," she began, "if it's money—"

"It's not. I promise."

"All right then. You get back into bed and rest. Call if you get worse or you need anything."

"I'll be fine. I just need to sleep."

After hanging up, Erin stood staring at the phone for a long moment. It seemed as though she'd been telling more and more lies recently. Her guilty thoughts were interrupted by the sound of the doorbell. She ran to the door and threw it open without bothering to check to see who it was. Suddenly Ashley was in her arms, kissing her. Erin barely managed to get the door closed and locked before Ashley pulled her into the bedroom.

The last time they'd made love, Erin had wanted to prolong every moment of the pleasure, but this time they couldn't get to each other fast enough. Before she could fully comprehend what was happening, Erin found herself in bed on her back with Ashley kissing her wildly. Fingers fumbled and tore at buttons. In the frenzy a button popped off and pinged across the floor, hitting the wall. Erin's shirt ended up shoved up around her neck as Ashley sucked first one nipple and then the other. She felt the button on her shorts being released. A moment later, the shorts were around her ankles and Ashley was between her legs.

Erin opened her eyes slowly. The afternoon sun felt hot on her feet. It took her a few seconds to orient herself and remember what had happened. A movement beside her made her smile. Ashley was here. They still had the afternoon, night and most of the following day to spend together. She turned and curled herself around the sleeping form.

"Hey, sleepyhead," she whispered.

Ashley made a soft mewing sound as she stretched. "I can't remember the last time I slept so well," she said as she turned into Erin's arms. "Why do I feel so safe with you?"

"Because you are safe," Erin replied as she stroked Ashley's long chestnut hair.

After several minutes, Ashley raised her face to Erin's and kissed her. As the kiss deepened, Erin pulled Ashley beneath her and this time they made love slowly. Erin discovered she loved making love in the bright afternoon light where she could see every inch of Ashley's beautiful body.

Afterward they snuggled and dozed in each other's arms. When Erin woke, she lay quietly listening to Ashley's slow, easy breathing. There were so many things about this woman that she didn't know. Would there ever be enough time to ask all her questions? One of the things she was dying to know was what had happened between Jess and Ashley during the week? She was afraid to ask, fearing it would ruin their perfect afternoon.

"Are you awake?" Ashley asked, surprising her.

"I thought you were sleeping," Erin said.

"Catnapping," she murmured.

"I could get used to this," Erin said and kissed Ashley's hair.

"I think I could too," Ashley agreed. "What's bothering you?"

Erin started to deny that anything was bothering her, but her curiosity won out. "What happened this week? Did you tell her you wanted out?" The minute the question was out she could tell it had been a mistake by the sudden tension in Ashley's body. "You don't have to tell me if you don't want to," she added quickly. She kept quiet as Ashley slowly relaxed.

"Leaving Jess is more complicated than you think," Ashley started slowly. "If I'm ever going to get away from her, it has to be her idea or at least she has to think it is."

"How can you make her think it's her idea?" Erin asked confused.

"The easiest way would be for her to meet someone else and dump me, but she doesn't seem to have much interest in anything other than an occasional one-night stand. I still don't know what I'm going to do." She reached down and pulled the sheet over them.

Erin tried to imagine what it would be like to be in Ashley's situation. How would she handle it? *I would leave. There's no way I'd put with that.* She suddenly remembered how scared she had been that night when she thought the cop pulling her over was Jess Lawler. Maybe she wouldn't handle it so well either, she realized.

CHAPTER FIFTEEN

"Someone's at the door. Erin, wake up."

The alarm in Ashley's voice brought Erin fully awake. The security lights on the unit across from her lent a soft glow to the bedroom. "What's wrong?" she asked as she sat up.

"It's the doorbell. Someone is ringing it."

Erin flipped on the bedside lamp and grabbed her shorts and shirt off the floor. As she pulled them on, she noticed that Ashley was pale and shaking. She brushed Ashley's hair back. "Hey. It's all right. It's probably just some kid selling something for school." She kissed Ashley's forehead. "I'll be right back." The doorbell rang again as Erin ran into the living room. A small twinge of concern nibbled at her courage. Did Jess come home early and find Ashley gone? She shook off the doubt. Even if Jess had come home early, she wouldn't know where to find Ashley. *Jess doesn't know I even exist*, she reminded herself. Still she took the time to peek through the peephole. When she saw the face on the other side, she muttered a soft curse and opened the door.

Diana took one look at her and stepped back. "I guess you've changed your mind about the party," she said quietly.

As Erin fumbled for something to say, she was sure she saw a flicker of hurt in Diana's eyes. She couldn't very well tell Diana that she had forgotten all about the party or even why she had forgotten. "I'm not feeling very well," she answered lamely.

"All right," Diana replied as she stepped back further. "I'm sorry I disturbed you." She looked Erin in the eye and said, "I guess you should go back to bed." Without waiting for a reply she turned sharply and disappeared down the hallway.

Erin stepped out to call her back, but it was too late. She had already disappeared into the stairwell. After going back into the apartment, Erin slowly closed the door and locked it. She felt bad about hurting Diana's feelings, which she was positive she'd done. As she went back toward the bedroom, she recalled the blonde who had spent the night with Diana. *Why should I feel bad that I'm spending the night with my girlfriend?* she fumed. Diana should understand that this was more important than attending some party with a bunch of people she didn't even know.

"Who was it?" Ashley asked when Erin came into the bedroom.

"It was nothing," Erin replied. "Just my neighbor letting me know she was leaving."

Ashley was watching her closely. "Do your neighbors normally let you know when they go out?" she asked suspiciously.

"Well, no." Erin could hear the defensiveness in her voice. "We sort of watch out for each other's place, and if we're going to be away overnight we try to let each other know." It scared her how easily the lie rolled off her tongue.

Ashley's demeanor changed as she reached over and pulled Erin down to the bed. "Do you spend a lot of nights away from home?" she asked coyly as her fingers began to work their way beneath Erin's shirt.

"Of course not." *I'm always here waiting for you to call,* she added silently.

Ashley kissed her and soon Erin's clothes were back on the floor. As they made love again, Erin couldn't shake the look of hurt in Diana's eyes. *You don't owe her anything*, she kept telling herself as she rolled Ashley over and slipped a hand between those long, beautiful legs.

Erin waited until Ashley was asleep before easing out of bed and pulling her clothes on. After tiptoeing out of the room, she eased the bedroom door closed. She and Ashley had spent the day in bed making love and she was hungry. The clock on the stove indicated it was almost midnight. Before turning on the lights, Erin looked out the window down into the parking lot. Diana's Jeep wasn't in its usual spot. She stood at the window for several seconds, thinking about Diana, before making her way into the kitchen. A quick glance in the refrigerator reminded her that she needed to go grocery shopping soon.

"There you are."

Erin looked over the refrigerator door. Ashley was standing at the bar. Her hair was mussed from sleep and her cheeks held a new glow. "I'm sorry I woke you. I thought I'd make a sandwich or something."

Ashley stepped into the kitchen wearing nothing but a thigh-length T-shirt. "Come over here and sit down." She patted a chair at the small kitchen table. "Let me make you something."

"You don't have to do that," Erin protested. "I can—"

Ashley gave her a quick kiss. "I want to. Please, sit down."

Erin nodded and did as asked. It felt odd to sit in her own kitchen and let someone wait on her.

"Erin," Ashley chided. "Your refrigerator seems a little on the empty side." She peeked over the door and shook her head. "How does scrambled eggs and toast sound?"

"That's fine." Erin pointed out the cabinet where the cookware was. She thought about the food from the picnic, but in truth scrambled chicken eggs sounded a lot better than fish eggs.

"The next time I come over, I'll stop for groceries on the way," Ashley said.

"The next time?" Erin asked, almost afraid she had not heard her correctly.

Ashley dropped butter into a skillet and watched it melt. "We've been so busy"—she gave Erin a wicked smile—"I didn't get a chance to tell you. One of the guys Jess works with bought a small place at Rockport. That's where they've gone fishing this weekend." She cracked four eggs into a bowl and whipped them with a fork. "Anyway, the place needs a lot of work, and Jess, along with a couple other members of their gang, is going to help him. So, she'll be going to Rockport for the next few weekends to work on the place and at least one weekend out of the month after that to fish."

Erin couldn't stop the sappy grin that stretched across her face.

Ashley began to laugh. "Look at that smile."

Erin walked to the stove and took Ashley into her arms. "Thank God for great fishing and crappy construction." She kissed Ashley and held her close. For the first time she had an inkling of what it would be like to have someone in her life permanently and she liked the way it felt.

Ashley pulled away slightly. "I thought you were hungry."

"I am," Erin insisted as her hands pushed beneath Ashley's T-shirt.

"I think you'd better start the toast while I finish the eggs," Ashley suggested.

Erin groaned as she stepped away.

"After all, we have the rest of the night and all day tomorrow and I want to make sure you have plenty of strength." Ashley leaned over and nipped the back of Erin's neck.

Happier than she had been in ages, Erin made the toast and poured them each a glass of juice. Rather than eating at the table, they moved into the living room and sat on the couch. From the gusto with which they both dug into the eggs, it was obvious to Erin that they had both been hungry. It was around twelve thirty when she heard the door to the stairwell close. Diana was home. Without thinking she stepped to the window and looked down into the parking lot.

"What's wrong?" Ashley asked, her eyes wide with concern.

Erin watched her from the window and realized that Ashley's fear of Jess was always hovering just below the surface. "Nothing's wrong. I was just making sure that was Diana coming in."

The look in Ashley's eyes changed from fear to jealousy. "You seem to keep pretty close tabs on this woman. Who is she exactly?"

Erin sat back down on the couch. "I told you who she is. She moved in across the hall. As I said, we sort of keep an eye out for each other."

"Is she a lesbian?"

"I think so."

"You think so?" Ashley pushed.

"Okay, yes, she's a lesbian but I don't see what—"

"Why did you lie to me?" Ashley stood suddenly, causing Erin to draw back.

"I didn't lie," Erin lied.

"Yes, you did. You tried to hide the fact that she's a lesbian. Is she cute? Are you sleeping with her?" Ashley took a step toward her.

"Now hold on," Erin protested as she raised her hand to stop her.

Ashley's screams tore through the room as she dropped to the floor and covered her head, sobbing loudly.

Frightened by the sudden outburst Erin jumped up and tripped over the edge of the coffee table. As she fell back, her feet became entangled in the table's legs and toppled it over, sending their empty plates and glasses tumbling onto the floor. The melee caused Ashley's sobs to double in intensity. Erin scrambled up and almost cried out as a sharp pain shot through her ankle.

"Ashley, it's all right," she said as she tried to reach out to the sobbing woman.

Ashley merely pulled herself into a tighter ball.

A sudden pounding on the door made Erin turn sharply. When her injured right foot hit the floor it failed to hold her weight and she fell against the large, overstuffed chair. The pounding on the door intensified and Erin could hear Diana yelling, asking if she was all right.

"Diana, it's okay. Just give me a minute," she hollered as she tried to reach Ashley. When she put a hand on Ashley's shoulders, the sobbing woman practically crawled under the couch. Diana was still pounding on the door. Unsure of what to do about Ashley, Erin hobbled to the door as quickly as she could and released the lock. Diana nearly knocked her down when she rushed in.

"Are you okay?" Diana demanded as she spun from Erin to take in the rest of the room.

Erin glanced back at the hysterical Ashley and the overturned table.

"What happened?" Diana asked.

"I'm not sure. We were talking one moment and the next minute all hell broke loose."

A sharp rapping on the floor alerted Erin that they had disturbed her downstairs neighbor, Mr. Griswold.

"Oh, Christ," she muttered as she limped toward Ashley. Griswold would call the cops for sure.

"What's wrong with your foot?" Diana asked.

"Never mind that. We've got to get her quiet before old man Griswold calls the cops."

"Ashley," Erin said softly. "Please, you have to stop crying and tell me what's wrong."

"What's wrong with her?" Diana asked as she came around the overturned table.

"I think she thought I was going to hit her," Erin replied miserably. The look of shock on Diana's face caused Erin to rush on. "I wasn't going to," she insisted. "We were talking and I just raised my arm like this"—she demonstrated—"and she freaked out."

Diana nodded slowly. "I think someone else has hit her before."

"They have."

Erin watched as Diana knelt beside Ashley and without touching her began to talk. "Ashley, my name is Diana. You're safe here. No one is going to hurt you. Erin wasn't trying to hurt you. Ashley, can you hear me? Will you sit up please and let us help you back to the couch?"

Ashley's sobbing seemed to lessen.

"Can I help you up?" Diana asked. "Take my hand and let me help you, Ashley." She waited for Ashley to respond. Several seconds ticked slowly by before Ashley began to gradually raise her head. After some gentle coaxing, Diana was able to get Ashley seated on the couch.

Erin slowly released a long breath.

"Erin, come over hear and sit by Ashley while I run back to my apartment."

Careful to test her ankle before putting weight on it, Erin moved around the table and sat beside Ashley. Diana left.

"I'm so sorry." Ashley sobbed as a wave of chills shook her body.

Erin eased an arm around her and pulled her close. "It's okay. I'm sorry I scared you. I didn't know . . . I didn't realize." Tears stung her eyes. "My God, Ashley, I'd never do anything to hurt you," she whispered. "I love you. Don't you know that?"

Ashley began to sob harder just as Diana came back into the apartment.

"What did you do?" Diana demanded in a soothing voice that totally contradicted the stern look she sent Erin's way.

"I was only talking to her," Erin insisted.

"Well, stop it! You just sit there and hold her."

Erin did as she was told.

"Ashley," Diana began, "I have a sleeping pill that I think you should take. It's an over-the-counter product. You need to rest."

Ashley nodded and Diana led her into the bedroom, leaving Erin on the couch feeling rather shell-shocked.

When Diana returned, she motioned to Erin's ankle. "Let me have a look at that."

"I never realized you were a Florence Nightingale reincarnate," Erin said, feeling a little peeved that Diana had reprimanded her earlier.

"In college I worked as a team leader for a teen summer camp. Each year we went on a two-week wilderness trek. Trust me, I

91

learned a lot about First Aid." She examined Erin's ankle. "It's not broken. I think it's only a nasty twist. Take it easy and don't plan on playing in any volleyball tournaments anytime soon."

"How is she?" Erin asked, staring toward the partially closed bedroom door.

"She'll be fine. She's sleeping." Diana righted the coffee table and began to pick up the scattered dishes.

"You don't have to do that," Erin said as she scooted off the couch to help.

"Get back on the couch and rest your ankle while I put these in the dishwasher."

"Are you always so bossy?" Erin asked. "Besides, it's feeling better already."

Diana looked at her thoughtfully for a moment. "Yes, I guess I am." She went into the kitchen and stacked the dishes in the dishwasher.

"You're pretty honest, too."

"Speaking of which, I'm glad to see you're feeling better."

Erin lowered her head. "I'm sorry about that. I didn't mean to lie, but I couldn't very well tell you that . . . that—"

Diana held up her hand. "Please, spare me the details." She looked at her watch as she came back to the couch. "It's almost two. You should try to get some sleep."

Erin shook her head. "I'm not sleepy."

"Yeah, I know what you mean." Diana turned to study Erin's television. "Is that a DVD player?" she asked.

Erin acknowledged that it was.

"I rented that new Harrison Ford movie. Would you like to watch it over here?"

While Diana went to get the movie, Erin hobbled over to the bedroom door to check on Ashley, who was sleeping soundly. This was not the weekend she had envisioned a few hours earlier. As she stood watching her, she realized that Ashley had most likely not told her the truth about Jess. She was no expert on physical abuse but felt certain that one isolated incident wouldn't cause the traumatic reaction Ashley had experienced tonight. That sort of terror came from repeated abuse.

There was a soft knock at the door before Diana entered with a movie and a bag of freshly popped popcorn.

CHAPTER SIXTEEN

Erin's eyes opened slowly. She was on her couch. As she sat up she noticed that she was covered with the quilt her grandmother had given her just before she died. She normally kept it in the closet on the shelf. Why was it over her? Slowly the events of the previous night filtered through her tired brain. She glanced toward the bedroom door that was still partially closed. Ashley must still be sleeping. The last thing Erin remembered was watching the movie with Diana. She must have gone to sleep during the movie, and Diana had covered her with the quilt before leaving. The popcorn bowls had been cleared away. She swung her legs off the couch and tested her ankle. It was a little stiff, as Diana had said it would be, but it no longer hurt to walk on it. After folding the quilt, she tiptoed into the bedroom and returned it to the closet.

"What time is it?" Ashley asked in a voice deep with sleep.

"It's only a little after seven. You should try to sleep some more."

Ashley patted the bed beside her. "Come back to bed."

As Erin slipped beneath the covers she realized that Ashley didn't know she had slept on the couch.

"Why do I feel so groggy?" Ashley murmured.

"It's probably the sleeping pill."

"Sleeping pill?" Ashley sat up slowly. "God, it wasn't just a dream, was it?" Tears began to course down her cheeks. "I'm so sorry you had to see me like that." She started to get out of bed. "I should leave."

Erin placed a tentative hand on Ashley's back. "There's nothing to be embarrassed about. It's all over with now. Come back to bed." She rubbed small circles across Ashley's shoulders. When Ashley continued to sit on the side of the bed, Erin continued, "I love you, Ashley, please don't leave."

"Don't say that," Ashley whispered harshly. "You don't know me. How can you love me?"

"I've asked myself the same question, and I don't know the answer. I only know it's true."

"You wouldn't love me if you really knew me."

Erin didn't know how to respond. She sat up and wrapped her arms around Ashley's waist. "Don't leave. We still have the day and I want to spend it with you."

"Sex is all you ever think about," Ashley snapped.

Erin swallowed the pain of Ashley's words. "We don't have to make love. We can get dressed and go out to breakfast, or go for a walk, whatever you want to do. I simply want to spend time with you."

"Why can't you just leave me alone and stop clinging to me?"

Stung by the harsh words, Erin pulled away, confused. "I'm sorry. I didn't mean to upset you."

Ashley flew off the bed and began to pull her clothes on. "Why are you such a wuss? I must have been crazy. If Jess knew about you, she would rip you apart."

Anger crept up Erin's spine, but the memory of last night's fiasco kept her from showing it. "I'm going to make us some breakfast."

"Don't bother," Ashley said snidely.

Afraid she was going to lose her temper, Erin climbed off the bed and went into the kitchen.

She could hear Ashley slamming things into her overnight bag. To block out the noise, Erin started the dishwasher before turning her attention to wiping down the already clean countertops. A few minute later, Ashley stormed out of the bedroom with her bag. Without a word she left, slamming the door behind her.

In a fit of frustration, Erin hurled the dishcloth across the floor. She absolutely did not need this crap. When she walked over to pick up the dishcloth she saw the tousled bedclothes. Was it her imagination or did the room reek of sex? She grabbed the sheets off the bed, crammed them into the basket with the rest of her dirty laundry and headed down to the laundry room. At such an early hour, no one was using the machines. There were four washers and she sorted her clothes into three of them. While they washed she went back to her apartment and took a long hot shower. By the time she stepped out of the shower she had worked herself into a new bout of anger. This time she was angry at herself for letting Ashley push her into an argument. As she dressed, she tried to tell herself that any rational person would have reacted as she had. Well, maybe they wouldn't have flung a dishrag across the floor, but she felt certain she had a right to be upset by Ashley's accusations. She threw open as many windows as possible to air out the apartment and went back down to put her laundry in the dryer.

By one that afternoon, Erin was in the parking lot of the Pick and Pull junkyard. The young guy who greeted her was dressed in pressed jeans and a white T-shirt that Erin could only stare at. She wanted to ask him how he stayed so clean working there. Instead she pointed to her fender. "I need to find a piece to replace this," she said as she showed him the damage.

"What happened?" he asked.

"Someone hit me while I was at work."

He shook his head as he leaned over to study the fender. "There's no damage to the bumper or grill. It was probably an

SUV that hit you. One of those with the tire mounted on the back door. The tires are on a metal armature that swings out. It was probably the armature that got your headlight." He looked the truck over. "Is this an 'eighty-four model?"

"Yeah."

"There should be at least a few of these out there." He nodded toward the junked cars. "Let me go check."

Erin stood by the truck as he ran inside to check his inventory. A few minutes later, he returned with the exact location of two different wrecks she could pull the part from. "I guess you can take the parts off by yourself." It was a statement rather than a question.

Erin nodded as the guy studied the damage once more.

"You know you're going to have to straighten this dent out before the chrome will fit on there correctly. If you don't, every time it rains water is going to get down in there and cause it to start rusting."

Erin looked at the old truck. "Well, I certainly don't want her to start rusting," she replied, feeling tired.

"No, you don't. It won't be hard to fix. I can let you borrow my tools, if you like."

"What would I have to do?" Erin asked.

"You just drill a little hole here," he pointed to the center of the small dent. "Then you put in a pulling tool and pull on it until the dent pops out. After that you use a hammer to bang it out smooth, put filler in the hole and slap on some paint."

"That's all?" Her attempt at sarcasm appeared to be lost on him.

"Yep, that's all she needs."

"Do you mind if I put the parts on here, just to make sure they fit and everything?"

He shrugged. "You won't be in my way. Let me know when you're done and we'll settle up then."

Before she could say anything else, he headed back into the office.

Erin shook her head as she removed her toolbox from the truck and went in search of the replacement parts. The first wrecked truck was exactly where he had told her it would be but unfortunately someone had already removed the reflector. The trim was still intact so she opened her toolbox and went to work on removing it. Afterward, she made her way over to where the second truck was supposed to be. She had a little more trouble locating it, but her persistence paid off. The reflector was still intact. As she worked on removing the part, she thought about the instructions the guy had given her for popping out the dent. They sounded simple enough. She wondered if she'd be strong enough to pull out the dent. After getting the reflector off, she removed the headlight lamp and the signal light bulb. Maybe she'd be lucky and they'd work. If not, all it would cost was her time. She put away her tools and headed back to her truck.

When she arrived she was surprised to find that the damaged parts where already off and lying on the ground beside her truck.

"I popped that dent out for you," the guy said from behind her.

"Thanks, I appreciate that."

"I love these old beauties," he said as he patted the Ford's hood. "It hurts me to see one damaged."

"It belonged to my grandfather. He bought it new and used it until he died."

"You should restore it."

Erin gave a small snort. "I can barely afford to keep it running. There's no way I can afford to restore it."

He nodded in understanding as another car pulled into the lot. "See you later," he said as he left to help the new customer.

Erin examined the area where the dent had been. She had to look close to find it. There was a small patch of filler where he had patched the drill hole. She went to work replacing the new parts. Working kept thoughts of Ashley at bay. When she finished she checked the lights and felt like cheering when they both worked. There was an added bonus in the fact that the filler had been hidden by the chrome trim.

She went to find the guy to pay him. He was on the phone but waved to indicate he would be right with her. The office was hot and stuffy, so she went back out to admire her handiwork.

"She looks almost as good as new," the guy said as he joined her. "How come you know how to do that?" he nodded at the repairs.

Erin shrugged. "I don't know really. I've just always been good at stuff like that."

He nodded knowingly. "Some people are," he agreed.

"How much do I owe you?"

He rubbed his chin. "Tell you what. Since you let me pop that dent out for you, let's call it even, but if you ever decide to sell her, I get first dibs."

Erin blinked. "I should be paying you for fixing the dent."

He chuckled. "Oh, no, ma'am. Like I said, I love these babies." He patted the fender. "It really does hurt me to see one of them damaged."

Erin tried to argue again but he waved her off. She thanked him and drove away.

On the way home she began to think about how she had repaired the truck. For as long as she could remember she had enjoyed working with her hands. When other kids were playing with toys, she would be taking apart an old clock or playing with a block of wood. That was what she did best. Some of her best memories were of working in her father's workshop. She could still remember how good it felt when they finished restoring a piece to its original beauty. As she got older and more skilled, he taught her how to create the beautiful dovetail joints common in quality antique furniture and how to make replacement pieces for the delicate inlays found on some pieces. A wave of loneliness hit her. She missed being able to see her parents on a regular basis. She considered driving to Austin, but it was already so late that she wouldn't be able to spend much time with them. Besides, she still needed to go to the grocery store, and she needed to iron a few clothes.

CHAPTER SEVENTEEN

Diana's Jeep wasn't in the parking lot when Erin pulled into her usual spot. She had purchased more groceries than she should have, but she felt justified because she'd saved so much money at the junkyard. After getting out she took a moment to admire the repairs she'd done on the truck. Seeing them again gave her a feeling of accomplishment. She took her time in gathering the first load of groceries. Now that she was here, she wasn't eager to go back to her apartment. She thought about putting the groceries away and then going to see Mary and Alice and show them the truck, but she barely had enough gas to get to and from work the following week. The long trek from the parking lot and up two flights of stairs with groceries was the only real drawback of living where she did. The heavy bottles of juice forced her to make more trips than she would have liked. On the final trip in she closed the door and locked it.

She noticed the blinking light on the answering machine and

stood watching it for several seconds. Without checking she already knew it was Ashley. Part of her wanted to hit the erase button, while another part longed to speed across the room to play the message. Ashley's anger frightened Erin. Never having been around rage like that, she didn't know how to cope with it. She walked over to the machine. There were three messages waiting. Her finger hovered over the play button. What would Ashley's mood be? Would she still be angry? She pressed play and gave a deep sigh of relief when she heard Mary's voice asking if she was feeling better. The second call was from her mother, informing her that her oldest brother Tom and his wife, Edith, were expecting their first child. The third call was a hang-up. Torn between disappointment and an odd sense of relief, Erin began to put the groceries away. She was almost finished when there was a knock at the door.

Erin froze when she saw Ashley standing on the other side of the door. For the briefest moment, she considered pretending she wasn't home, but the desire to talk to her was stronger. As soon as she began to open the door, Ashley slipped inside.

"I'm sorry about the way I left this morning. I was so embarrassed and upset," Ashley said. "The thought of you and that other woman seeing me like I was last night was too much."

"There's nothing to be embarrassed about. I shouldn't have lost my temper. I didn't realize it would upset you so." She held out her hand to Ashley. "We need to talk."

Ashley shook her head. "I didn't come here to talk. I want you to take me right here." To Erin's astonishment, Ashley pushed her shorts down and kicked them to the side before reaching for Erin. "Take me, now," she whispered urgently as she grabbed Erin's hand and pushed it between her legs.

"Ashley," she said as she pulled her hand away and tried to slip out of Ashley's clench. "Wait a minute."

"Do you have any toys?"

Confused by the sudden turn in conversation, Erin blinked. "You mean like Monopoly? I have a deck of cards and—"

101

"Never mind," Ashley barked, "Use your fist."

"My fist?" Beads of sweat popped out along Erin's hairline as she realized what Ashley was wanting. She licked her lips nervously. This was way beyond her limited vanilla sex life.

"Will you stop wasting time? We have to hurry."

Erin nearly passed out when Ashley turned and bent over the back of a kitchen chair and spread her legs.

"Now, Erin, do it."

Erin glanced at her hand and made a fist before looking back at Ashley. What the hell was she supposed to do? She had read about fisting but hadn't thought about real people actually doing it.

"Erin, please, baby. I need you." Ashley's hips began to move provocatively.

Erin moved behind her and gently slipped a finger into Ashley. She was shocked by how wet Ashley was.

"Don't tease me. Please." The plea was drawn out into a long almost wail-like supplication.

Erin looked longingly at the case of water sitting on the floor beside the refrigerator. Her throat so dry it ached. She tried to speak but nothing came out. She cleared her throat again. "I don't know how," she said, embarrassed.

"It's not like you need a frigging manual," Ashley snapped as she reached back and grabbed Erin's hand. "Tuck your thumb inside your palm, like this and point your fingers like that," she instructed as she molded Erin's hand into shape before bending back over the chair.

Erin made a tentative attempt.

"Harder," Ashley demanded as she pushed back onto Erin's fingers.

When Erin's now wet hand slipped into Ashley, she experienced a sudden vision of watching her grandfather deliver a calf that was breech. Stunned that such an image would come to her at this moment, Erin banished it and tried to focus on what she was doing.

"Close your hand," Ashley gasped as she pushed herself back on Erin's hand.

As if in a dream, Erin watched her arm as it slowly moved in and out of Ashley. Her stomach felt like a cement mixer stirring up the multitude of emotions churning through her—fear, curiosity, a twinge of desire and a strange sense of power. Ashley's moans of pleasure sparked a primitive desire in Erin and she found herself growing wet. Her heart began to pound and her breathing changed as she increased the tempo of her thrusting. With her free hand she reached around Ashley and slipped her fingers between Ashley's legs. Results were almost instantaneous.

As Ashley's climax grew in intensity, the rickety chair she was leaning over bumped into the flimsy dining table, making it inch across the kitchen floor. A bag of oranges were jostled off the table. Erin watched as the bright orange fruit hit the floor and rolled into a pattern that reminded her of a chart of the solar system. As the table continued its raucous dance, Erin had no choice but to follow along.

Less than ten minutes later, Erin was trying to collect herself as Ashley began to dress. Unable to depend on her rubbery legs any longer, she slipped to the floor and rested her back against the end of the bar.

"Don't be angry with me," Ashley whispered as she leaned over and kissed Erin's forehead. "I had to have something to get me through the week."

Sweating and trembling from the experience, all Erin could manage was a small nod. After another short hug, Ashley jumped up.

"I know it's rude to come and run, but I have to get home."

And just like that Erin found herself sitting alone. She stared at the dining table that was now resting against the wall. In previous sexual encounters she had never minded the scent of her lover on her hand, but now the smell made her feel queasy. The room spun when she tried to stand so she could wash up. She eased herself back down and rested her forehead against her knees, letting her hands fall to her sides. *What just happened here?* she wondered.

After several minutes she managed to get to the bathroom and scrub her hands and arms. The effort seemed to sap the last of her strength. She barely made it to the bed before collapsing. Her stomach gave an uneasy twist when she thought about the way Ashley had rushed home. She pushed it out of her mind as she closed her eyes and slept.

It was a quarter after seven when Erin finally woke up on Monday morning. She had slept straight through the night. Rather than feeling refreshed, her head felt heavy and her movements were sluggish. Ashley's scent seemed to ooze from her pores. A hot shower and several vigorous scrubbings did little to help. Since she didn't have to be at work until eight-thirty, she had plenty of time to fix breakfast, but nothing appealed to her. She finally forced herself to swallow a small glass of orange juice before heading out the door.

As soon as she got to work, she went straight to her desk rather than going to the break room to catch up with the other early birds. When Mary found her a few minutes later she was almost asleep.

"Are you still feeling bad?" Mary asked.

Erin slowly raised her head and tucked her hands beneath the desk, afraid that Mary would be able to smell Ashley's scent. "No. I guess I'm just tired."

"You should have let me take your truck over Saturday morning and fix it."

"I did it yesterday. I was feeling okay then."

"Must be having some kind of a relapse," Mary said as she peered into Erin's eyes. "Why don't you take a sick day and go home?"

"I can't afford to. That week I was out sick with the flu is still hanging out there." The company gave them sick pay, but if you had two or more occurrences within a twelve-month period, you were counseled and it affected the shift bids. Erin didn't want to end up working nights again.

"I hate this damn company," Mary muttered. "I swear if it wasn't for the health insurance I'd quit today." She patted Erin's shoulder. "Try to hang in there."

Erin tried to nod but wasn't sure she had succeeded. In a daze, she signed onto the system and tried to focus on the stack of orders in front of her. As the morning crawled by, she began to wonder if she did indeed have some terminal illness. When it was time for break, she waved Mary off and took a nap at her desk. It seemed like only seconds passed before Mary was shaking her awake.

"Here," Mary said, pushing a Styrofoam cup into her hand. "I know you don't like coffee, but I put a lot of cream and sugar in it for you. Maybe it'll help perk you up."

"Thanks," she mumbled as Mary left to go back to work. Erin opened the cup and sipped it tentatively. By the time she had finished the coffee, she was feeling somewhat better. When lunch rolled around, she managed to eat a bowl of soup and had another cup of coffee. She was still tired but she felt a little better. "You may have found a miracle cure," she told Mary as they walked back to the office.

"You're probably just tired from being sick this weekend," Mary reasoned.

Erin needed to talk. She longed to tell Mary what was going on but knew it would only start an argument. So she went back to work instead.

The afternoon slipped by slowly. By five o'clock Erin was wondering if she'd be able to drive home. Apparently Mary was worried too.

"Let me drive you home," Mary said as she waited for Erin to shut her system down.

"I can drive," Erin assured her. "Besides, I don't want to leave my truck here overnight."

"We can go in your truck. I'll call Alice from your place and have her swing by there to pick me up."

"I appreciate the offer, but my apartment is less than fifteen minutes away. I'll be fine."

"All right," Mary agreed hesitantly. "You be careful."

"Yes, Mother," Erin drawled.

"Watch it," Mary warned playfully.

When Erin arrived home, she put on a long shirt and went straight to bed. She had barely fallen asleep when the doorbell rang. She covered her head with a pillow, determined to ignore whoever it was. It rang a couple of more times before it quit and her phone started ringing.

"All I want to do is sleep," she mumbled as she fumbled for the phone.

"Why aren't you answering your door? Is there someone in there with you? Open this door right now." The statement was followed by an insistent pounding.

Confused, Erin sat up. "Who is this?" She stopped as she recognized the voice. "Ashley? Is that you?" Her stomach began to hurt.

"Were you expecting someone else?" Again she pounded on the door.

"Hold on." Erin went to open the door. Now she remembered why she hated cell phones.

As soon as she opened the door, Ashley flew in and dashed past her. Erin tried to keep up as Ashley ran into the bathroom. Dressed in a skirt and blouse, Ashley looked different, more professional maybe.

"Where is she?" Ashley insisted as she stormed back into the bedroom and pulled the closet door open.

"There's no one here but us," Erin said as she lowered herself onto the edge of the bed.

"Then why didn't you answer the door?"

"I don't feel well. I was sleeping when you rang the bell."

Ashley's demeanor instantly changed. "You're sick. Oh, my poor baby. What's wrong?" She placed her hand against Erin's forehead.

"I'm just tired."

"Tired, but I slipped away so I could be with you."

"I'm sorry," Erin said regretfully.

"I can make you feel better," Ashley cooed. "I brought you something." She smiled as she reached into a canvas bag she was carrying and pulled something out. "Hurry and put it on." She thrust the item into Erin's hand.

Erin looked at the object. *What the heck is it?* she wondered. *What are all of these straps for?* As the straps straightened out into their intended position Erin froze. She had read about this. Suddenly she threw the dildo and harness to the floor.

"I don't feel like doing this now," Erin said as she backed away from the contraption.

"I need you," Ashley protested. "You have to do this for me. Please," she whispered as she pulled her skirt off.

"Ashley, we have to talk," Erin said as she watched Ashley pick up the harness.

"There will be plenty of time to talk later. Right now, I need this." She shoved the harness into Erin's hand. "Now show me what you have."

Less than twenty minutes after she had been awakened by the doorbell, a stunned Erin was once more alone in her apartment.

CHAPTER EIGHTEEN

Ashley came by Erin's apartment on Tuesday and Wednesday afternoons. Both times she refused to take time to talk and each time she arrived with the offensive canvas bag.

Despite her limited sexual experience, Erin had never considered herself a prude. She tried telling herself that under different circumstances she might not have found the dildo to be so offensive, but the speedy one-sided sexual encounters and Ashley's speedier departure felt sordid. Each time after Ashley left, Erin felt used and wrung out. All she wanted to do was sleep. She didn't feel like eating and deep bruises encircled her eyes. Sonia had called her up to her desk to ask her if she was sick. When Erin admitted that she hadn't been feeling well, Sonia suggested that Erin schedule a doctor's appointment.

By Thursday afternoon Erin was determined that the thirty-minute sex blitzes had to stop. When Ashley and her canvas bag arrived again around five thirty, Erin was ready.

"No," she said, holding up her hands. "I don't like this. I don't like the way it makes me feel."

Unfazed, Ashley slapped the bag into Erin's hands. "Hurry up. I don't have time to argue. I have to get home."

Erin flung the bag back to her. "Then go home."

Clearly shocked, Ashley looked at her. "Why are you being so mean?"

"I'm not trying to be mean, but this has to stop."

"You said you loved me."

Careful not to make sudden moves that would frighten her, Erin reached for Ashley's hand. "I do love you. That's why I want to spend time with you. I enjoy talking to you."

"We can talk during the weekend."

Erin had almost forgotten that Ashley had told her Jess would be out of town for the next few weekends. The thought of an entire weekend with Ashley sent Erin's stomach into an uncomfortable roll. "How are you managing to get away every evening?" she asked in an attempt to stall.

Ashley shrugged. "I told her I'm working late."

"Aren't you worried that she might call and check on you?"

"No. I said I'd be working in the conference room and couldn't be reached." Again she extended the bag. "Now, put this on."

Erin flinched. "I'm not in the mood."

"I can get you in the mood." Before Erin could move away, Ashley had her pinned against the counter.

"Stop it."

"Oh, now I understand. You think I've been neglecting you. That's what this is all about." Ashley pushed her hands between Erin's legs.

"Ashley, I said stop."

When Ashley continued pawing at her, Erin shoved her away. "Damn it. When I say stop, I mean stop."

Ashley's eyes flared. "You're just like all the rest." Without warning, she slapped Erin so hard that Erin lost her balance and fell. Before Erin could comprehend what had happened Ashley was on her knees beside her. "I'm sorry," she cried. "Oh, baby, for-give me. I didn't mean to."

Erin pushed her away and stood. "Get out."

"I won't do it again," Ashley pleaded.

"I said get out."

Ashley wrapped her arms around Erin's legs in a death grip. "Please, don't make me leave. I swear I'll never do it again."

It took all of Erin's strength to pry Ashley loose. "You're right about that because you won't have the chance to hit me again." She pulled the sobbing woman up and pushed her toward the door. "Leave and take this damn thing with you." She tossed the bag to her. "I don't ever want to see you again." She opened the door and tried to force Ashley out.

"You can't do this," Ashley yelled as she grabbed onto the door to keep from being shoved outside. "Why are you making me leave? You said you loved me."

Erin eased up on her struggle to close the door. "Ashley," she said finally. "I'm sorry, but that's no longer true. I can't love some-one who treats me the way you've been treating me. And then you hit me. I can't live this way."

"But I like being with you. You're going to make Jess leave me alone."

Too stunned to speak for a moment, Erin could only stare at her. "That's the reason you're seeing me?" she managed to whis-per. "You think I can make Jess leave?" When Ashley didn't answer, Erin took a deep breath to ease the aching in her chest. "I agree you need to get away from Jess. I'll do whatever I can to help you find someone who can help you. There are places you can go. There are shelters you can stay in. But I don't want to see you like this anymore."

Ashley snatched her arm away from Erin. "Fuck you," she spat. "I don't need your help and you're a lousy fuck."

"Then there's nothing left for us to say. Good-bye, Ashley." Erin closed the door and locked it quickly. As soon as she did, Ashley began to pound on it, demanding and then begging to be let back in. Erin leaned against the door, trying not to cry. How could she have been so stupid to get mixed up with this woman? Mary and Alice had tried to warn her, but she hadn't listened. Ashley began to hurl curses through the door. Erin covered her ears and slid to the floor, praying that Diana wasn't home or that Mr. Griswold, the neighbor downstairs, wouldn't hear the commotion and call the police. The assault on the door intensified. It shuddered under the onslaught. Erin wondered how long it would be able to stand up to Ashley's anger.

Through the din, Erin heard the squeal of the stairwell door opening. Either someone was coming to investigate the ruckus or Diana had arrived home.

Erin stood and tried to see who it was by looking through the peephole, but they were still too far down the hallway. As she strained to see, she heard the muffled sound of Diana's voice. Ashley started screaming obscenities at Diana. Erin watched in horror as Ashley hurled the canvas bag at Diana and disappeared from view. A moment later, Erin heard the stairwell door slamming against the wall. She watched as a startled-looking Diana came into view holding the canvas bag. Erin nearly died when Diana peeked into the bag before quickly clasping it shut. She saw her hesitate before tapping on the door.

"Erin, it's Diana. Are you all right?"

Erin leaned against the door and began to sob.

"Open the door. Please. I'm worried about you."

Erin prayed that she would be struck dead. When higher powers ignored her she released the lock and slowly opened the door. She saw the look of shock on Diana's face when she saw her.

"Are you okay?" Diana asked quietly.

Erin turned and made her way to the overstuffed chair. She had never been so humiliated in her life.

Diana came into the room and closed the door. She discreetly placed the canvas bag on the floor beside the door.

"Would you lock that, please?" Erin wrapped her arms tightly around her body and curled into the chair.

After locking the door, Diana perched on the edge of the couch. "Do you want to talk about it?"

"What's to talk about? She hit me and I told her to leave."

Diana exhaled slowly and folded her hands into her lap. "Are you hurt? Physically, I mean."

Erin shook her head. "I just feel like such an idiot."

"Why?"

She sat up suddenly. "I've been chasing after her for months like some kind of love-starved kid." A harsh laugh punctuated the statement. "Hell, I even told her I loved her. Can you believe that? Why didn't I see there was something wrong with her? How could I have allowed the past three days to happen?"

"You mean she hit you before?"

Erin hung her head. She couldn't tell Diana what had transpired with Ashley during the last few days. A heavy silence filled the room until Diana finally stood.

"My Grandmother Garza had a wonderful home remedy that she swore by. It seemed to cure everything from a mashed finger to a broken heart. I just happened to keep a small stock in my freezer."

"What is it? I could use a couple of bottles."

"If you feel like walking across the hall, I'll show you."

Erin looked up suspiciously.

Diana shook her head and wiped the hair away from Erin's forehead. "Come on. I think it'll do you good to get out of here for a while."

At the door, Erin couldn't stop herself from peeking out first to make sure Ashley wasn't lying in wait for them.

When they were safely locked inside Diana's apartment, Diana removed a container from her freezer and held it up. "Homemade *molé*," she declared. "Give me time to cook some chicken and simmer it with this and everything will look a little brighter."

Whether it was the shock of the last hour wearing off or Diana's kindness that triggered the tears, Erin couldn't say. When she collapsed onto the couch into a crying wreck, Diana simply held her.

When the tears slowed, Diana handed her a box of tissues and left the room. When she returned she pressed a glass into Erin's hand. "Drink this. It's brandy. It'll make you feel better."

With a prayer that it would work its magic quickly, Erin took a gulp and gasped as the alcohol burned her throat.

"Hey, not so fast," Diana warned.

Erin held the glass out. "More."

"Erin," Diana started but stopped. "I'll be right back." When Diana returned she had the bottle and another glass with her. She sipped from her glass as Erin downed two more shots.

Erin closed her eyes and relished the feel of the fiery liquid hitting her empty stomach. She held out the glass for another shot. As the alcohol ate away her inhibitions, she began to talk. "I told her I loved her and I thought I did, but recently everything started changing."

"Changing how?"

"Well, first off, you know she spent last weekend here. Jess was out of town. She was going to be out of town for the next few weekends. So we were going to have a lot more time together, but Ashley got all weird."

"What do you mean?" Diana asked as she set her glass down.

The alcohol was beginning to hit Erin. She tried to clear the haze enough to think. "It started Sunday morning. It was almost as if she tried to start an argument. She called me a wuss when I tried to talk to her."

"It bothered you when she called you a wuss?"

"Yeah, a little, but she didn't stop there. She kept on until she got mad and left. I thought it was all over between us. Then, Monday evening she showed up and insisted—" She inhaled sharply.

Diana waited patiently.

Erin considered waiting and talking to Mary, but the thought of trying to tell Mary about what had occurred on Monday evening made her extend the shot glass again. She downed the brandy and took a deep breath. "When she came in Monday, she didn't want to talk. She just wanted to . . . to . . ." She looked at Diana and cleared her throat before adding, "You know."

"She wanted to make love," Diana offered.

Erin hesitated. "Yeah, sort of, but it felt different. She was more demanding and she wanted me to do different things than we had done before."

Diana poured herself another shot before replying. "There's nothing wrong with adding variety to your sex life."

"I didn't mind what she wanted so much." The alcohol loosened her tongue. "It was okay, after she showed me how. I didn't like the way she—" Erin stopped. Even with all the alcohol she had consumed, she couldn't bring herself to tell Diana what had happened. "It was the desperation that bothered me. It was the way she wanted me to hurry up so that she could go home. As soon as . . . it was over, she left." She shook her head. "It was like she was watching the clock the entire time I was . . . you know . . ."

"Do you want my honest opinion?" Diana asked when Erin fell silent.

"Yeah."

"It sounds as though you're feeling guilty about the affair. Your guilt is making the sex seem repulsive."

Erin ran a thumbnail along the outer leg seam in her jeans. "That's how it felt," she replied.

"I think you need to talk to Ashley. Maybe she thinks she's doing what you want. Have you tried to tell her that you're not interested in these afternoon quickies?"

"When she brought the . . ." Erin glanced at Diana and remembered that she had looked inside the canvas bag after Ashley had shoved at her. She swallowed hard. "When she brought the bag, I tried to tell her I didn't want to use it, but then I did anyway."

"If you didn't want to, why did you?"

Erin felt her neck grow warm. "I don't have a lot of experience," she admitted. "It seemed so important to her. I don't know why I did it anyway. Maybe I was afraid she'd leave. I don't know what's wrong with me. I didn't really mind the . . . the thing so

114

much. I mean, if that's what she wanted. I just felt . . ." She searched for a word that would describe how she had felt.

"Used?" Diana asked softly.

Erin's head snapped up as the proverbial light came on. "Yes. That's it. I don't think she wanted me to make love to her. It was almost like she was trying to . . . to punish herself for something and she was using me."

"I can't tell you what to do," Diana began, "but I've sort of been where you are now. All I can tell you is that sometimes we have to make choices that aren't easy."

Erin frowned. "What do you mean?"

Diana patted Erin's knee. "That's the part you have to find out on you own." She stood up. "Would you like to sit in the kitchen and talk to me while I cook?"

Before Erin could answer, Diana had already disappeared into the kitchen. An awkward silence fell between them when Erin came into the tiny dining room adjacent to the kitchen and sat down.

Diana finally broke it. "Did you find out anything about whether or not your company had a tuition plan?"

"They have a plan, but I don't think I'm really college material."

"I think you're wrong, but it's your choice." Diana put a bowl into the microwave. "Maybe all you need is a different job."

"I don't really mind the job I have now. I just need to make more money," Erin countered.

"Can you ask for a raise?"

"No. We have a union and everything revolves around the contract."

"What about transferring to another job within the company? Is there a position you're qualified for that would pay better?"

Erin shook her head.

"All right." Diana gave it a moment's thought. "Maybe you should consider getting a second job. A lot of people I know have a second job." Diana glanced over at her as she pulled a cooking pot from the cabinet. "This might be the perfect time for you to think about taking on a second job. You'd be so busy you wouldn't have time to think about . . . other things."

Erin liked the idea of a second job. "What could I do?"

"Think about what you really like to do. Let me give you an example. My sister loves video games and when she needed extra money she got a job as a sales clerk in one of those shops that sells them. She's a manager there now and has quit her other job." She filled the pot with water and placed it on the stove before turning to Erin. "You can't tell me that there's absolutely nothing you're good at or that you enjoy doing."

"I like restoring antiques," Erin admitted.

Diana placed her fists on her hips and stared at Erin. "Are you any good at it?"

Erin shrugged. "I guess so. I've been helping my dad since I was a kid."

"There you go. You could do something like that. There are a lot of antiques stores here. Surely someone is looking for help."

A flicker of excitement tickled Erin's stomach. "Do you have a phone book?"

By the time dinner was ready, Erin had compiled a list of antiques stores that were located within a reasonable driving distance of the apartment complex.

116

CHAPTER NINETEEN

The following morning Erin called in sick to work.

"Have you made a doctor's appointment?" Sonia asked when Erin requested the day off.

"Yes," Erin lied. "I'm going in this afternoon." She prayed Sonia wouldn't insist she bring in a note from the doctor.

"We're really swamped here, but I know you haven't been feeling well. I appreciate your continuing to come in."

Erin felt bad. She knew the unit was behind on keying since they had cut out the overtime. "If you need me, I might be able to make up my time tomorrow," she offered.

"No. You take care of yourself. You'll be a lot more effective if you're well."

Erin turned off the phone before crawling back into bed. She slept until a little after one that afternoon. When she awoke, her body was sore and her mouth felt like it was lined with cotton. After brushing her teeth, she took a long, hot shower, carefully keeping all thoughts of Ashley and the last few days at bay. The pounding spray began to ease the muscles in her neck and back. By the time she stepped out of the shower her skin was a deep pink and the bathroom looked like a sauna. She wrapped herself in her favorite fluffy robe.

The list of antiques stores she intended to call was lying on the nightstand. Before she could change her mind, she picked up the phone and began dialing the numbers on the list. No one was looking for help. Determined not to let the slight setback get her down, she made her way to the kitchen for some food. As she prepared a sandwich she kept thinking about antiques. The more she thought about them the more it made sense. Restoring antiques was the one thing she was really good at. There had to be a way she could put her talent to use. She knew the answer would come to her eventually; she just needed to give it time to process.

With her food and juice in hand she settled into her favorite chair and turned on the television. She flipped through the channels. One of them was hosting a marathon of *The Golden Girls*. She tried to concentrate on the show, but in her peripheral vision she kept seeing the canvas bag. She turned more in the chair so she couldn't see the bag, but it kept bothering her. Finally, she went into the bedroom and got dressed. Afterward, she grabbed a trash bag and slipped it over the canvas bag before tying it tightly and dumping it in with the rest of her garbage. She grabbed her keys, then headed for the Dumpster. As she walked toward the back of the complex, she could hear kids shouting and laughing. It was Friday afternoon and they were coming home from school. When she reached the Dumpster she raised the heavy lid with one hand and swung the garbage bag over the rim. The lid gave a nice satisfying thud when she released it. A vague sense of relief came with the sound. On the way back to her apartment she wondered if her parents had plans for the weekend. Maybe she would call them. She could drive up to Austin tomorrow morning and spend the night with them. It would give her a chance to talk to her father. Maybe he would have an idea about how she could best put her restoration talents to use. Feeling better than she had in days, Erin took the back stairs into her building. She considered asking Diana if she'd like to go to the movies tonight. By the time she stepped into her hallway she was almost smiling.

The smile died when she found Ashley standing outside her door with an overnight bag at her feet.

"Hi," Ashley called out. "I left work early."

Erin stopped short. "What are you doing here?" she asked, unable to believe her eyes.

"It's Friday. I'm spending the weekend, remember?"

"You can't be serious." She shook her head. "Ashley, you aren't welcome here. I don't want to see you anymore. I thought I made that clear last night."

Ashley waved her off. "Oh, I know you were upset last night, but we can work that out. Look what I brought."

Erin stepped back, terrified of whatever new sex game Ashley had thought up.

Seeing her reaction, Ashley began to laugh. "Stop being silly. It's only some movies," she said, holding up a bag from Blockbuster.

"I don't care what it is. You have to leave." Erin was beginning to realize that Ashley's mental state might be in worse shape than she had thought. She wondered if she could get into her apartment without Ashley following her.

"There's no need for me to leave," Ashley insisted. "Jess is in Dallas until Sunday afternoon. We have all weekend."

Erin rubbed her forehead. "Dallas? I thought . . ." She shook her head. "Look, I don't know how else to say this. I don't want to see you anymore. I don't want you coming over here or calling me. Do you understand that?"

Ashley stomped her foot. "Stop being so pissy. I told you I was sorry about our little argument. Are you going to hold it against me forever?"

"Little argument," Erin said disbelievingly. "You hit me. I don't call that a little argument."

"Oh, please. It was barely a tap. I didn't even close my hand. Now, open this door. I'm tired of standing out here."

"I told you to leave."

"Is this about her?" She nodded toward Diana's apartment. "Is that it? You've got someone else on the side and you're tired of me?"

"This has nothing to do with anyone else. This is about you. I simply don't want to see you anymore. I want you to leave me alone."

"What if I don't?"

The smile Ashley gave her made the hair on the back of Erin's neck stand up. She answered with the first thing that popped into her head. "Then I'm going to call the police. If I have to, I'll file whatever charges I can against you." She braced herself for Ashley's anger.

Ashley's response was not what Erin had expected. She started laughing and continuing until she was laughing so hard she could barely stand.

"I don't see anything funny about this," Erin said, beginning to get angry.

Ashley wiped her eyes. "Oh, you are priceless. Do you think that little threat will stop me from coming here, if I truly want to?"

"Why don't we find out?" Erin challenged as she pulled her keys from her pocket.

"You won't really call the police," Ashley said.

"You stand right there and watch." Erin pushed past her and slipped the key into the lock.

Ashley reached out and caught Erin's arm. "You can't do that. Your call will go into the north substation. That's where Jess works. The officers there know me."

"Then I suggest you leave. Now," she added.

Tears filled Ashley's eyes. "But what will I do all weekend? Jess is gone."

"Maybe this would be a good time for you to try and get some help for yourself," Erin said quietly.

Ashley's arm swung up, but Erin was ready and was able to grab it. "Leave, please."

Erin stood outside her door and watched until Ashley disappeared into the stairwell. As soon as she was inside her apartment, she locked the door and dialed her parents' number. When their answering machine kicked in she hung up. She would wait a while and then call them back. If it wasn't too late, maybe she would drive up tonight. She went to her bedroom, took down a small suitcase and began to pack. Her phone rang before she could finish. Afraid it was Ashley she checked the Caller ID before picking up. It was the apartment manager.

"Ms. Fox," he said as soon as she answered. "There has been a problem with your truck."

"My truck?"

"Yes, one of the other tenants just called to report that she saw a woman busting your windows and—"

Erin didn't hear the rest; she was already running out the door.

CHAPTER TWENTY

A small crowd was standing around Erin's truck when she arrived. They parted to let her through. Mr. Tyler, the apartment manager, was off to the side talking on his cell phone. Rage unlike any she had ever experienced filled her when she saw the shattered driver's side glass and windshield.

"I saw who did it," a tall, painfully thin woman said. "It was a woman. She had long hair and was carrying a small suitcase."

Erin slowly walked around the truck checking for other damage.

"I yelled at her to stop, but she ran off," the woman said as she followed along behind Erin.

"Thank you," Erin replied automatically. In her mind she was ripping Ashley Wade to shreds.

Mr. Tyler came over to join them. "I've called the police. They should be here any moment." He turned to the woman. "Mrs. Alexander, if you wouldn't mind waiting until they arrive. They'll need your statement."

Erin leaned against the truck and tried to control her anger. She heard the manager urging the crowd to go on about their business. As soon as he had shooed them away, he came back to where Erin was standing. "Ms. Fox, I can't tell you how sorry we are that this happened. The security cameras caught it all on tape, and I'll certainly turn everything over to the police." He smoothed his thin hair. "Do you have any idea who might be angry at you?"

"How do you know it was directed at me?" she snapped.

"Well, no one else's vehicle was damaged."

"Maybe that was because Mrs. Alexander frightened her away before she had a chance to."

"Well, yes, I suppose that could be." He moved back to stand beside Mrs. Alexander and a heavyset man dressed in a uniform with *Sierra Water* stitched over the breast pocket.

When the police officer arrived he asked Erin to wait while he took statements from Mrs. Alexander and Mr. Tyler. She was sitting on the tailgate of her truck when he returned.

"A witness saw a woman bashing in your windows with a baseball bat," the officer said. "Do you have any idea who might have done this?"

"I think it was Ashley Wade," she replied as she hopped off the tailgate. She removed the scrap of paper from her wallet and handed it to him. "That's her address."

The officer looked at the address for a long moment before handing it back. "How do you know Ms. Wade?"

"We've been dating for the past three months." Her stomach tightened when the officer released a long sigh and began to tap his pen against the pad. Did he know Ashley and Jess were a couple?

"I see," he finally replied. "What makes you think she might have had something to do with this?"

"Because I told her I didn't want to see her anymore. She got angry."

"I see," he said again.

123

Erin noticed he was no longer writing anything down. "Are you from the north substation?" she asked.

He glanced up. "Yes. Why do you ask?"

She shrugged. "Just curious."

"Are you willing to drop the charges if Ms. Wade pays for the damage?"

"No. I want this on record, in case she continues to harass me."

He rubbed his cheek. "How well do you know Ms. Wade?" He blushed slightly. "What I meant was, how much do you know about her personal situation?"

Suddenly she felt scared. Was it true that cops stuck together? Was it possible that this guy already knew what Jess was capable of and was trying to protect Ashley? Maybe she should be thinking of Ashley as well. What Ashley had done was inexcusable, but if Jess found out about the affair, Ashley might be in real danger. "Who will see this report?"

"Are you worried about anyone in particular seeing it?" he asked.

Erin poked at the asphalt with the toe of her shoe. If he didn't know what was going on between Jess and Ashley and she said too much it might make things worse. Finally, she shook her head. "No. I was just wondering."

"If you're worried that we'll call your family or place of employment, we don't do that anymore."

Erin looked at him. "I'm out to my family, and the majority of my coworkers know I'm gay. I'm not worried about that." She rushed on before he could say anything. "Can I get a restraining order or something?"

"Has she been abusive toward you?"

She felt certain that the things this man saw on a daily basis would make Ashley slapping her sound petty. "She hit me once."

"Has she threatened you directly with a lethal weapon or talked about using one?"

"No."

"Has she threatened to harm you in any way?"

"No."

124

"Then you probably don't have much of a chance. Texas law requires that you must prove there has been abuse. There have to be witnesses either to the actual abuse or the results of it. You know, like medical reports, police reports, pictures of the damage, that sort of thing. Then you have to go before a judge and convince him that the probability of danger—"

Erin held up her hand to stop him. "I get the picture." No wonder women were so reluctant to ask for help.

"You never answered my question," he reminded her. "Are you willing to drop the charges if you're compensated for the damage?"

Erin swallowed her fear. Ashley must be terrified now. Flashes of the past few days whipped through her mind. The mental images were accompanied by the sense of shame she had felt after each of these evenings. She shoved the thoughts away. Now was not the time to go soft. She had to eradicate Ashley from her life "No. I intend to press charges."

He nodded. "Someone will be in touch with you as soon as we contact Ms. Wade," he said before pointing toward the damaged windows. "You might want to tape some plastic sheeting over that, just in case it rains."

Erin thanked him and went back to her apartment to hunt for something to cover the damage. She was taping garbage bags over the bashed windows when Diana pulled in.

"What happened?" Diana asked as she came over to the truck.

"Ashley got mad at me and took it out on my windows."

"Did you report it?"

"Yeah, and I feel like a heel for doing so. Maybe I shouldn't press charges if she'll pay for the damage."

"Why?" Diana held the edge of a bag as Erin tore off a strip of duct tape. "Erin, this is serious."

"I know, but if Jess finds out, I don't know what she'll do to Ashley."

"Aren't you worried that Jess will come looking for you because you intend to press charges?"

Erin felt the blood leave her face. "Well, I honestly hadn't thought about it until you brought it up."

Diana let go of the bag. "I'm sorry. But seriously, shouldn't you be thinking about that?"

Erin taped down the last loose section of the bag. "Unless Ashley tells her, I don't think Jess will find out. If you think about the number of police reports that go through a substation, the odds of her ever seeing it should be low." Erin was trying to sound braver than she felt.

CHAPTER TWENTY-ONE

Erin and Diana walked up the stairs toward their apartments together.

"You're home a little earlier than usual, aren't you?" Erin asked.

"My last class is my free period. I didn't have any appointments today, so I skipped out early."

"Thanks for listening last night. It really helped a lot," Erin said as they stepped into the hallway.

"I'm glad I could help." Diana sorted through the various keys on her keychain. "What are you going to do?"

"I was thinking about going to Austin to see my parents, but now I guess I'll be getting my truck fixed. That seems to be how I'm spending my weekends recently." Erin removed her keys from her pocket. After waving good-bye, Erin went inside her apartment. She needed to look at her insurance policy to see if her thousand-dollar deductible applied to glass breakage.

The phone rang moments after she went in. It was her mom, calling her back.

"I was just calling to see how you guys were," Erin said.

"When are you coming to visit?" her mom asked.

"I might come up next weekend if I don't have to work. I'm sort of looking for a second job."

"If you need money, your dad and I could help some."

"It's nothing serious," Erin said. "I want to get the transmission repairs paid off and get a little money put away in the bank. I don't like having a credit card bill."

"You sound like your father."

"I'll take that as a compliment," Erin said with a laugh.

They talked for a while longer about her brothers and the good news about Edith's pregnancy before her mom had to hang up to fix dinner.

Erin pulled out her auto insurance policy and read through it. After several minutes, she put it away, disgusted. It was going to cost her a fortune to have the windows replaced. She wondered if Mary knew how to replace a windshield. Erin's mechanical endeavors had never involved replacing a window. She reached for the phone but stopped. If she called, Mary would want to know how the windows had gotten knocked out and Erin wasn't up to a lecture. Too tired to deal with the issue anymore, she decided to wait until morning before making a decision on whether to turn it over to the insurance company or try and tackle it herself. Wanting to take her mind off the problem, she took the antique lap desk out. After spreading out some newspapers on the kitchen floor, she started to work on it. She lost track of time as she carefully sanded the delicate nooks and crannies of the scrollwork. By the time she had finished the first piece, her legs were beginning to cramp from sitting on the floor for so long. As she stood and slowly worked the kinks out of her muscles she thought of her father's old workshop with envy. She dreamed of a day when she would have a small place of her own with a workshop. At her current salary, it would never be as nice as her dad's, but given time she could still set up a nice shop. After getting a glass of juice from the refrigerator she went back to work. She had only been at it a short time when the doorbell rang. She glanced at the clock on the stove and was amazed to see it was after six. When the bell rang again her stomach tightened. Surely Ashley wouldn't be brazen enough to come back after what she had done to her truck.

Erin crept to the door and peeked through the peephole. She let out a small squeal when she found an eye looking back at her.

"Erin Fox, I'd like to talk to you, please," a woman's voice called out.

Erin's knees began to knock. Even without seeing anything other than the quick glimpse of the eye, she knew it must be Jess Lawler. A sharp pounding on the door made her jump back.

"Would you please open the door and let me in? My name is Jess Lawler. I need to talk to you."

Erin debated whether she should call the police or not. What would she tell them if she did call? All Jess had done so far was knock on the door, and there wasn't a law against that. As she continued to try and figure out what to do, Jess pounded on the door again.

"Would you open the door? I know you're in there." The pounding was much louder this time.

"What do you want?" Erin asked through the door.

"I told you I need to talk to you."

"Well, talk. I'm listening." Erin heard a frustrated sigh from the other side of the door.

"I can't talk through this door. Now, please open it."

Erin glanced at the flimsy security chain. "I'm not opening the door."

There was a single loud rap and then silence. When Erin couldn't bear the silence any longer, she peeped out again. All she could see was a portion of Jess's side. She was apparently leaning against the wall beside the door.

"I need to talk to you about Ashley," Jess said quietly. "I want to ask you to drop the charges. I'll pay for the damage to your truck."

Erin's mind quickly processed the words. Was it a trick to get her to open the door? It would certainly help her a lot if she didn't have to pay for the cost of the repairs. When there was no further pounding on the door, Erin slowly unlocked it.

Jess Lawler was a lot bigger than Erin had anticipated. One look at the woman who stood over six feet tall and Erin knew she had made a mistake in opening the door. She started to slam it shut but Jess grabbed the door and easily pushed Erin inside.

Erin looked around for a weapon but nothing seemed adequate.

"Sit down," Jess ordered. "I just want to talk to you."

To Erin's amazement, Jess strode to the couch and sat down. Still not convinced, Erin remained near the door.

"Would you please sit down?" Jess asked as she pointed to the big overstuffed chair.

Erin slowly made her way over to the chair but couldn't bring herself to sit down in it properly. She perched on the arm instead.

Jess shook her head and sighed but apparently decided Erin's gesture was good enough. "I would like for you to drop the charges against Ashley. I'll pay for whatever damage she caused."

"How did you know about the windows?"

Jess leaned back and Erin noticed the circles under her eyes. "Ashley told me and then I received a call from a friend of mine."

"Was it the police officer who took the report?" Erin asked.

"Yes. We work together." She studied Erin closely. "I guess you know that I'm a cop."

Erin could only nod.

"I've already called a shop that will replace the windows. They'll come out tomorrow morning and do the job here. All you have to do is sign for the work and drop the charges."

"Is Ashley okay?" Erin felt a little braver now that Jess had leaned back.

A pained expression flitted across Jess's face. "She'll be fine."

"Did you hurt her?"

Jess looked at her confused. "Hurt her? Why would I hurt her?"

Erin stood. "If you've beaten her again, I'll call the cops this time myself." Before Erin could react Jess was on her feet and looming over her.

"What the hell are you talking about?" she demanded as she leaned menacingly toward Erin.

Erin swallowed the fear that threatened to close her throat. If this Neanderthal was going to kill her, she was at least going to have her say first. "I think you're despicable," she said in a voice much fainter than she would have liked. "If you love her, how could you beat her? And if you don't love her, why can't you just let her go so she can have a decent life?" Bewildered, she could only watch as a stunned-looking Jess Lawler collapsed onto the couch, then dropped her head into her hands. As much as she would have liked to think that her words had been so powerful that they had pummeled this woman to her knees, Erin knew that wasn't the case. She had the strongest sense that she had missed something important.

When Jess looked up, she seemed much older. Her voice shook when she spoke. "I've never struck Ashley."

Erin looked at her disbelievingly.

"Yes," Jess said, "I have a bad temper, and sometimes it gets a little short, but I swear to you, I would never strike her."

"She said you hit her with a chair. Who do you think I'm going to believe?" Although a part of her was wondering if she really could believe Ashley.

"Are you having an affair with Ashley?" Jess asked bluntly.

Erin blinked in confusion. How much did Jess know? "What did she tell you?" she hedged.

"That you cut her off in traffic. She said she was so angry that she followed you here and smashed your truck's windows." Jess watched her closely. "That's not true, is it?"

When Erin didn't reply Jess simply nodded and folded her hands into her lap. Erin stared at the woman's large hands and was shaken by the strong sense of gentleness they conveyed. She wasn't fooled about their strength. Those hands could easily choke the life out of her.

"You're not the first, you know," Jess said softly. "There have been others. Lots of others."

"Why do you stay with her?" Erin tried to control the queasiness building in her stomach. She had been such a fool.

Jess looked at her for another long moment before answering. "Because I love her, and I keep hoping that someday she'll get better."

"Get better?"

Jess looked down at her folded hands. "Ashley is—" Her voice broke. She cleared her throat and tried again. "She's bipolar and that's all you need to know," she said gruffly. "Will you drop the charges?"

Erin hesitated. Could Jess be telling the truth? That would explain Ashley's erratic behavior. Finally, she nodded. "Yeah. I'll drop the charges."

Jess removed a piece of paper from her pocket and handed it over to Erin. "If you'll call this number and ask for Officer Brian Johnson, he'll take care of everything."

Erin took the sheet and looked at it without really seeing it. "Is Ashley okay?" she asked quietly.

"She will be. She's been off her meds for a while. I've been so busy I hadn't noticed."

"Maybe if you spent more time at home instead of running off with your drinking buddies this wouldn't have happened."

Jess stood slowly and made her way toward the door, where she stopped and turned back. "Not that it's any of your business, but I haven't had a drink in almost six years. I don't have time. I didn't notice Ashley was cutting back on her meds. I've been working two jobs in order to try and pay off the credit card bills she runs up every time she has one of her episodes." She opened the door. "Thanks for dropping the charges," she said as she left and closed the door softly behind her.

Erin remembered the picnic and the horrendously expensive items Ashley had brought. Were those items part of the debt Jess was trying to work off? More confused that ever, Erin slowly locked the door.

CHAPTER TWENTY-TWO

Erin continued to sit on the chair arm for several minutes thinking about what Jess had told her. Was she telling the truth about Ashley or lying to protect herself? She knew nothing about bipolar disorder. The phone rang. Still thinking about Ashley, Erin answered without checking to see who was calling. She regretted the lapse as soon as she heard Ashley's voice.

"Just answer yes or no," Ashley said in a loud whisper. "Is Jess there?"

"Ashley, Jess has already—"

"Don't say my name!" she screamed, so loud Erin jerked the phone away from her ear.

"It's all right. Jess isn't here. She left."

"Are you okay? Did she hurt you?"

"No. She didn't hurt me."

"What did she want? What did she tell you? Whatever it was, it's a lie. Jess always lies to people. She wants everyone to think it's me and not her, but you know better. You know I'm right, don't you? You can see that Jess is trying to make everyone think I'm crazy."

Erin ran a thumbnail along the edge of the counter, tracing the smooth edge of the tile. She didn't know who to believe. Before she could answer, Ashley began talking again.

"I wish you were here. I want you so much now, I ache."

Erin tried to ignore the tingle that ran through her body at Ashley's words. Memories of how Ashley had felt when they made love added a warm glow.

"Can I come over?"

Erin snapped out of her reverie. "No. I meant it when I said I don't want to see you again."

Ashley laughed softly. "Why are you being so mean to me?"

"For starters, you busted my truck windows."

"I was only trying to get your attention."

"Well, you succeeded."

"You should come over and punish me. That's why I did it, you know." Her voice had taken on a sultry silkiness. "I wanted you to come over and punish me."

Erin tried to ignore the slight trembling that raced through her body. "I have to go. Please don't call here again." She hung up before Ashley could protest. The phone began to ring again almost immediately. Erin stared at it, willing it to be quiet. She jumped back when the answering machine kicked in and Ashley's voice suddenly filled the room. The raw sexuality in it pushed Erin back until she bumped into the table.

"If you won't come over to help me, I'll have to take care of it alone."

Was she talking about suicide? Terrified, Erin leapt for the phone. She was about to pick it up when a long drawn-out sigh engulfed the room. She had heard the sound before. It was the sound Ashley made when she climaxed. Erin tried to make herself hit the stop button on the machine, but her arm suddenly felt as if it were made of lead.

"Did you like that, baby?" Ashley's silky voice whispered. "It was nothing compared to what you do for me. Please, come over here and touch me. Please."

Erin's hand came to life and slapped the power button to the answering machine. The room swirled around her, and her legs no longer seemed strong enough to support her weight. She slid into a dining room chair before lowering her head between her knees. After taking several deep breaths she began to feel better and slowly sat up. As she tried to tell herself she was over Ashley Wade, she couldn't deny the strong feelings of desire that left her feeling weak and shaky.

The phone rang again. With the answering machine off, the phone continued to ring long after the normal four times. When it stopped ringing the silence left behind was deafening. Erin's nerves tingled with trepidation as she waited for the phone to ring again. When it did, she jumped up and grabbed her truck keys, desperate to escape the phone. As she started out the door, she remembered the busted windows. She couldn't leave. *Stop being a dunce*, she told herself. *All you have to do is turn off the phone.*

Erin remembered she was supposed to call and tell someone she was not going to press charges against Ashley. She found the number Jess had given her and called it. When the guy came to the phone and she told him she was dropping the charges, he didn't question her decision, so she assumed he had already spoken with Jess. After hanging up, she turned off the phone and sat on the couch where she tried to make sense of everything that Jess had told her. Was she lying? If Jess wasn't lying then Ashley was. Maybe they were both telling half-truths. Erin went to the computer and signed on. She did a search for bipolar disorder and started skimming the different sites. A lot of them were ads for various medications, but she finally spotted one that explained the condition as a brain disorder causing a person's mood, ability to function and energy to shift between extreme highs and lows. She scanned through a list of symptoms indicating mania or depression. As she read her stomach tightened. The symptoms for episodes included euphoric moods, increased energy, restlessness and spending sprees. Her breath caught as she scrolled down the list and saw the last entry in the list: increased sexual drive often accompanied by provocative and aggressive behavior. It looked as though Jess had been telling the truth. Erin sat looking at the screen for several minutes, wondering why she hadn't realized sooner that something wasn't right with Ashley. When she looked back over the time they had shared it seemed so obvious. The way Ashley could never sit still. Her mood swings. Erin shut the computer off and grabbed her keys. She needed to get out of the apartment. She couldn't drive her car, but she could walk.

Erin was opening the door to the stairwell when Diana called out to her.

"Are you okay?" Diana asked. "You blew right past me. I'm not sure you even saw me."

Erin shook her head. "Sorry. I guess I was thinking about something else."

"If you're headed downstairs I'll walk with you," Diana offered.

"Hot date?" Erin asked more out of courtesy than interest.

Diana chuckled. "The last hot date I had was in August. The air conditioner in her car stopped working on the drive over to pick me up. Besides, do I look like I'm dressed for a hot date?"

Erin glanced over and saw that Diana was wearing an old pair of cut-offs and a T-shirt. She chuckled before asking, "What about the blonde the other night? She looked pretty hot."

"Blonde?" Diana frowned before saying. "Oh, that blonde. I guess you're right. She is hot. I hadn't really noticed."

"Oh, come on. You're not blind."

"I am when it comes to my sisters-in-law."

It was Erin's turn to frown. "You spent the night with your sister-in-law?"

Diana gave her an amused look. "And why were you noticing who spent the night at my place?"

Erin's cheeks burned. "I just happened to be looking out the window when you two pulled into the parking lot, and I . . . um . . ."

She cleared her throat. "I just happened to notice her car was still there the next morning."

"I see. Well, what you 'just happened' to not know is that my brother, Raul, is in Iraq and Heather, his wife, was having a bad night. I invited her over and we spent most of the night watching old home videos and talking about him."

"Sorry, I didn't mean to be so nosy."

"That's all right." They had reached the bottom of the stairs. "You're looking sort of blue," Diana pointed out.

Erin shrugged. "I was just going for a walk."

"Great," Diana said enthusiastically. "Then you can come with me."

"Where are you headed?"

"Come on, I'll show you." She started jogging off.

Erin gave up and followed her. When Diana jogged out of the complex parking lot and headed down the sidewalk, Erin caught up with her. "Where are we going?" she asked.

"Nowhere in particular. Just follow me," Diana said.

Ten minutes later they jogged into a park and Diana slowed her pace to a walk. "Wasn't that great?"

Erin struggled to catch her breath as sweat poured off her. "I'll tell you tomorrow when I'm able to talk again," she panted.

"Oh, stop it. You did great. I'm the one who almost died. I haven't been jogging in over a year."

They continued walking until they reached a park bench where they both collapsed.

"God, we're pathetic," Diana said as she stretched her legs out. "It's Friday night and we're sitting in a park drenched in sweat with nothing but sore legs to show for our efforts."

Erin laughed. "It could be worse. It could be Saturday night."

Diana chuckled. "That's true."

Erin leaned back and realized that despite her wobbly legs, she felt better than she had in weeks. The sun was setting low into the west. It would soon be dark.

"Listen to that bird," Diana marveled.

"It's a Carolina wren," Erin replied.

Diana turned to her. "You can tell what type of bird it is just by listening to it?"

"My parents are avid birders. A lot of our family vacations revolved around birds."

"What's that one?" Diana asked as a different bird began to sing.

"That's a mockingbird and if you'll listen real close, way back over there"—Erin pointed toward a brushy area—"you'll hear a cardinal. It's making a sort of chipping sound."

Diana's face lit up as she smiled. "You're right. I hear it." Suddenly a streak of red flashed as the cardinal flew to a tree near them. "Look at him. He's beautiful."

Erin watched as he cocked his head from side to side, watching them. "If you like birds, you should go to the Aransas Wildlife Refuge," she said.

"Where is it?"

"Down on the coast, a little east of Aransas Pass."

"Let's go." Diana jumped up.

"Right now?"

"Sure, why not? Do you have something you have to do this weekend?"

"Well, no, I don't have plans, but—"

"Then why shouldn't we go? It'll be fun."

Erin thought about spending a long, lonely weekend in her apartment and found herself agreeing. "Yeah, why shouldn't we go?"

"Great, let's get going." Diana started jogging off.

"Please tell me you plan on driving and not jogging all the way down there," Erin called after her.

CHAPTER TWENTY-THREE

After taking a quick shower, Erin packed a small suitcase. From the top of her pantry she took down an ice chest and filled it with bottles of juice, some fruit and what was left of her milk. In a plastic bag she packed a box of cereal and several packages of ramen noodles. The hotel and gas would be a big enough expense; she couldn't afford to pay to eat out as well. As she packed she told herself she should be feeling guilty about the expenses, but she couldn't bring herself to feel any guilt.

"It's me," Diana called out as she knocked on the door.

Erin grabbed her things and opened the door. "Perfect timing," she said as she locked her door. She smiled when she turned and saw that Diana was also holding an ice chest and some plastic bags.

"Let's get out of here before we come to our senses," Diana urged.

They ran down the stairs, neither seeming to remember the wobbly legs they had been suffering from earlier. When they reached the parking lot Erin faltered for a moment when she saw her truck. Jess had told her they were supposed to replace the glass the following morning.

Diana stopped short. "Oh," she said sadly. "I forgot about your truck. You were going to get it fixed tomorrow."

Jess had said all Erin needed to do was sign for the work. She glanced toward the office. "Can you wait just a minute? I may be able to take care of this."

Diana nodded as Erin set her bags down beside the truck.

Erin ran to the office and was glad to see that Mr. Tyler, the apartment manager, was still there.

"Did you get everything settled with your truck?" he asked when he saw her.

"Yes. Thank you. I was wondering, are you going to be here tomorrow?"

He nodded. "Yes. I normally take Mondays and Wednesdays off."

"Could I ask a favor of you?"

He frowned before asking what she needed.

Erin quickly explained that someone would be out the following morning to replace the windows in her truck but that she wasn't going to be able to be there during the day. She wondered if he could possibly sign for work.

He shook his head vehemently. "Goodness, no. I couldn't take on that responsibility. I'd have no way of knowing whether you'd be happy with the workmanship or not."

"All they need is a signature verifying that the glass was installed," Erin said, although she had no idea what he would be signing. "The person responsible for the damage is paying for the work. All you'd need to do is sign. These are professionals. There won't be anything to worry about."

He hesitated.

"Please, I would really appreciate it."

"All right, but if there are any problems I don't want you

coming back in here complaining to me, and understand that I'm doing this as a favor to you personally. It has nothing to do with being the manager of the complex. If you have any problems, you can't go filing complaints about me."

"Of course not. I understand," she said, backing out of the office quickly. "I really appreciate your doing this," she called as she slipped out the door and ran back to Diana's Jeep. "Let's go," Erin said. "Before he changes his mind."

"Changes his mind?"

"I'll explain later." Erin threw her bags into the Jeep. Within minutes they were driving toward the interstate.

"What was that all about?" Diana asked when they were underway.

Erin quickly explained.

"Do you think they'll let him sign?"

Erin hesitated. She had thought about them not doing the work if she wasn't there. She shook her head. At that moment, she didn't care. "I can take a bus to work if they don't get it fixed. I really can't stand the thought of spending another weekend in that tiny apartment." As soon as the words were out of her mouth she started worrying. If the windows weren't repaired right away, would Jess back out on the deal? After all, Erin had already dropped the charges against Ashley. As she pondered the possibility, she decided that Jess Lawler didn't seem like the kind of woman who would go back on her word. Feeling better, she leaned back into the seat and started to relax. The Jeep still had that new-car smell. Compared to her old truck it seemed liked a luxury ride. "Does this fancy vehicle have a radio?" she teased.

Diana pushed a button and music blared from every direction. "My brother Carlos installed it for me."

"How many brothers do you have?" Erin shouted over the music.

Diana lowered the volume. "There are four of us, two boys and two girls."

141

"Where do you fall in the ranks?"

"Carlos is the oldest, then me, and Rosa, and Raul is the baby. What about you?"

"I have two brothers. Tom is the oldest. I'm second and Andy is the youngest."

"You mentioned your parents moved to Austin, right?"

As they drove through the night they talked about their families and about growing up. The tension in Erin's shoulders slowly eased as the miles between herself and Ashley continued to grow.

It was almost midnight by the time they stopped in Rockport and found a motel with a vacancy sign flashing. Diana unfastened her seatbelt and hopped out of the Jeep. "I'll get a room and we can work out the details later." She disappeared before Erin could protest.

While Diana was inside, Erin checked her wallet and found fifty-two dollars in cash and her credit card. She did a quick calculation on what half of the room and gas expenses would amount to. Then she added a few dollars more for the unexpected and estimated that at bare minimum the weekend would cost her about one hundred and fifty dollars. She experienced a moment of doubt about her hasty decision for the getaway. Maybe she should have stayed home and made sure her truck was taken care of. She could have saved herself the additional expense. Her shoulders began to tighten and she found herself wondering when she was ever going to get the card paid off. "Stop it," she scolded. "I work hard. I deserve this weekend." She took a deep breath and allowed herself to stop fretting over money. If she had to, she'd get an extra job to pay off the card, but for this one weekend she intended to have fun.

Diana was soon back. "I have some good news and what you might consider bad news," she said as she cranked the engine.

"Bad news first," Erin said, expecting to hear there were no vacancies after all.

"They only had one room left and it was a single."

"Oh," Erin replied quietly.

When she didn't say anything further, Diana continued, "The

142

good news is the room is a king-size kitchenette and the woman felt so bad about not having two standard rooms, she gave us the kitchenette at the same rate as a standard room."

Erin couldn't concentrate on what Diana was saying about the room. She was busy trying to interpret the strange reactions she had experienced when she heard they'd be sleeping in the same bed. She had taken it for granted that they would share a room, but certainly not a bed. Initially she'd been relieved that a room had been available, but a little disappointed when Diana said she'd tried to get two rooms. What was it she felt when one bed was mentioned? Surprise, yes. Discomfort, maybe. She started slightly when she realized what the emotion was—excitement.

A thin bead of sweat dampened her hairline as she pushed the thought away. There was absolutely no way she would allow herself to think of Diana as anything other than a friend. The fiasco with Ashley had taught her that she was better off alone. She needed to get her own life in order before she could consider bringing someone else into it.

"Would you rather look somewhere else for a room?" Diana asked.

Erin shook her head. "No, this is fine."

They drove around to the back and were thrilled to discover that their room faced the water. A full moon painted silver ribbons across the water's surface. As soon as Erin stepped out of the Jeep and breathed in the balmy salt air from the Gulf of Mexico, she experienced a sense of coming home. A collage of memories engulfed her. Memories of the times she and her family had spent here. Every summer her father would place his plumbing business in the hands of his crew for two or three weeks and take his family to the coast. They would rent a house near the water and for a while their lives revolved around birds, fishing and everything fun.

"I'd forgotten how much I love this place," she said as she took another deep breath of salty air.

"Look at that moon," Diana said. "It lights up the entire bay."

They reluctantly made their way inside.

In looking around the room Erin noted it was very similar to their apartment, just on a smaller scale. The door opened onto a small sitting area. Beyond that, near the window, was the bed across from the obligatory dresser with television combo. The kitchenette ran across the back wall and the bathroom was in the far corner.

Erin tried to act normal, but she couldn't keep her eyes from straying to the bed. *This is silly*, she told herself. *We're both adults. This shouldn't be the cause of any concern.* With a new sense of determination, she strode to the bed.

"Which side do you prefer?" she asked nonchalantly.

"The side farthest from the door," Diana replied. "That way, if a mad axe murderer breaks in during the night, I'll have more time to run away."

Erin laughed. "That's the silliest thing I've ever heard."

"Maybe so, but I'll bet you think about it before you fall asleep tonight," Diana said as she rushed over and placed a book on the nightstand.

Erin pointed to the book. "Is that like marking your territory?"

"You have to admit that it's quicker and neater than peeing on it," Diana said.

Erin shook her head and started unpacking her suitcase.

CHAPTER TWENTY-FOUR

As soon as she finished unpacking her things, Erin went to the large front window and gazed out over the water.

"Would you mind going for a walk?" Diana asked. "I'm so wound up; I'll never get to sleep."

They strolled along the roadway, following the water's edge, wordlessly. It seemed to Erin that she had a memory for nearly every section of this old road. There by that pier was where she had caught her first flounder. Over there by those large concrete pieces was where Tom fell and broke his arm while trying to sneak up on a Great Blue heron.

"Where's the beach?" Diana asked, interrupting Erin's musings.

Erin glanced at the murky water that splashed up against the narrow strip of grassy land. "We'll have to drive over to Port Aransas if you're interested in sandy beaches. I'm sorry I didn't mention there's no real beach in Rockport. When we came down here, swimming wasn't a big deal for us."

"It's not a big deal. I just thought it was strange not to see a beach." They walked a while longer.

"There's Fulton Harbor," Erin said pointing. "I used to spend hours there fishing."

"I've never been fishing," Diana said.

Erin looked at her in amazement. "You're joking."

Diana shook her head. "No, I'm not. I wouldn't even know how to hold a fishing pole."

"Would you like to learn?"

Diana's nose scrunched. "I don't think so. I have no desire to pick up worms."

"You don't fish with worms here. Or at least, I don't," Erin said.

"What do you use?"

"Either lures or shrimp."

"Shrimp?"

"Yeah. You can use live or dead shrimp."

Diana shuttered. "I can't see myself picking up a live shrimp."

"They won't hurt you."

"They certainly won't if I don't pick one up," Diana replied.

"Would you mind walking out on the pier? I just want to see if the fish are biting tonight."

"You mean there are people out there fishing now?"

"There probably are. I always preferred fishing at night. It's a lot cooler and the fish seem to bite better then." When they arrived at the pier, Erin felt a tingle of excitement as she stepped onto the wooden walkway. "I don't know why I quit coming down here," she said. "There's a charge if you're going to fish. I'll run in to let them know we're just going to walk out on the pier." She left Diana standing on the pier as she went into the small bait shop. The old man behind the counter could have been the same guy who was there when she was a kid. His battered old cap and grizzled beard hid most of his face. He was watching a small black-and-white television and started to stand when she came in.

"Is it okay if we just walk out to have a look around?" she asked.

He waved her off. "Suit yourself."

"What's biting tonight?"

"Mainly skeeters," he replied and scratched his arm to emphasize his meaning.

Erin thanked him and stepped back outside. Diana was leaning over the rail of the pier.

"What do you see?" Erin asked as she went over to join her.

"Water."

Erin rolled her eyes. "You're as funny as the old guy inside. You two should get together and form a vaudeville act."

Diana's laughter flowed over the water.

"Let's go see what's biting," Erin said.

They started down the pier.

"These lights here"—Erin pointed to the lights that hung over the water—"help draw the fish in."

"How?"

Erin looked at her. She had never wondered why the lights were there. "I guess they attract bugs and the fish are coming up for the bugs. I've never really thought about why. It was just always a big deal to fish by a light."

"I can see there's a lot of skill involved in this sport," Diana said with a touch of sarcasm.

"Hey, as far as I'm concerned, fishing is about fun. I leave all the hard stuff to the professionals. I don't worry about water temperatures or wind velocity. The only thing that I care about is whether or not the fish I catch is big enough to keep."

At the end of the pier another pier teed off from the main walkway. Here they found four men and two women scattered along the rail. They drifted closer to the two women.

"Those fishing poles are huge," Diana murmured.

"Saltwater rods are bigger than freshwater rods," Erin answered softly. She pointed toward a bench in the center of the pier. "Let's sit down and watch for a while."

They had barely gotten seated when a high-pitched squeal filled the air. Instantly all of the people fishing came to life.

Erin pointed to the short heavyset woman near them. "She's got a fish on the line."

"Where is it?" Diana asked, jumping up.

Erin swallowed a laugh and took hold of Diana's arm. "It's still in the water. She has to bring it in."

They watched as the woman fought the fish. She would reel it in and suddenly the fish would make a run, causing the reel to scream as the line ripped off it.

"It must be pretty big," Erin said as her heart began to pound with excitement. She longed to be in the woman's place. It had been years since she had fought a large catch.

Despite Erin's best intentions of not crowding the woman, she and Diana were soon leaning over the railing straining to catch a glimpse of the fish.

"There it is," Diana screamed gleefully as a large silvery flash zipped across the top of the water.

The woman was vigorously reeling the excess line in and Erin held her breath. If the fish were to suddenly change course or jump, she would probably lose it, but the fish made a lethal mistake and fought the line. The woman eased up on the drag and patiently waited until the fish had worn itself out. Within a few minutes, she was able to easily reel it in to where the other woman waited with a long-handled net. It took both of them to bring the fish over the rail.

As soon as the fish hit the pier, Erin and Diana raced over for a closer look.

"It's a Red," Erin said in awe. "It must weigh close to thirty pounds."

The woman who had reeled it in laughed and said, "The way my arms are shaking it felt like twice that."

The second woman whipped out a small metal tape measure. "Twenty-six and a half inches," she announced loudly. Cheers and whistles of appreciation from the other fishermen echoed along the pier.

"You ready?" asked the woman who had held the net.

The other one nodded and before Erin had time to process what they were doing, the fish was heaved over the rail, back into the water.

Diana gave a small squeal of protest and turned to Erin. "Why did they throw it back?"

"We fish strictly catch-and-release," replied the woman who had caught the fish. "He was much too beautiful to kill." She tilted her head. "Don't you think so?"

Diana glanced toward the water where the fish had disappeared and then back to the woman. "You're right. I guess I got caught up in the moment."

The woman smiled. "It's easy to do." She glanced around the pier. "You're not fishing?" she asked.

"No," Erin said. "We just stopped by to see if anything was biting."

The second woman laughed. "Well, you got here just in time," she said as she picked up her pole and started checking the rigging.

"We should go," Erin suggested as the women settled down to fishing again. It seemed to her that Diana was a little hesitant to leave. "Did you want to stay a while longer?"

Diana shook her head. "I was just thinking that maybe we could come down here again soon, and you could teach me how to fish."

"Sure."

"Besides the pole, what other equipment would we need?"

"That depends on how into it you want to get. You can fish with a stick and a piece of string with a hook and weight tied to it."

Diana glanced back toward the women. "Could I catch a fish that big?"

"You might, but those big Reds are not as common as they once were."

"Could you have thrown it back?" Diana asked.

"In a heartbeat," Erin said without thinking. "If you don't throw them back, you have to clean them. Trust me when I say that cleaning fish is not fun."

Diana scrunched her nose again. "Ugh, point taken."

Erin glanced at her watch. It was after one a.m. "It's late. If you want to get to the wildlife refuge early tomorrow—or rather, this morning—we'd better get some sleep."

"Have you ever caught a fish that large?" Diana asked as they left the pier.

"No. The biggest fish I ever caught was a twelve-pound flounder. I was about sixteen, I guess, and Dad had to help me bring it in."

"Did you keep it?"

"Yeah, but Dad did the fish-cleaning then. I still don't know how to clean a flounder."

They rehashed the exciting episode on the way back to the motel. While Diana was in the bathroom, Erin gathered her night-clothes, an old pair of shorts and a long shirt. As soon as Diana came out, Erin rushed in and took her time brushing her teeth and preparing for bed. When she came out she was relieved to find that Diana was already sleeping soundly.

CHAPTER TWENTY-FIVE

Erin awoke to the smell of coffee. She rolled over and squinted at the clock. It was only a little after five.

"I didn't think you were ever going to wake up, sleepyhead," Diana called cheerfully.

Erin sat up and found Diana sitting at the table with a cup in front of her. "Didn't we just go to bed a couple of hours ago?" she asked.

"Yes, but you said we had to get an early start if we wanted to see birds," Diana reminded her. "Since I can't do anything without my morning coffee, I decided I'd better get a head start."

Erin noticed Diana's hair looked wet. "You've already showered? What time did you get up?"

"I'm one of those lucky people who don't need a lot of sleep. It's hell on girlfriends, but great for getting things done."

Erin nodded as she rolled out of bed and gathered her clothes. "Give me a few minutes and I'll be ready to go," she said as she headed toward the bathroom. The shower helped wake her up and by the time she was dressed, she was looking forward to the day. When she came out, a bowl of cereal and a glass of juice were waiting for her.

"I didn't pour the milk," Diana said as she poured herself another cup of coffee. "I assumed you wouldn't want soggy cereal."

"You assumed correctly," Erin said as she took the milk from the refrigerator.

"How did you sleep?" Diana asked as they sat down at the table.

"Like a rock. I didn't hear anything."

Erin liked the fact that Diana sipped her coffee in silence while Erin ate her cereal. She always needed a few minutes in the morning to get her body jump-started. After having lived alone for so long, it was difficult for her to wake up and start talking right away.

After eating, Erin washed the dishes and they were soon on the road, headed to the wildlife refuge. As they were driving Erin suddenly remembered she didn't have binoculars. "Do you by any chance have a pair of binoculars in here?" she asked.

"I don't even own a pair." Diana glanced at her and grimaced. "I guess it would make bird-watching easier."

"We'll still be able to see some of the larger birds, but the smaller ones may be a problem. We'll have to be quiet and get as close to them as possible."

When they arrived at the wildlife refuge, Erin suggested they park the Jeep and hike along one of the trails.

They had been on the trail for a few minutes when Diana cleared her throat. "Erin," she began in a serious tone. "There's something I think I should tell you."

Erin suppressed a groan. The birds were singing and the early-morning sun was painting the sky glorious shades of pink and blue. It was too beautiful to spoil with conversation, especially if it was going to be bad news. She didn't want anything to ruin their weekend. "Okay," she replied, bracing herself.

"I'm getting married."

Erin's jaw dropped. She had not been prepared for that bombshell. She stared at Diana, unable to think of anything to say.

After what felt like an eternity, Diana began to giggle. She was soon laughing so hard she could barely stand.

"What's so funny?" Erin demanded.

"April Fool's!" Diana cackled.

It took Erin a moment to recover. She had forgotten it was the first of April. In an attempt to hide the shock she had felt, she rolled her eyes. "I can't believe you still play that childish game."

"You're just saying that because I got you," Diana said as she practically skipped down the path.

Erin finally gave in and laughed. "Okay, I admit it. You did get me."

"You should have seen your face." Diana chuckled again. "It was priceless."

Erin stopped short and shushed her.

Diana stopped and watched her with anticipation. When she couldn't stand it any longer she asked, "Do you hear a bird?"

"No," Erin whispered. "I thought I heard something in the woods over there." She pointed to her right.

"What did you hear?"

"It was a coughing or a weird growling sound."

"It was probably just someone else out here looking for birds," Diana replied.

"No." Erin turned her ear in the direction of the sound. "It was different."

Diana planted her fists on her hips and sighed. "It's too late to try and pull an April Fool's joke on me now."

Erin silenced her with a wave. "There it is again. Did you hear it?"

"You're just trying to scare me to get even with me for—" Diana stopped as a low rumble crept out of the woods. "What was that?"

Erin looked at her. "That's the noise I've been talking about."

She took Diana by the arm and started walking. "I think we'd better move on."

"Don't you want to know what it is?" Diana glanced over her shoulder.

"Not particularly."

"You're not even a little bit curious?"

Erin stopped and looked at her. "If you're that curious, I'll be happy to wait for you right here."

There was soft rustling of grasses. This time it came from the other side of the road.

"I can't stand not knowing what it is," Diana admitted.

Erin was about to suggest it was a javelina when a loud vibrating growl filled the air. Almost immediately another one bellowed from a different direction. Erin was trying to pinpoint where the sounds were coming from when she heard what sounded like something being dragged.

"Oh, crap!" Diana yelped and pointed toward the grass.

Erin turned to see an enormous alligator headed straight toward them. "Run!" she screamed.

As they whirled, a second gator appeared from the opposite direction. Erin pushed Diana toward one of the towering old oaks that dotted the area. "Up the tree," she yelled.

Diana was already moving.

Erin didn't look back as she ran for the tree. The low-growing limbs provided them with a ladder-like passage up the tree. As soon as she felt like she was high enough to avoid the alligators, She looked down and nearly fell out of the tree when she found the larger of the two directly beneath the tree. The smaller gator was about eight feet away. They seemed to be assessing her.

"Get up here," Diana insisted.

Erin looked up and found that Diana had taken up residence on a large limb about five feet above her. She carefully made her way up to where Diana sat. "Well, at least you found out what was making the noise," she said with a nervous laugh.

Diana looked at her and shook her head. "I thought bird-watching was supposed to be boring and sedate."

They sat looking down at the gators. One was well over seven feet long and the other only slightly smaller.

"Where did they come from?" Diana asked.

"There's an alligator pond near the visitors' center. We drove past it," Erin said. "I never thought about it, but I guess gators can go wherever they like."

"Aren't they supposed to stay near water?"

Erin glanced around. From their perch they had a nice view of the surrounding area. "Look around," she said. The wooded area only extended a hundred yards or so on either side of the path. The land on both sides dropped off quickly into a marsh.

"Maybe they'll hurry up and crawl back over there," Diana said. "How long can they stay out of the water?"

Perplexed, Erin looked at her. "You're the teacher. What do I know about alligators?"

Before Diana could respond, a loud vibrating bellow filled the air as one of the gators arched his neck upwards sharply and slapped his gigantic tail. They watched in fascination as the smaller one began to slowly back away. The more aggressive gator pushed his advantage and lurched forward. With frightening speed the smaller reptile whipped around and disappeared back into the woods.

One of those weird facts Erin didn't know she even possessed slowly surfaced as she watched the sunlight dance on the alligator's knobby back. "They bask in the sunshine for hours," she said slowly.

"What?"

"Alligators are cold-blooded. They warm themselves by basking in the sun."

Diana looked down in horror. "Are you telling me we could be stuck up here until he decides he's warm?"

Erin shrugged. Why had she chosen this particular path? There were plenty of others she could have taken. She tried to inject some humor. "Look at it this way. We're high enough that if a bird flies by, we won't need the binoculars." To her relief Diana began to laugh. Soon they were both laughing.

As two hours crawled by and their reptilian friend showed no signs of moving on, Diana began to squirm. "You're not going to believe this," she said finally. "I have to pee."

Erin sighed. "I've been trying not to think about it, and now that you've mentioned it I have to go too."

"How much longer do you think he's going to stay there?"

"Maybe he'll leave when the sun moves over enough to make this spot shady."

"I don't think I can wait that long," Diana said. "He looks like he's asleep. Couldn't we try to sneak away?"

Erin looked around, studying the area. "Did you see how fast he shot across that road? I'm not sure I'm in any hurry to challenge him to a footrace."

Diana jiggled her foot. "I've really got to go. Why did I have that second cup of coffee?"

Erin carefully shifted around until she was facing the opposite direction. The limbs of the old oak branched out to surround a half dozen other trees. "We might be able to crawl along those limbs," she said, pointing, "until we reach that other tree. If we're quiet he might not pay us any attention."

"Do you think we can make it over there?"

"Only one way to find out," Erin said as she began to work her way over to the next limb. "Follow me and be as quiet as you can." She slowly worked her way from limb to limb. Sometimes she would be forced to climb higher, other times lower. It took her several minutes to reach an area where the limbs of two of the trees intersected at the proper angles. She waited for Diana to catch up. "I'm going to climb out onto that limb and then lower myself down that one," she said, gesturing. "Don't follow me until I say so. Those limbs aren't as big as these are."

Diana studied Erin's route. "You be careful," she urged. "That limb looks sort of puny."

"Careful is my middle name," Erin muttered as she slowly lowered herself from one limb to the other. As soon as her toes touched the lower limb, she realized her mistake. The distance between the two branches was farther than it appeared. She was stretched full-length between the two and at some point she would have to let go of the oak. Once she released her grip, it would be almost impossible for her to maintain her balance. If she fell there was an eight-foot drop to the ground below.

"What's wrong?" Diana asked.

Erin swallowed. "It's farther than I thought. I can't let go," she admitted.

"Oh." It had clearly taken Diana a moment to realize what Erin meant. "Can you pull yourself back up here?"

"No." Erin's arms were beginning to tremble. She closed her eyes and gritted her teeth.

"Let me help you."

"No! The limb can't hold both of us. It'll break."

"What should I do? You can't just keep hanging there."

Erin didn't respond. It was taking all her energy just to hang on.

She heard a rustling sound above her. "What are you doing?" she whispered.

"Be quiet," Diana hissed. "I'll hurry as quickly as I can."

Erin forced her eyes open and looked up for Diana, but she wasn't there. "Where are you?" Her fingers were beginning to burn. She tried to shift some of her weight to her feet, but she was too short. *Oh, to be two inches taller*, she lamented. She lowered her head in time to see Diana drop out of the oak tree and land less than eight feet from the gator. Erin held her breath and watched the animal as Diana sprinted to the tree Erin now balanced on. The alligator made no indication that he had heard anything. The bottom limbs on this tree were much higher than those on the old oak, and Diana was clearly having problems. Slipping down the trunk for the second time, Erin realized Diana wasn't going to be able to climb the tree. Just then the gator slowly raised his head, and Erin knew she had to do something. With a quick prayer, she took a deep breath and let go. For a moment she seemed to hang in space, and then her feet were coming down and she was falling. Her toes slipped off the branch. As she fell past the limb, she grabbed onto it for dear life. The momentum of the fall forced the limb downward and she heard the sickening crack as the wood gave way. Somewhere below she heard Diana scream. As Erin was hurtled toward the tree trunk all she could think about was the alligator attacking Diana. The ground was rushing toward her at an alarming rate. She knew she was about to be slammed against the tree trunk. Closing her eyes, she let go. She landed hard on her back. The impact knocked the breath out of her. The next thing she knew Diana was standing over her.

Erin gasped for air, terrified that the alligator would come tearing after them. She fought to sit up but Diana kept pushing her down. Erin saw Diana's lips moving and struggled to make sense of what she was saying. Finally the words ate through her terror.

"The gator," Erin tried to shout. But the words came out as a hoarse whisper.

"It's all right. You scared him off with all that racket you made." Diana pushed the hair back from Erin's face. "Stop moving around. Are you all right? Did you break anything?"

Erin stopped struggling and slowly assessed her condition. She was half buried in a deep layer of leaves and the rotting mulch of decades. Her arms hurt from dangling for so long, and her hip ached where she had landed on a rock or something hard, but other than that she seemed intact. "I think I'm okay." She sat up slowly.

"Easy does it," Diana said as she helped Erin stand.

Erin took a tentative step and then another. She moved her arms about and twisted her torso. "I'm okay," she said with a wide smile of relief.

"Are you sure?" Diana persisted.

Erin nodded as she continued to move about. "Yeah. I'm fine."

Suddenly Diana slapped her on the shoulder and stalked off.

"Hey. What was that for?" Erin yelped as she followed her.

"For scaring me half to death," Diana yelled over her shoulder. "I was coming to help you."

Erin caught up with her and put a hand out to stop her. When Diana spun toward her Erin was shocked to see tears in her eyes.

"I thought you had killed yourself," Diana said as she quickly brushed her cheek then ran off toward the Jeep.

CHAPTER TWENTY-SIX

Erin slowly followed Diana back to the Jeep. When she arrived Diana was sitting on what looked like an old hitching rail that had been erected to keep cars from driving onto the trail.

"I'm sorry I scared you," Erin said as she stood off to the side. "I didn't do it on purpose."

"I know." Diana continued to stare at the ground at her feet. "I apologize for overreacting. I thought you had broken your back or neck."

Erin rubbed her hip. She suspected that whatever she had landed on was leaving a nasty bruise. "I'm fine." Neither of them spoke for several moments. Uncomfortable with the silence, she cleared her throat. "If you want to leave, I understand." She made a slight waving motion with her hand. "This wasn't exactly how I planned to show you the refuge."

Diana gave a small chuckle and then began to laugh nervously. "Can you image what we must have looked like sitting up there in that tree?"

"I can't believe he ran off because of a little noise."

"A little noise," Diana exclaimed. "It sounded like the entire tree was coming down. I thought we were both goners."

Erin laughed. "When that limb broke, I nearly peed my pants."

"You scared me so badly I almost forgot I had to go," Diana said as she stood. "I don't know about you, but I think I'd like to try a different trail."

"I have an even better idea," Erin said as she started toward the Jeep. "There's a sixteen-mile auto loop. Why don't we save the trails for another day and do the drive today?"

"I'll vote for that."

"Come on. There's a restroom at the observation tower."

As they drove along the loop they spotted several birds. Most were too far away for them to see well without the aid of binoculars. When they reached the observation tower they both made a beeline to the restroom before beginning the climb to the top.

"The whooping cranes usually leave around the end of March," Erin said as they made their way up the steep inclined walkway. "But we might get lucky and still see one."

"What's so special about them?"

"I have to warn you. I'm a little fanatical about these birds."

"I'll take my chances," Diana said as she took Erin's arm.

Erin tried to ignore the ripple of pleasure that Diana's touch brought. "I'll try to give you the short version. In the nineteen-fifties the whooping crane was almost extinct. There were less than twenty of them still living. The government and conservation groups worked to save the flock. Today the flock that migrates between the refuge here and Wood Buffalo National Park in Canada has grown to about one hundred and ninety-four birds." She smiled when she heard Diana gasp in astonishment.

"They fly all that way?"

"Yeah. Like I said, they leave here around the end of March and get to Canada in late April. At the end of September, they migrate back here. They glide on the wind currents and can stay aloft for up to ten hours."

"That's amazing," Diana replied, clearly in awe.

When they reached the top of the observatory, Erin stood at the rail and slowly surveyed the marshland below.

"What am I looking for?" Diana asked as she shielded her eyes from the sun.

"They're a big white crane with black wing tips and red on the head and cheeks." As Erin continued searching she added, "I read somewhere that a blood sample is required to identify the gender of a whooping crane."

"No wonder they were almost extinct," Diana said.

Erin grinned. "Are you always such a comedian?"

"Listen, I'm trying to be good. I let the wing tips go."

"My father wears wing tips," Erin replied.

"Aw, see what you did?" Diana scolded. "That was my line."

"I was trying to save you from having to resort to such an old joke," Erin said.

"You're too sweet."

"I try." She stopped suddenly and pointed. "I think I see one." She moved to the spotting scopes provided and swung it toward the spot. It took her a minute to find it, but as soon as the large bird came into view she felt the same sense of wonder she had felt the first time she saw one as a child. "Come and look," she urged Diana.

"Wow," Diana gushed when she had the bird in sight. "It's beautiful. I didn't expect it to be so big." They continued to watch the bird until it flew away. "Just think," she said as they watched the crane glide across the marsh. "It may be leaving for Canada right this minute. We may have seen it start its journey."

Erin watched until it disappeared out of sight. She liked the thought that they had witnessed the beginning of its migration. As she turned to face Diana, she caught her breath. The sun was glistening off of Diana's raven black hair and highlighted the thin aristocratic features of her face. Erin turned away quickly before Diana caught her staring. "There's a lot more to see along the auto route, if you're ready."

As they drove the paved road, Erin began to relax and enjoy herself. As before, the lack of binoculars limited their viewing, but the pleasant drive allowed them to shake off the scare with the alligator.

When they came back around to the picnic area, Diana parked in the shade of a large oak, then removed an ice chest from the back. "I packed us a lunch while you were in the shower."

"Good. All that adventure has given me an appetite." They sat at one of the picnic tables.

"I hope you like peanut butter and jelly sandwiches," Diana said. "I raided your stash and found some apples and juice."

"That sounds great."

They relished the sandwiches and fruit as if it were a gourmet meal.

After tossing her apple core away, Erin sighed. "That's the best peanut butter and jelly sandwich I've ever had."

"I'll bet you say that to all the girls," Diana teased.

"You make it sound like there've been scores of women."

"Don't tell me there haven't been."

Erin shook her head. "I'm a woman of extremely limited experience."

"Why do I find that hard to believe?"

"Maybe you're judging me by your own record," Erin said.

"Touché," Diana grabbed her chest and pretended to collapse.

A loud series of calls sounded overhead.

"What are those birds?" Diana asked.

"Titmice," Erin responded before looking up.

Diana looked at her and smiled. "Are you pulling my leg?"

"No, ma'am, I'm not. Those feisty little gray birds are tufted titmice, or titmouse if there's only one of them."

Diana burst into laughter. "Now I know you're teasing me."

"I am not."

They watched the birds as they flitted from limb to limb.

"This is proving to be an extremely educational day," Diana mused as she glanced at Erin. "I'm glad we came." When she took Erin's arm there was nothing sexual about it.

"Me too," Erin agreed as they continued to study the birds.

CHAPTER TWENTY-SEVEN

It was after two before they left the refuge. As they drove back toward town, they kept talking about their day. Erin was certain it was a day that would remain in her memory for many years to come. She was fairly certain she'd be feeling the bruise on her hip for quite a while also.

When they came into the edge of town, Diana pointed to a sign. "Look. Someone's having a yard sale. Let's go."

Erin agreed and they turned down the lane and followed the signs. When they reached the house, they found several other cars already there. "It's so late, there probably won't be anything good left," she said as they got out of the Jeep.

"Oh, you never know. There's that whole thing of one man's junk is another man's treasure."

Erin wasn't sure she agreed but didn't argue. She was pleased to see a lot of items still left. "I guess they don't get the number of people here that we do in San Antonio," she whispered.

As they walked around the yard, Erin spied a small rectangular table that drew her interest. When she saw that it sat on three downward-turned splayfeet, her heart began to pound. Despite its being covered with decades of grime, she was positive she knew what it was. She examined the table carefully. *It can't be real*, she told herself as she brushed away some of the cobwebs and ran her hand along the turned baluster support. Decades of grime and wax buildup was embedded so thickly that it felt almost smooth. Someone had attempted to peel away a scrap of what appeared to be old newspaper. The remaining paper was firmly embedded in the grime. She studied the top and found no visible signs of gouges or splitting in the wood, but she couldn't be sure until she cleaned it. She crossed her fingers, hoping the fifty dollars in her wallet would be enough to buy the piece.

When she caught the attention of the young man in charge of the sale she tried to appear nonchalant. "How much do you want for this table?" she asked when he approached.

Diana walked up just as he did. "Erin, you're not serious. That thing is hideous."

The man frowned at Diana before turning his attention to Erin. "I've been asking ten, but it's getting late and I don't want to keep any of this stuff. If you want it for seven bucks you can have it."

Erin's hand shook as she pulled out her wallet and handed him a five-dollar bill and two ones.

"You don't want that thing." Diana said. "My dad can help you find a nice one."

"This one is fine," Erin replied. As she picked the table up to leave she started feeling guilty. The man had no idea what he was selling for seven dollars. She stopped. "Wait a minute," she called out to him.

He shook his head and waved her off. "No refunds. All sales are final. Paint it with some white paint and it'll look brand new."

Erin smiled and shrugged. "I tried," she whispered to Diana.

They put the table into the back of the Jeep and drove away.

"I shouldn't have said that about the table," Diana apologized.

"No. You shouldn't have," Erin said, unable to keep the huge grin off her face.

"I can't believe you're so happy to have it."

"I have reason to believe that beneath all that grime is a very old tilt-top side table."

Diana glanced at the table through the rearview mirror. "How can you tell? It's so filthy."

"I can clean it up and restore it."

"Are you sure?"

Erin nodded. "If everything was as easy to read as birds and wood, life would be a lot easier."

Diana didn't look convinced. "You definitely know birds, but I'm going to withhold judgment on the furniture, because that is one ugly table."

They spent the rest of the trip back into town talking about the birds they had seen. When they reached the motel, Erin took the table inside to examine it closer. She itched to start working on it but warned herself to be patient. Her father's motto was that the real secret to restoring old furniture was ten percent elbow grease and ninety percent patience.

"You really like that thing, don't you?"

Erin rubbed her hand over the wood. She didn't know the period the piece belonged to, or even the year it was built, but she did know it was old and had been built with skill and love. "You wait until I've cleaned it up. You'll be singing a different song then."

"I'll take your word for it," Diana replied with an edge of skepticism in her voice. "Right now, I'm starving."

"Me too."

Diana went to the refrigerator and glanced inside. "Our choices are peanut butter and jelly or jelly and peanut butter." She peeked over the opened door. "What sounds good to you?"

Erin stared at the table for a moment. "Let's go out and eat. I feel like celebrating."

Diana closed the refrigerator door and came over to look at the table. "Is it really that special?"

Erin smiled. "Yeah, I think it might be."

After some discussion, she learned that Diana loved seafood. Erin suggested they go to the Boiling Pot to eat. She hadn't been there in a few years and hoped it was as good as she remembered. When they entered, Diana slowly took in the crayoned walls and the tables covered with butcher paper. Erin was happy to see that Diana looked more curious than put off by the strange décor. It was still early enough that the place was empty except for a couple who was sitting on the patio. A waitress seated them and took their drink orders.

"What's good here?" Diana asked.

"They have a special that I think you'll enjoy," Erin said. "It's sort of their trademark. If you're up to a little adventure, that is."

Diana's eyebrows arched in curiosity. "Adventure, huh?" She drummed her fingers lightly on the table. "We survived the alligator, so I guess I can handle it."

When the waitress returned, Erin placed the order.

"No one will ever believe us when we tell them an alligator chased us up a tree," Erin said as she ripped the paper covering off a straw.

"You have to admit it's not something you hear about happening very often."

Erin chuckled.

"I can't believe how hungry I am," Diana said before sipping her beer.

"I don't think that will be a problem much longer."

Before Diana could respond two waitresses arrived. One carried a stainless steel pot that she dumped onto the paper-covered table. The second waitress arrived with bowls of melted garlic butter, a warm loaf of bread and small wooden mallets. She tied large plastic bibs around their neck.

Erin's mouth watered as she eyed the mound of potatoes, corn-on-the-cob, slices of sausage and a delicious variety of crab legs.

"I'm not sure I know what to do with this," Diana said. "Where's the silverware?"

"Right here," Erin said as she wiggled her fingers.

"We're eating with our hands?"

Erin picked up a snow crab leg and used the mallet to open it. After a quick dip into the butter she popped it into her mouth.

Diana chose a crab leg and gave it a tentative rap. Erin began to wonder if maybe this had been a bad idea. Diana put a little more muscle behind the mallet and extracted a long succulent strip of crabmeat. She followed Erin's example of dipping it into the butter before tasting it. As soon as she began to chew, she closed her eyes and moaned in appreciation. "That was so good," she said.

"They use a special Cajun boil."

The women dug into the food with gusto, and soon a large mound of cracked shells littered the sides of the table.

"I'm so full I can barely move," Diana said as she leaned back. "And there's still food left."

"All I see left is potatoes, corn and a little sausage," Erin said as she used the mallet to push the leftovers around.

A waitress returned with small bowls of water, a slice of lemon and a small terrycloth towel.

"Is that a fingerbowl?" Diana asked in amazement.

"Hey, this is a classy place," Erin deadpanned. "Rub the lemon on your hands. It'll remove the fishy smell." After demonstrating she rinsed her hands off in the bowl and dried them on the towel.

Diana gave her hands a sniff. "It works."

As they left the restaurant, Diana gave Erin's arm a quick squeeze. "Thank you for suggesting this place. That was fun."

"I wasn't so sure you were going to like it," Erin admitted.

"At first I was a little skeptical, but that was so much fun, I may throw all my silverware away when I get home."

"That would add a whole new dimension to eating soup."

"Okay, I'll keep the silverware," Diana conceded. She stopped and pointed. "Is that a marina?"

"Yeah. Would you like to walk over there?"

"Oh, I'd love to take a walk. I really did eat too much." As they headed toward the marina, Diana gave a long sigh. "I hate to leave here. I never realized all of this was here. Can we come back again soon?"

Erin pushed away the thoughts of money and smiled. "Sure. Maybe next time we could even do some fishing."

Diana seemed to give the suggestion some thought. "I think I might be willing to give that a try." She linked her arm through Erin's and they continued to walk.

CHAPTER TWENTY-EIGHT

They left Rockport the following morning. On the trip back they were both enchanted with the riotous display of wildflowers along the highway.

"I can't believe we missed all of this when we drove down," Diana said as they drove past a particularly spectacular patch of bluebonnets and yellow buttercups.

"It was so dark we couldn't see them. I had forgotten how pretty the wildflowers can be out this way."

They chatted all the way back to San Antonio and the miles flew by quickly. When they pulled into the apartment complex, Erin held her breath until she saw the light reflecting off the new windows in her truck.

"They fixed them," Diana said happily. "I was worried." She parked next to the truck.

Erin got out and examined the repairs. Everything seemed fine.

"If you'll carry the table, I'll get your bag," Diana offered.

As they climbed the stairs to their apartments, Erin experienced a stab of something akin to regret. "I had fun this weekend," she said when they reached the landing.

"Me too. Thanks for going. I know it was a bad time for you to leave, but I think we both needed the time away."

Erin smiled and nodded. She had managed to keep thoughts of Ashley at bay throughout most of the weekend. That all changed as soon as they stepped into the hallway. Even before she reached her door Erin could see that something was wrong. She set the table down and slowly moved forward.

"What's wrong?" Diana asked.

Erin stared at the shiny padlock that now secured the door. It took her a moment to notice the damaged wood of the doorjamb.

Diana gasped. "Oh, my God! I've been robbed!"

Erin turned and noticed that Diana's door also had a padlock on it. Neither of the women spoke as they stared at the busted doors. Erin didn't want to accept the suspicion that was beginning to germinate.

"I guess we'd better go see if Mr. Tyler is in," Diana said as she set the bags down.

They went to the office together and found an extremely unhappy apartment manager awaiting them. As soon as he saw them he jumped to his feet and stormed toward them.

"Ladies," he began before they could speak, "I can't tell you how upset I am by all this. It's been a madhouse since Friday night with all the calls and people coming in looking for you."

Erin frowned. Who would have been looking for her? She started to speak but Tyler launched back into his tirade.

"Ms. Fox, this will simply not do." He glared at Erin. "I don't know what's going on and quite frankly I don't want to know." He paused to give her a chance to fill him in. When she didn't, he glared harder. "I've spoken to the owners and I'm sorry, but we have no alternative. I'm officially giving you notice that you have five days to evacuate the apartment. We can't have this sort of behavior—"

Numb, Erin let the news bounce off of her. The alarm clock would go off any moment now and all of this would be nothing but a bad dream.

"You can't cancel her lease," Diana protested. "It's not our fault that someone broke into our apartments. Maybe the owners should be thinking about improving security rather than placing blame."

He held up a hand. "We most certainly can issue an eviction notice. From the description that Mr. Griswold gave, it appears to be the same woman who vandalized vehicles in the parking lot Friday." He hesitated slightly. "If you were to consult a lawyer you might possibly find that you would be entitled to a couple of more days, but rest assured we are totally within our rights to evict you." He fussed with his hair. "After all, we do have the safety of our other tenants to think of."

A spark of anger snapped Erin's head up. "My truck was the only one damaged Friday. No one else was involved. What happened exactly?" she asked.

Mr. Tyler looked pained as he took a deep breath. "Mr. Griswold called me very late Friday night to report the noise in your apartment. Let me add that this is not the first time he has called complaining about the noise from your apartment," he said, nodding toward Erin. "Of course I was concerned, since I knew you were supposed to be out of town and I told him so, but he insisted the noise was coming from your apartment. I, of course, got dressed and started over to investigate and he called me back, saying the disturbance was getting louder. He informed me that he was going to come up and stop it himself." Tyler waved his hand. "I tried to stop him, but that man is impossible."

Erin could sense he wasn't finished with his story, so she waited for him to continue.

"Anyway," he went on, "Griswold told the police that when he pounded on your door, Ms. Fox, a young woman ran out of Ms. Garza's apartment and practically attacked him. She actually accused Mr. Griswold of"—he placed his hand over his mouth and coughed softly—"of having an affair with you." He looked directly at Erin and smirked.

"So you called the police?" Diana asked.

"Most definitely. I had no way in which to contact either of you. I can only assume you were off somewhere together." He glanced back and forth between them. When they neither confirmed nor denied his assumption he gave a small clucking sound. "It is completely within my authority and responsibility to inform the authorities. I am, after all, the manager."

"Did they catch the woman?" Erin asked.

He scrunched his lips into a prim pout. "No. Unfortunately by the time I arrived, she had already escaped. Griswold was unable to subdue her."

"Do you have the key to the padlock on our doors?" Erin asked. "I'd like to get into my apartment now."

He turned without answering and went to his desk. When he returned he had two keys and an envelope. He handed a key to Diana. "I have to warn you, Ms. Garza, that you have been given fair warning. We will not tolerate this sort of trouble. If there is any further trouble, you will also be asked to leave. You're responsible for the necessary repairs to your apartment. I personally inspect all repairs to ensure they're properly done."

"This had nothing to do with her," Erin said. "She doesn't even know the woman who did this. That woman has . . . some problems and probably wasn't even aware of what she was doing."

"I'm not interested in excuses," he replied as he handed her a key and the envelope. "Here's your eviction notice. As I said you have five days. If you want to hire a lawyer, you are certainly within your rights. I've also enclosed a letter informing you that the cost of repairs will be deducted from your deposit. If there are any remaining monies, a check will be forwarded to you." He turned to Diana. "You'll be responsible for the cost of repairing the damage to your apartment as well. If you want to press Ms. Fox for reimbursing you, that will be something you'll have to handle on your own."

A slow anger began to swell in Erin. She wished she could punch the smug bastard. Instead she turned and left.

"I'm really sorry you got dragged into my mess," she said to Diana as they walked back to their apartments. "I'll certainly reimburse you for damages." Even as she made the offer she didn't know how she would ever make good on it.

"This wasn't your fault and you don't have worry about me. My father insisted I take renter's insurance. I'm sure I'm covered. What are you going to do? Where are you going to live?"

"I can stay with friends until I find another place," Erin said, knowing she could turn to Mary and Alice for help.

They walked in silence. When they reached the hallway they stopped and stared at the damaged doors.

"Maybe we should do this together," Diana suggested.

Erin nodded and slipped the key into the padlock on her door. She had thought she'd be prepared for the sight, but the mess inside stopped her cold. Furniture was overturned. A leg on the old coffee table was broken off. Cushions on the chair and couch had been ripped open and the stuffing strewn everywhere. Chards of dishes and glassware glittered like scattered jewels. The television screen was broken and her computer was lying on the floor. The printer was across the room in several different pieces. Her small stereo, a birthday present from her parents, looked as though it had been used as a battering ram.

In the kitchen bottles of juice and condiments had been taken from the refrigerator and smashed against the walls and floor. Tears rolled down her cheeks as she moved around her demolished home. When she stepped into the bedroom and saw the shattered mirror on the antique dresser that she and her dad had restored she went numb. She grabbed onto the bedroom door to keep from falling as she surveyed the damage. The bed linens had been ripped to shreds and the mattress slashed open. The lamps appeared to have been thrown against the wall. Her meager wardrobe was now nothing more than a pile of torn rags. She found her grandmother's quilt in a heap across the room. She grabbed it up and lovingly inspected every inch. There were a couple of rips along the ruffled edge.

"I can help you fix that," Diana murmured.

Erin nodded before stumbling into the bathroom. It was as though she had stepped into a different room. This was the only area of the apartment that had escaped Ashley's onslaught. The order of the room left Erin feeling disoriented. She turned. A pale and shaking Diana was standing behind her. They made their way back toward the kitchen. It was then that Erin saw the answering machine lying on the floor. The red light was calmly blinking. Drawn to the only thing that still seemed to be intact, she picked it up and hit the play button and gasped when she discovered she had eighteen unheard messages.

Suddenly Ashley's voice filled the air. "Where are you?" she demanded.

Shocked by the all too real sound of Ashley's voice, Erin hit the erase button and kept hitting it as Ashley's voice poured from call after call. Without warning the voice changed from Ashley's to Erin's mother.

"Erin, what's going on? Some woman keeps calling here demanding to know where you are. She won't leave her name. Are you in some sort of trouble? Please call us as soon as you get in."

Diana slipped her arm around Erin as the next message began. It was Ashley and Erin hit erase. Then it was Mary.

"Hey, it's Mary. What the hell's going on? Someone—I think it's Ashley Wade—keeps calling here asking for you. Where are you? I thought you were sick. Call me. I don't care what time it is. Just call."

There were more messages from Ashley intermixed with two other messages from her mom. Erin could hear the growing concern in her mother's voice. But when she heard the message from Sonia, her supervisor, Erin's legs began to shake. "This is Sonia. I'm calling because someone has called the office three times today looking for you and then she called my cell num—" The message

175

shutoff as the tape came to its end. In the silence that followed, Erin realized her life would never be the same.

"How did she get everyone's phone numbers?" Diana asked.

Erin started to shrug but remembered the small notebook of phone numbers she had always kept by the phone. Ashley must have found it. "I have to call my parents," she mumbled. "They'll be worried sick by now."

"I'll leave you alone."

"No. Please don't leave. I know you want to check on your place. I'd rather you didn't go alone, but I really need to call Mom and Dad. I promise I'll only be a minute."

Diana nodded. "Take all the time you need." She glanced at the devastation around them. "I'm going to wait for you in the hallway."

Erin's father answered the phone before the first ring was complete. Her mom was on the extension and they were both talking to her at once. It took her a moment to calm them enough to allow her to partially explain.

"I'm okay," she began. "I went to the coast with a friend Friday night and we just got back."

"Who is this woman and why does she keep calling?" her mother asked.

Erin took a deep breath. "Are you guys going to be home this weekend?" she asked. "This is sort of complicated and—"

"Erin Janelle Fox," her mother snapped, "I have no intentions of waiting until the weekend to know what's going on with you."

"I understand. That's not what I meant." She stopped and steadied her breathing. "I'm really sorry that you've been so worried. I have to do something right now, so can we compromise? I'll call you back in an hour and tell you everything that's going on. I promise that I'm all right and that I'm in absolutely no sort of danger. I have a friend here with me if you'd like to ask her."

"Yes, I would," her mother said.

"Noreen," her father cut in. "If Erin says she's fine, then she's fine."

Erin's heart hurt when she heard her mother sniff and the extension disconnect.

"Erin," her father began in a tone that left no doubt he wasn't fooling around, "you call your mother back or I'll be driving down there *tonight*."

"Yes, sir. I will."

"You are okay, aren't you?"

"I'm fine." *At least physically*, she thought.

She hung up the phone and found Diana was sitting on the floor in the hallway, staring at her apartment door.

"Ready?" Erin asked.

Diana nodded slightly and stood. The journey across the hallway seemed to take forever. As Diana opened the padlock on her apartment door, Erin braced herself for the devastation she knew they'd fine.

Diana stood with her hand on the doorknob for a long moment before stepping back. "I'm afraid to open it," she whispered.

"Let me," Erin said. She couldn't remember ever feeling so bad about anything in her life. After a deep breath, she turned the doorknob and pushed. The door opened slowly. She looked inside and her jaw dropped. The room was the same as it had the last time she'd been there for dinner. Nothing was disturbed. She motioned Diana inside. "It's okay," she said, laughing nervously.

Diana's eyes grew wide. "You mean it?" she whispered.

Erin nodded, too relieved to speak.

Together they hurried to the bedroom and back to the kitchen. Other than the busted door, there was no other evidence of any damage and nothing seemed to be missing.

CHAPTER TWENTY-NINE

"I don't understand," Diana said as they stood in her living room. "Why did she break in and then not disturb anything?"

Erin shrugged. "Maybe she was too exhausted after trashing my place." She tried to smile but was too tired to pull it off.

They stood in silence for a long moment. "I should go back over and call my parents. I don't know how I'm going to explain this to them."

Diana put a hand on Erin's shoulder. "Just tell them the truth. From everything you've told me about them, I think they'll understand."

"Yeah. They will." Erin went to the door. Their bags and the table were still sitting in the hallway. She picked up Diana's bag and brought it in.

"You're welcome to stay over here tonight if you'd like," Diana offered.

"Thanks, but I need to get everything cleaned up and see if I have anything left to pack." When she thought of Sonia's call she felt ill. Would she still have a job come tomorrow morning? Since she had called in sick to work on Friday morning, going to the coast that night probably wasn't a smart move on her part. She picked up the table and her bag and went back to her apartment.

Before she could call her parents her phone began to ring. She approached the phone slowly. Part of her wanted to confront Ashley and demand an explanation, while a more rational part of her understood that it was Ashley's illness that was responsible for the damage. A short-lived sense of relief washed over her when she saw Mary's name flashing on the screen. This call would be almost as bad as talking to her parents. She realized that Alice and Mary would have been worried about her.

"Are you okay?" Mary asked as soon as Erin answered.

"Yes, I'm fine."

"We'll be there in twenty-five minutes. Don't you dare leave." Mary hung up before Erin could protest.

Erin slowly dialed her parents' phone number. This time her mom answered first and her father was on the extension. She gave them a severely sanitized version of the story with Ashley, conveniently leaving out Jess and both cases of vandalism. She was still talking to them when she saw Mary's car pull into the parking lot. "Mom, I need to do some laundry. I'll see you guys this weekend."

"Call us before you leave," her father said.

Erin barely had time to hang up before there was a pounding on her door. As soon as she opened it, Mary and Alice barged in, clearly ready to read her the riot act. At the sight of the place they stopped dead.

"What in the hell happened here?" Mary asked.

Erin wondered if she could simply will herself to disappear. "Ashley." Her throat seemed to close around the word, forcing her to cough.

Alice was quickly by her side. "Oh, you poor thing. Mary, get her a glass of water."

Mary started into the kitchen but stopped when she saw the

empty cabinets. "Um . . . there don't seem be any glasses that aren't—"

"I'm fine," Erin replied.

The three of them were silently surveying the mess when there was a knock at the door. Erin stiffened. Could it be Ashley coming back?

Mary shot across the room before Erin could respond. From the way she threw the door open, Erin was certain it was a good thing that the visitor wasn't Ashley.

A shocked Diana recoiled. She was carrying two large grocery bags. "I went to buy some trash bags. I thought I'd help you clean up," she said to Erin.

"Now there's a woman with a brain," Alice declared as she pushed Erin and Mary out of the way and helped Diana in with the bags.

Alice began assigning tasks with the efficiency of a drill sergeant. They had barely gotten started when there was another knock at the door. Erin was the closest to it and opened it. Work inside ceased as they all stood staring at Jess Lawler. To Erin, Jess looked as though she had aged ten years since she had seen her on Friday. Could it really have only been two days earlier when Jess had first come to the apartment asking her to drop the charges against Ashley?

Erin stepped back, stunned by the surge of anger that ripped through her. Jess took the movement as an invitation to enter. Upon seeing the apartment she broke into tears.

"I'm so sorry," she kept whispering as Alice tried to calm her.

Erin's anger dissipated as quickly as it had surfaced. Jess wasn't responsible for any of this. There was no one to blame but herself. She was the one who got involved with Ashley, even after Mary and Alice tried to warn her.

When Jess finally calmed down everyone went back to work. Jess worked alongside them.

It was almost nine thirty that night before Mary, Jess and Erin hauled the last of the garbage bags out to the nearly full Dumpster at the side of the complex. This was actually the second Dumpster.

They had already filled the one out back a couple of hours earlier. There hadn't been much sorting to do since Ashley had literally ripped everything to shreds. Most of the cleaning consisted of sweeping up the debris.

Erin was so tired she could barely put one foot in front of the other. She didn't argue when Mary stopped at one of the picnic tables and motioned for them to sit down.

At first no one spoke and then Jess began. Erin listened as Jess explained how she had been called by one of other cops at the sub-station to let her know there was an APB out for Ashley's arrest. Jess had found her hiding in the closet of their bedroom. Ashley had been so violent that Jess had no choice but to call for help. Ashley had been taken to the hospital and placed under a suicide watch.

"The hospital wouldn't listen to anything I said," Jess said. "They called her parents in Arizona." Her voice broke. She stopped and took a moment before continuing. "They flew in Saturday afternoon. They're trying to get all this mess straightened out, so that they can take her back to Arizona." She paused again. "They're going to . . . to . . . have her locked away in one of those places. They won't let me take care of her."

Mary put an arm around Jess's shoulders. "You can't do it alone. I know it's hard for you to watch them take her away, but maybe it's for the best. If they can get her the help she needs. I know you tried your best. Nobody can say you didn't."

"Even my best was never good enough," Jess replied bitterly. "There were times when I thought she had it licked. She'd be taking her meds like she was supposed to and everything would be good between us." She looked at Mary. "You know what I mean."

Mary nodded.

"Then she'd start thinking she could do without the meds and—" She shook her head. "I gotta get going. I have to be back at work in a couple of hours." She stood up to go and Mary followed her. They talked quietly for a moment before Mary gave her a quick hug.

When Mary returned she sighed. "Life's a strange thing. When

181

Jess and I used to run around together, she was always so confident about everything. She was good at sports. Women flocked to her like bees to honey." She gave a short humorless chuckle. "I sort of looked up to her, wanted to be like her. Who would have ever thought?" She sighed again. "We'd better get back inside before Alice comes looking for us."

Erin looked up and saw Diana waving to them. "Too late," she said.

"We've ordered pizza," Diana called out.

Erin waved an acknowledgment as Diana went inside.

"She seems nice," Mary said, nodding toward Diana.

"She is." Erin glanced at Mary. "Don't go there," she warned.

Mary gave her a look of innocence. "What are you talking about?"

"I'm not ready to even think about seeing anyone."

"Hey, I just said she seems nice. I didn't suggest you rent a U-Haul." She stopped suddenly. "Dang, Erin, I didn't mean anything—"

Erin grabbed Mary's arm and gave it a gentle squeeze. "I know that. Come on. Let's go get something to eat. I just realized I'm starving."

CHAPTER THIRTY

As they ate, Erin sat on the floor and eyed her apartment. Nothing much was left. As she surveyed the meager remnants of her possessions, she kept thinking about Ashley. A part of Erin wanted to hate her for all the damage—both physical and emotional—that she had caused, yet a deeper part of her just hurt. What Ashley was going through now must be hell. Erin wondered how much Ashley was aware of. Did she even know what was happening to her? Had she realized what she was doing when she trashed the apartment? Or was it all like a dream to her? It must be terrifying to be locked up. A small shiver ran down Erin's back. She fought the thoughts off and looked at the broken leg on the coffee table, which could be repaired. It wouldn't be great, but it would work for a while. Alice had assured her that the couch and chair could be reupholstered, but the television, stereo and computer were shot. Her mattress and box springs were down by the Dumpster. At least the bed frame was intact. She hoped her father would be able to help her replace the glass in the mirror on the dresser, which had received a couple of deep scratches along with several minor ones. She could fix those. All of her clothes except what she had taken to the coast and two pairs of jeans were now in the trash. There were no dishes left. A couple of pots had survived with nothing more serious than a ding or a missing handle. The old table in the dining room was still standing and three of the four chairs were useable. Ashley had apparently overlooked the antique lap desk Erin had been restoring for her mother. It had been in a box in the closet. Other than those few items Erin had nothing. Suddenly it hit her that she soon wouldn't even have a place to stay, and she began to shake. She considered the possibility of moving to Austin to live with her parents. It went without saying that they would be there to help her in any way they could. The idea evaporated as quickly as it had appeared. She wasn't ready to make that move yet.

"Erin, you can stay with us until you're able to get new furniture," Alice said.

Erin leaned against the bar and tried to control her shaking limbs. The others were sitting at the table. "I'll be fine here," Erin said. She didn't feel like being around anyone.

"You can't stay here," Mary and Diana said together.

Erin tried to control her irritation. She knew they were only trying to help.

"What are you going to do after Friday?" Diana asked.

Erin glared up at her. She hadn't talked to Mary or Alice yet. Now they would really have a cow.

"What's going on Friday?" Mary asked. Her suspicious nature was on full alert.

Diana waited for Erin to speak.

As soon as Mary and Alice found out about the eviction, they would insist she stay with them and she didn't want to become a burden. Mary was clearly still waiting for an answer. Erin knew she didn't have many choices so she gave up. "I'm being evicted."

"What?" Mary and Alice gasped in unison.

"The apartment manager gave me a five-day eviction notice."

"Can he do that?" Alice asked.

184

Erin shrugged. She would feel better if she could rant and rave about his unfair treatment, but she couldn't. "I don't blame him," she admitted. "His job is to take care of the place and the tenants. He told me I could hire a lawyer, but I can't see where it'd do much good. I'd have to take time off of work. In the end, I'd still probably have to move, plus I'd owe the lawyer."

They were all silent for a moment.

"You'll come and stay with us until you're back on your feet," Alice insisted.

Erin wanted to protest, but she knew she really didn't have any other options unless she wanted to move to Austin with her parents. "Thanks. I'll find a place as soon as I can."

Mary and Alice quickly waved away her concern. "There's plenty of room," Mary insisted.

Diana stood up and rubbed her lower back. "I should get going. Tomorrow is a workday."

They all agreed. Erin's body ached as she pulled herself upright and walked to the door with Diana.

"I'm sorry if I spoke when I shouldn't have about the eviction," Diana said. "I didn't think."

"That's okay. I was just trying to avoid the inevitable." She followed Diana into the hallway.

"Despite all this, I really enjoyed the weekend," Diana said.

"Too bad we had to come back to this, huh?"

Diana looked at her for a moment. "I'm going to miss having you as a neighbor."

"The apartment will be rented out soon enough."

Diana pushed a lock of hair away from Erin's forehead. "It won't be the same."

"No, I'm sure it'll be much quieter," Erin said in an attempt to lighten the mood.

"Can we still get together occasionally?"

"Sure. Mary and Alice only live about twenty minutes away. I'll give you their address and phone number before I leave."

"I'd like that." The usual sense of comfort that existed between them suddenly disappeared.

Erin struggled to think of something to say, but nothing came. She licked her lips and slipped her hands into her pockets.

"I'll see you," Diana said with a small sigh.

"Yeah, sure." Erin rushed back into her apartment.

"Is there anything you want to take with you tonight?" Mary asked.

Erin looked around. "I'll take the table and that box." She pointed to the table she had purchased at the yard sale and the box containing the antique lap desk. She added to her bag the two pairs of intact jeans they had found beneath the wreckage in the bedroom. She would have to do laundry tonight. Alice took the bag from her and Mary picked up the box. Without looking back, Erin grabbed the table. "I'm ready." As they headed down the hall, she heard the soft sounds of music coming from Diana's apartment. Her steps faltered, but she quickly recovered. She had nothing to offer anyone. As they walked down the stairs she refused to allow herself the luxury of feeling sorry for herself.

After putting her things into the back of her truck, Erin followed Mary and Alice out of the parking lot. A horn blared at her as a car swung into the opposite lane. She had pulled out in front of it without even seeing it. Shaken by the near miss, she focused all of her attention on their taillights. By the time she pulled into their driveway, she was ready to weep with exhaustion.

They helped her unload her things. As soon as they were inside, Alice insisted on putting fresh bed linens on. "No one has slept in that room in months. The sheets will smell musty after all that time."

"They're fine," Erin assured her. "I need to do some laundry, though."

"Mary, you show her how to start that cranky old washer," Alice said, pulling fresh sheets from the hallway linen closet.

Erin started to protest, but Mary took her by the arm. "Come on. I learned a long time ago that it's easier to just let her have her way. Once she makes up her mind there's no changing it."

It was almost midnight before Erin was finally alone in her new home. The bedroom was much larger than her old bedroom, and the adjoining bath was almost twice as large as the one in the apartment. She grabbed a clean T-shirt and went to take a hot shower, hoping it would help her relax. Rather than relax her, the shower only seemed to make her more alert. She crawled into the bed and stretched out before starting a mental list of things she needed to do. Tomorrow afternoon after work, she would start looking for a second job. She would flip burgers if necessary. As soon as she had enough saved for a deposit she could start looking for another apartment. She could buy used furniture a little at a time until she had what she needed. What then? She sat up. Then she would be right back where she was before meeting Ashley. She crawled out of bed and began to pace. That was not where she wanted to be. *What do I want?* she asked herself as she pounded her fist against her forehead. She was still wrestling with her demons when she heard Mary and Alice begin to stir a little after six.

CHAPTER THIRTY-ONE

Erin was in the process of signing on to the system when Sonia approached her.

"I need to talk to you," Sonia said. "Sign off and meet me in the small conference room."

Erin nodded and glanced over at Mary, who was watching them, her eyebrows raised in inquiry. Erin shrugged and shook her head as she shut down her machine.

When she reached the conference room, Sonia was waiting for her. She motioned to a chair across from her and asked Erin to sit. "I thought we should talk."

Erin's stomach began to hurt. This didn't look good.

"Don't look so scared," Sonia said. "I'm not firing you."

Erin gave a weak smile, but for some reason the words didn't give her much comfort.

Sonia opened a folder and spread out several sheets of paper. Erin recognized them as the daily stat sheets they received. "Your work has been slipping the last few months," Sonia began. "Your process errors are up and your keystrokes are down significantly." She folded her hands and looked at Erin. "What's going on?"

Erin swallowed. She liked Sonia. She was a good manager and knew her job, but Erin didn't feel comfortable discussing her private life with her. "Nothing," she replied.

Sonia sighed and leaned back in her chair. "I know you're a very private person. I try to respect that, but when your work starts dropping off, I have to get involved. Can you understand that?"

Erin nodded. "I just have a lot of things on my mind. I'll do better."

"That's what you told me when we last spoke. Things haven't improved." She leaned forward slightly. "Do you want to keep working here?"

Erin's head snapped up and for a long moment the two women stared at each other. For the first time, Erin really saw Sonia—not as a taskmaster who dictated her every move from nine to five every day, but as a forty-something woman who was as trapped in this job as she was. There were streaks of gray beginning to appear in her dark hair, and circles beneath her eyes. When Erin looked closer she sensed a heaviness about Sonia that reeked of unhappiness. "Are you happy?" Erin asked.

Sonia blinked at the question. "We're not here to discuss me," she sputtered.

Erin tried to put her feelings into words. "I need this job," she said. "Do I like it? No. But I don't hate it exactly either. It's sort of like going to the dentist. I don't like doing it, but the alternative is worse." She rubbed her cheek. "Do I want to keep working here?" she asked aloud and realized she didn't have a definitive answer. "At this point in my life, I don't have a choice." She waited for Sonia to tell her to leave. When she didn't, Erin pushed her luck. "Do you ever wish you were doing something else?"

Sonia smiled slightly before answering. "Of course, I used to. Everyone does."

"What did you want to do?"

"I think I would have made a great wedding planner." She blushed slightly. "My husband says I have a talent for what he calls the 'foo-foos.'"

"Why don't you do it?"

Sonia looked at her and shook her head. "You're still so young." She stopped and, for a moment, Erin didn't think she was going to continue, but she finally gave a small sigh and said, "I have three kids. Gary, my husband, works for a small landscaping company that doesn't offer health insurance. We depend on my job to provide healthcare coverage."

"Couldn't you do it in your spare time?"

"I work at least fifty hours a week here and have three kids. Spare time is a luxury that disappeared a long time ago."

At that moment, Erin made up her mind. She was going to find a way out. If it meant going to college, then she'd stop whining, buckle down and do whatever it took. "I'm sorry about those phone calls." She took a deep breath. "I've had a few problems," she admitted. "I think the worst is over. I'll start doing better."

Sonia studied her. For a moment she seemed on the verge of saying something, but then began to gather up the stat sheets. "Good. If there's nothing else, you can go on back to your desk."

Erin stood to leave.

"By the way, the home office has approved our requests for overtime. I'll be announcing it later today."

"I'll take all I can get."

"I appreciate it. Just sign the request sheet when it comes around."

Erin nodded and left. She couldn't help but notice that it was several minutes before Sonia returned to her desk.

When break time rolled around, Mary waited until she and Erin were alone on the stairs before asking her about her meeting with Sonia.

"She just wanted to talk to me about my stats. They still aren't up where she wants them to be." Before Mary could pursue the subject, Erin quickly changed the subject. "That shed you have out back, is there room in it for me to work on that table?"

"Sure. We just store the Christmas decorations and some other junk out there. If you want I'll help you clear out a corner this afternoon."

"Thanks, but I think I'll be working overtime."

"Overtime?"

"Yeah, Sonia mentioned that they had received approval."

"Oh, damn," Mary muttered. "She'll start riding my butt again to work overtime."

Erin opened the stairwell door. "Just tell her I'm working your hours. I'm going to sign up to come in at seven. Maybe I'll even be able to stay later in the evenings. I'll have to wait and see how much she'll approve."

Mary frowned at her. "You know, you don't have to kill yourself. You can stay as long as you like."

"I know, but I want to do it." They walked into the noisy cafeteria. As she grabbed a bottle of juice, Erin felt a touch of her old self returning. If she could put in at least two extra hours a day plus Saturdays, she'd be able to start looking for an apartment in about a month.

When the overtime sheet was circulated, Erin signed up for a seven to seven shift and an additional eight hours on Saturday. She wasn't surprised when Sonia came by her desk a while later.

"Is this right?" Sonia asked, holding the sheet out to her.

"Yes."

"That's twenty-eight hours of overtime a week. Are you sure you can handle it?"

"I'm positive." She held her breath as Sonia thought about it. If she could maintain the hours, she would have the money for a deposit in a little over three weeks.

"I'm going to give you a tentative approval," Sonia replied. "If I see your stats dipping, I'm going to cancel the request."

"Okay," Erin replied, knowing that nothing short of a disaster was going to stop her from working the extra hours. "Can I start today?"

Sonia made a notation on the sheet. "You can work until seven today if you'd like."

After work that day Erin went clothes shopping and picked up a couple of items she needed for the table. It hurt her to add yet another expense to her credit card, but it couldn't be avoided. Afterward she called her parents. She was grateful her father answered. She told him she wouldn't be able to drive up for the weekend and explained that she was working overtime. Her father assured her that he understood but reminded her to call her mother or to at least e-mail her. She agreed to e-mail since it was cheaper than calling. She could use the computer in Mary and Alice's kitchen.

Each weekday morning she was up at six, at her desk by seven and working until seven that night. When she arrived home each evening, she ate a quick dinner, washed her dishes and went to the small workshop where she happily tackled the challenge of restoring the table. On Saturday, she worked from seven until three-thirty. Mary and Alice were gone when she came in, so she changed and went straight to the workshop. Earlier in the week she had managed to get the mechanism that controlled the tilt top to work again and had started the slow, tedious process of cleaning the wood. One of the downward-turned splayfeet was completed and she had cleaned about halfway up the second. After pouring some of the cleaning solution into a tin can, she grabbed a handful of cotton swabs and moved the table to the open doorway and began to work. A slight glimmer of guilt prodded her about not going to see her parents today. There was still plenty of time for her to drive to Austin and spend the night with them, but she wasn't ready to face the concerned looks and questions she knew they would have. She would go to see them soon, she promised herself.

As the grime and thick wax buildup slowly gave way to her gentle coaxing, everything else receded and the tension in her shoulders began to ease. By the time she realized it was growing dark, she had finished the three splayfeet and was working on the turned baluster support. She moved the table back into the workshop and turned the light on. The baluster was the dirtiest area and would be the hardest part to clean. Her hand soon found a comfortable rhythm. The grime gave way in hairline increments. She fought the urge to start on the top. That was the section she loved working on most. *Patience*, she told herself. If the entire length was as bad as the section she was working on, it could take her over a week just to finish the baluster. Swallowing her impulse to hurry, she forced herself to concentrate on what she was doing. She thought about how pleased Diana would be when she saw the restored table. Thinking of Diana gave her another small moment of guilt. She had promised she would give Diana her new address and phone number. Something was holding her back. She missed talking to Diana and was eager to complete the table to show her, but each time she reached for the phone to call, she changed her mind.

Her neck was beginning to ache from the odd position she was in. She found an old piece of cardboard and turned the table upside down to relieve the stress on her neck. By the time Mary came out to check on her, she had cleaned almost a fourth of the baluster.

CHAPTER THIRTY-TWO

A wave of hot air rushed out of the truck when Erin opened the door. It was only the first Saturday in May, but the late afternoon temperatures were already reaching the uncomfortable stage. She sighed as she rolled the windows down and cranked the engine. She had lost track of the number of hours of overtime she had worked in the past month. With the extra income she was making she had been able to give Mary and Alice a few bucks to help with food and utilities. Plus, she'd managed to pay off her earlier credit card bill, in addition to the $100 additional charge that Tyler had billed her for a new door, locks and labor. It would be at least another month before she would have enough to begin looking for an apartment. Mary and Alice had been wonderful, and had gone out of their way to make her feel at home, but she was ready to move on.

The garage sale table was finished. It was more beautiful than she could have hoped for. The lap desk for her mother was almost finished, too. All that was left to do was to wax it. That wasn't the only thing she needed to do, she reminded herself. She still hadn't contacted Diana. She tried to pinpoint why she hadn't called but couldn't. She missed her and wanted to talk to her, but something was holding her back. Erin pushed the thoughts away and headed back to the house. There would still be time for her to work on the gift for her mom. She would be driving to Austin next Saturday morning. Tom and his wife, Edith, were coming in from Chicago.

When she arrived back at the house, neither Mary's nor Alice's car was in the driveway. Between working overtime and spending time in the workshop, Erin hadn't seen much of them. In fact, since moving in, she had seen less of them than before.

Erin poured a glass of juice before flipping on the television. After channel-surfing for several minutes she gave up and turned it off. She was too antsy to work on the lap desk. Without giving herself time to think about it, she dialed Diana's number. Since it was Saturday she didn't expect Diana to be home and was caught off-guard when she answered.

"I didn't think you were going to call," Diana said when she heard Erin's voice.

"I've been so busy and . . ." She let the rest of the thought go unspoken.

An awkward pause settled between them.

"I was wondering if you'd like to go out to dinner somewhere," Erin said. "I know it's late and you probably already have plans."

"I do, actually."

"Oh. Well, maybe some other time. I'll let you go."

"Erin, wait. Do you like Thai food?"

"Yeah."

"How about I meet you at Thai Taste at seven?"

"Sure."

After hanging up, Erin returned to the workshop. She whistled as she applied the final coat of wax to the lap desk. The piece had turned out better than she had expected. As she was leaving to go shower, her gaze fell on the table she had restored. She wrapped it in what was left of an old bedspread that Alice had given her to tear into work rags, then placed it in her truck.

Diana's car was coming into the restaurant's parking lot when Erin arrived. She pulled her truck into the space next to Diana's Jeep.

"Perfect timing," Diana said as she stepped out.

Erin could feel herself smiling like an idiot, but she couldn't stop it. She was really glad to see her. "I brought something to show you," Erin said as she climbed into the bed of her truck and unwrapped the cloth from the table.

"You bought yourself a nice table," Diana exclaimed when she saw the piece.

Erin smiled even brighter. "You like it?"

"Yes. It's beautiful."

"It's the table I bought at the garage sale."

"No, it's not. That thing was hideous."

Erin laughed. "It's the same table. I told you it could be restored."

Diana looked at her closely. "Are you serious? That's really the same table?"

Erin began to rewrap it. "It's the same one." She started to get out of the truck.

"You're not going to leave it sitting back here are you?"

"It's not supposed to rain," Erin said as she gazed up at the clear sky.

"Aren't you afraid someone will take it?"

Erin glanced back at the table. It hadn't occurred to her that anyone would bother with it. "I guess I shouldn't have brought it."

"No, I'm glad you did. I can't believe how beautiful it looks."

Erin began to uncover the table again. "I think it'll fit in the cab of my truck, if I tilt the top down."

"You can put it inside the Jeep while we eat," Diana suggested.

Concerned about the possibility of scratching the table's legs, Erin agreed.

"I've missed talking to you," Diana said after they were inside the restaurant and waiting for their food.

"I've been working as much overtime as I can and working on the table at night," Erin said as she fiddled with an empty sweetener packet. "How have you been?"

"Good. I've started my countdown to summer vacation. I know it probably sounds silly to you, but it's only twenty more days until school is out. I love teaching but I can't wait until that final bell of the year rings."

Erin smiled and nodded. "Alice has been floating around the house the last few days also."

They sat in silence for a moment.

"They rented your old apartment out."

"Really?"

"Yes. It's a woman with a small girl. She sort of keeps to herself."

Erin shook her head. "That place was so small. I can't image how crowded she must be."

"Have you heard anything else about Ashley?"

"No. I think Mary has seen Jess a couple of times. I sort of heard her and Alice talking one night, but they clammed up when I came in."

Diana nodded. "They seem like such nice women."

"They're the greatest. I don't know what I would have done without them. They always seem to be bailing me out of one jam or another. I just hope that someday I'll be as together as they are."

"I'm sure they weren't always so together. I think that's something that comes with age and experience."

"You seem to be settled and we're about the same age."

Diana made a small hissing sound. "Trust me, if it weren't for my family, I'd probably be living on the streets somewhere. You forget I lived with my sister for three months before I moved into the apartment. Shelly's parents were there to help us out after we came home from college." She shrugged. "Don't be so hard on yourself. You were doing fine. You don't strike me as the sort of person who will stay down long."

197

Erin's cheeks grew warm at the unexpected compliment. She hoped Diana was right.

After dinner they stood outside the restaurant. Neither seemed ready to call an end to the evening.

"Would you like . . ." they both started at once.

"You first," Erin said with a small laugh.

"I was going to ask if you'd like to go over to the bar for a while."

Erin hesitated. She hated the horrible smoke in bars, and the music was always so loud they wouldn't be able to talk.

"It doesn't have to be the bar. We could go to a movie or something," Diana added.

"A movie would be good."

They bought a paper from the box outside Thai Taste and spread it over the hood of Diana's Jeep.

"Oh, look. They're having a film festival of old horror movies at the Rialto downtown," Erin said, pointing out the ad.

Diana glanced at her watch. "*The Return of the Zombies* is going to start in thirty-five minutes. If we hurry we can make it."

"I'm not exactly sure how to get to the Rialto," Erin said.

"You can follow me or, if you'd rather, we can go together. That might be better since parking down there is a nightmare."

Erin glanced at her truck. "I guess it'll be all right to leave the truck here for a while." Until all the mess with Ashley, she wouldn't have thought twice about leaving the truck. "It'll be fine," she said as much to herself as to Diana.

"Will you be going to Austin for Mother's Day?" Diana asked after they were on the road.

"Yeah. We'll all be home. My brother Tom and his wife are coming in from Chicago and of course Andy and his wife will be there too." She shifted slightly so she could see Diana better. "What about your family? Is it a big day?"

A look of sadness crossed her face. "Everyone but Raul will be there."

"That's your brother in Iraq?"

"Yes. He was supposed to be coming home in June, but he thinks they're going to extend his tour."

"I'm sorry to hear that."

"We all miss him, but it's really hard on his wife, Heather. She seems so lost without him." She glanced at Erin. "They have this special bond." She shrugged. "I guess it's the same with all relationships, but I never felt like I had the same type of connection with Shelly."

"You mean because you weren't married?"

"No. It wasn't that. It's something deeper than anything a ceremony or a piece of paper offers." She was quiet for a moment. "Mary and Alice seem to have it. From the short time I spent with them that night, I sensed something."

Erin understood what she was getting at. "There is something special between them."

"Have you ever had that with anyone?" Diana asked. She slowed for a stoplight.

"No, but I hope to someday."

Diana nodded. "Me too." She gave a sudden burst of laughter. "Listen to us, we're making ourselves depressed. No more maudlin conversations tonight." She held out her hand and Erin shook it.

As she held Diana's hand in hers, she couldn't help but notice how soft and warm it felt. She ran her thumb across the back of Diana's hand before she realized what she was doing and let go.

"What's your favorite old movie?" she asked to fill the void that releasing Diana's hand had created.

"*Swamp Thing*," Diana replied without hesitation. "I saw it for the first time when I was around twelve. My brothers walked around the house making that horrible noise for days and every time I heard it, I'd get scared all over again."

They talked about movies for the rest of the way to the theater. They grabbed sodas and popcorn as they passed through the lobby. Erin was amazed to find the theater was already packed. She hadn't expected this many people to be interested in such an old movie. It took them a few minutes to locate two empty seats together. The opening credits began almost as soon as they were settled. Erin quickly lost track of the story line, because every time Diana got scared she grabbed Erin's hand or buried her head against Erin's shoulder. Erin spent so much time trying to interpret the flurry of sensations shooting through her that she missed most of what was going on in the movie. Diana didn't seem to notice the effect her actions were causing. Even after the movie was over and they were driving back to Erin's truck and discussing the movie, she kept reaching across and touching Erin's arm whenever she relived one of the scarier scenes.

By the time they reached the restaurant it was closed and Erin's truck was the lone vehicle in the parking lot.

"Thanks for going to the movie tonight," Diana said as she released her seatbelt.

Before Erin could respond Diana leaned across the seat and gave her a quick kiss. It was so fast that Erin had no time to respond.

Erin mumbled something about having a good time, then hopped out of the Jeep and scurried to her truck. She was almost home before she remembered she had left the table in the back of Diana's Jeep.

CHAPTER THIRTY-THREE

Later that night Erin lay in bed staring at the ceiling. She had given up any hope of falling asleep. There were too many thoughts running through her head, although she mostly kept replaying the kiss. *It didn't mean anything*, she told herself. It was just Diana's way. She was a very physical person. She was always touching Erin's shoulder or linking arms with her. It was a habit. That was it.

She sat up in bed. For Diana, touching was a mannerism and nothing more. Suddenly she felt miserable. She got up and made her way toward the kitchen for a glass of milk. She found Mary sitting at the table already with a glass of water.

"You're not old enough for the two a.m. wild monkey," Mary said as she motioned for Erin to join her. "What are you doing awake?"

"I don't know. I can't fall asleep."

Mary looked at her and made a small clucking sound.

"What?" Erin asked as she took a glass from the cabinet and poured herself some milk.

"When I was your age it was usually a woman who was keeping me up."

"When you were my age, it was Alice who was keeping you up," Erin replied with a knowing glance.

Mary smiled. "Well, you're right about that."

"What's keeping you up now?"

Mary gave a wide smile. "It's still Alice."

Erin made a face as she leaned against the counter. "Don't tell me any more. That's like talking to my parents about sex."

"What's your excuse?" Mary asked, ignoring Erin's comment.

Erin shrugged. "Nothing. I just couldn't sleep."

"Are you still worrying about money?"

"No. Not really. I mean, I wish I had enough to get out of your way."

"You're not in the way. We enjoy having you around. What little we see of you anyway. You work so much you're never here." She sipped her water.

Erin wanted to ask Mary's opinion of the kiss but was afraid she'd sound silly.

"You came in later than usual," Mary commented. "Hot date?"

Erin hesitated a moment too long and Mary pounced on it.

"Ah, so now we get to the bottom of the problem. Who is she?"

"It's not that," Erin protested. "After Ashley, it'll be a long time before I'm ready to see anyone again."

"It seems to me that it's usually when we're not looking that we find something."

"That's bull," Erin muttered as she sat down across from her.

"Do you want to talk about it?"

"There's nothing to talk about. Diana and I went downtown to the Rialto to see a movie."

"And?"

"And nothing. That was it. We had dinner and went to a movie."

"So you had dinner, too."

"Well, yeah, but that doesn't mean anything except we were hungry."

"You're right. It probably doesn't mean anything. It's just interesting that you didn't mention it the first time." She sipped her water again.

Erin gave a sigh of exasperation. "I didn't say anything about it because it didn't mean anything. Just like the kiss didn't mean—" She stopped short.

"Oh, now we're getting to the good part," Mary said, rubbing her hands together. "Tell me about this kiss that didn't mean anything."

"Who's kissing who and what are you two doing up in the middle of the night?" Alice asked as she padded in.

Erin couldn't keep from smiling as she studied the Minnie Mouse pajamas that Alice was wearing.

"Erin was just about to tell me all about how she and Diana spent hours kissing—"

"It was one little kiss," Erin interrupted.

"Sometimes that's all it takes," Mary said.

Alice put an arm around Mary's shoulders and squeezed her. "Are you harassing poor Erin?"

"Yes, she is," Erin replied.

"I'm not harassing her. I was sitting here minding my own business when she wandered in here telling me tales of woe," Mary insisted.

"Well, it's late and I think we'd all better try and get some sleep," Alice insisted. "You promised me we could go antiquing tomorrow."

Mary rolled her eyes. "I'll be up in plenty of time to get you to the shops before anything opens." She turned to Erin. "We're driving up to Comfort tomorrow. Why don't you go with us? It'll do you good to do something besides work for a change." She stopped and gave Erin a sly smile. "Unless you're busy, of course."

"I'm not busy."

"Good," Alice said, patting Mary's shoulder. "It's all settled. Now everyone off to bed."

Mary stood as Erin picked up both glasses and took them to the dishwasher. "You could invite Diana to join us, if you'd like," Mary said.

"That would be a splendid idea," Alice agreed. "The four of us could go up and have a nice lunch somewhere."

"I'm sure she's busy," Erin said, but a part of her wished Diana wouldn't be busy.

"You could call her in the morning," Mary said.

Erin started toward her bedroom. "No. I'm sure you guys will want to get an early start and Diana will probably spend the day with her family."

Erin climbed back into bed and soon drifted off to sleep.

The clattering of dishes woke her. She rolled over and looked at the clock. It was almost ten. Normally Alice and Mary were so quiet she never heard them. She smiled when she realized this was Alice's subtle way of getting her out of bed. Erin took a quick shower before pulling on an old pair of blue jean shorts and a T-shirt.

The two women were just sitting down to eat breakfast when she came into the kitchen.

"Oh, you're awake," Alice said as she jumped up and grabbed another plate. "Come and have some breakfast."

Erin sat down and used a fork to spear a couple of the pancakes from the large platter in the center of the table. As she ate, Alice kept up a running commentary on the shops she wanted to visit and telling Erin all about the items she had found in the shops on previous visits.

They had finished eating and were putting the dishes in the dishwasher when Mary stopped and turned to Erin. "I almost forgot. I talked to Diana this morning and invited her to join us."

Erin almost dropped the glass she was holding. "You what?"

Mary gave her an innocent smile. "She seemed excited about going." She stopped and put a finger on her chin. "Of course, that was after she found out you'd be going also." She shook her head and added, "I'm sure that doesn't mean anything, though." She glanced at her watch. "She should be along any minute now."

Erin had the childish impulse to stick her tongue out at Mary. Instead, she excused herself to run back to her room. When she returned a few moments later, she was dressed in her best navy shorts and the blue and white striped shirt. Everytime she wore the shirt someone would comment on how flattering it was on her.

When she joined Alice and Mary in the living room she ignored Mary's not-to-subtle snickers.

CHAPTER THIRTY-FOUR

Diana arrived a few minutes later and any awkwardness Erin might have felt was lost when Alice began to hustle everyone out to her van.

"Should I take my truck in case she finds something?" Erin asked Mary as they crossed the yard.

"No," Mary said quietly. "The idea is that the less room we have, the less she'll buy." She gave her a sidelong glance. "Unless you and Diana would rather be alone . . ."

"Oh, shut up," Erin groused. She crawled into the van, and as soon as they were all settled, she leaned forward. "Alice, if you find anything that won't fit in the van, I'll be happy to loan Mary my truck to pick it up."

"Oh, you're so sweet," Alice began. "Mary, do you think they'll still have that beautiful armoire?"

Mary glared at Erin in the rearview mirror. "We'll have to check and see," she replied. "Don't get your hopes up, though. It was over a month ago that you first saw it."

Diana apparently hadn't missed the exchange between Erin and Mary and turned to Erin with a questioning look. Erin simply smiled and shook her head.

The awkwardness that Erin had anticipated feeling around Diana didn't materialize. In fact, they all seemed to enjoy the ride up into the Hill Country. The wildflowers were still splashing the roadsides with a multitude of colors and Alice kept them entertained with interesting tidbits of the area's history.

As they wandered from store to store Erin found herself studying the prices of furniture, all of which were way too steep for her, but the germ of an idea was planted.

"The table you restored is much nicer than anything I've seen today," Diana whispered as she caught up with Erin in one shop.

"I forgot and left it in your Jeep last night," Erin said.

"Yes, I saw it. I took it inside last night." Diana hesitated. "Erin, would you mind if I kept it for a few days?"

Erin shrugged. "Of course not. Why?"

Diana picked up a small vase and examined it. "I'd rather not say just yet, but I promise I'll take care of it."

"I'm not worried about that. I know you will."

"Thank you." Diana set the vase down and reached over to squeeze Erin's arm. Just as she did Mary came around the corner and saw them. Her knowing smile made Erin's face burn. Diana didn't seem to notice as she casually released Erin's arm and wandered off to look at something else.

They shopped until after two before going to a small café for a late lunch. Erin was pleased to discover that the food was not only good but reasonably priced as well. She and Mary watched in silence as Alice and Diana talked about the upcoming summer and their plans. After eating, they went to a few more shops before heading home.

"I'm so glad you thought to invite me," Diana said as she leaned her head against Erin's shoulder. "I can't remember when I've had so much fun. It's good to finally be making friends here again. I sort of lost track with most of the people I knew in high school."

Erin experienced a flash of regret that it hadn't been her idea to ask Diana to join them. She glanced up to see Mary give her a quick wink. Erin smiled back and allowed herself to relax. It was obvious that Diana only considered her a friend. Somewhere along the way on the drive back Diana fell asleep on Erin's shoulder. The warm sweet scent of her hair teased Erin's nostrils. At one point when she was certain Mary was too busy driving to notice, Erin allowed herself the luxury of breathing in Diana's fragrance. She liked the warmth of Diana sitting so near her.

Stop it! She gave herself a good mental shake. She didn't want to be involved with anyone. Without intending to, she twitched her shoulder. Diana startled awake.

"I'm sorry," she said, sitting up. "I can't believe I fell asleep." She looked so contrite that Erin felt like a jerk. When she moved away, Erin suddenly felt chilled despite the warm sunshine pouring through the windows.

The silence in the van no longer felt relaxing. Erin struggled trying to think of something to talk about, but everything seemed lame.

When they arrived back at the house, Diana said her good-byes and left. Erin stood watching the Jeep disappear.

"You know, sometimes, Erin, I wonder about you," Mary said as she took a bag from the back of the van.

"What did I do now?"

"Not a blasted thing. That's the problem."

Confused, Erin looked at her.

"Can't you see how much she cares for you?"

Erin held up her hand. "I've already told you. I'm not interested in starting a relationship. I like Diana as a friend. That's all I'm interested in right now."

"Well, unless I've gone completely senile, she's interested in a heck of a lot more." Mary headed inside with the bag.

Erin stood in the driveway for a moment then went around back to the workshop. It was only after she got there that she realized there was nothing left for her to work on. The lap desk was ready to take to her mother and Diana had the table. Not yet ready to go inside, she found a broom and began to sweep the floor. After she was finished she began to straighten the worktable. As she worked she thought about Diana and how often Diana found an excuse to touch her. Was it more than a habit? Could Diana be attracted to her? She scoffed at the idea and continued to tidy up. Mary didn't know Diana very well. She didn't know that Diana was just naturally a physical person. Erin stopped suddenly as a realization hit her. She had never seen Diana touch anyone else. Not once during the day had she taken either Mary's or Alice's arm as they walked alongside her. When she talked to them, she didn't constantly reach out to touch them. Erin leaned on the worktable. What if Mary was right? *Then I'd have to stop seeing Diana*, she realized with a start. As she went back toward the house, she made up her mind. If Diana was interested in anything other than friendship, she would stop seeing her. A deep sense of sadness came with the decision, but it couldn't be helped. She absolutely was not going to get involved with anyone for a long time.

The following Thursday night Erin was folding her laundry when the phone rang. Alice brought it to her. "It's Diana," she whispered as she passed the receiver to her.

Erin's heart began to pound. She had thought of Diana a lot during the past few days and it scared her. She looked at the instrument for a long moment before saying hello.

"I was wondering if you'd like to have dinner tomorrow night," Diana asked. Erin could hear the excitement in her voice.

"I can't. I'm going to Austin."

"Oh. I didn't think you were leaving until Saturday." There was a touch of disappointment in her voice.

"I changed my mind and decided to leave Friday after work," Erin lied. She wasn't leaving until Saturday morning, but the strange feelings she had been having for Diana recently worried her. She had a nagging sense that the more time she spent with Diana, the more the feelings would intensify.

"Do you think it would be all right if I came by for a few minutes now?"

Erin glanced at her watch. It was only a little after seven. "I'm not sure that would be a good idea."

There was a sigh of exasperation from the other end. "I just wanted to bring the table back." There was a slight pause. "You know, Erin, if you don't want to see me, all you have to do is say so. I'm a big girl. I can take a hint."

"It's not that," Erin hedged.

"Then what is it? You're like a faucet running hot and cold. One minute I think you like me and the next I feel like you're avoiding me."

Erin folded a pair of socks. Maybe Diana had a point. Perhaps it would be better for everyone if she defined their relationship now. She cleared her throat to speak but before she could say anything, Diana beat her to the punch.

"Forget about it. I'll bring the table by this weekend while you're gone." She hung up before Erin could respond.

Erin stared at the pile of laundry and wondered if she should call Diana back. *That would only make things more confusing*, she told herself.

She finished folding her clothes before saying her good nights and going to her room. She hadn't been there long when Alice knocked on the door. "You have another call."

Erin practically ran to the phone. When she heard a voice other than Diana's she experienced a stab of disappointment. It quickly changed to bafflement when she learned that the caller was Diana's mother.

"Diana showed me the table you restored," Mrs. Garza began. "I was wondering if you're interested in selling it."

Erin sat on the foot of the bed. "Sell it? I really hadn't thought about it," she replied.

"I believe Diana mentioned to you that I'm an interior designer, and I have a client who absolutely loves your table. He's willing to pay top dollar."

Erin licked her lips. "How much?"

210

When Mrs. Garza laughed it sounded like Diana's laugh. "Normally, the seller names a price and then we haggle, but since you're a friend of Diana's I guess I'll make an exception this time. He's authorized me to offer you four hundred dollars."

Erin nearly dropped the phone. She was glad they weren't discussing this face to face, because there was no way she could have disguised her reaction. She finally found her voice and was pleased by how calm she sounded. "I'll have to think about it," she said.

"Can you tell me if you have another offer?"

"No. I'm just not sure if I want to sell it." What Erin wanted was a chance to talk to her father. "Can I call you back on Monday and let you know then?"

"Certainly. Let me give you my number."

Erin took Mrs. Garza's number and promised to call her Monday evening. As she continued to sit on the bed she realized that if she was going to take the table home to show her father, she was going to have to call Diana and make arrangements to pick it up.

As she dialed Diana's number she wondered whether or not Diana would even take her call. When Diana answered and Erin explained why she was calling, Diana hesitated.

"My mom is here now. We were just leaving to go eat."

"Oh. Well, I could pick it up before I leave tomorrow afternoon."

"That won't work. I've already made other plans."

A stab of jealousy hit Erin. Diana was going out with someone else.

"Mom and I are going to Casa Linda. That's not far from where you are. If you like I'll bring the table with us and you can come by the restaurant and get it."

"Okay. What time?"

"We're almost ready to leave. So give us about twenty-five minutes."

CHAPTER THIRTY-FIVE

When Erin arrived at Casa Linda she made a slow circuit through the parking lot, searching for Diana's Jeep, before parking near the entrance. As she sat there waiting for them she thought about the money Mrs. Garza had offered her for the table. She didn't have a problem with selling the table. She only wanted to show it to her father to ensure she was getting a fair price. The money would certainly be welcomed. With the money she had saved from working overtime and the four hundred dollars from the table she was close to having enough for the first month's rent and deposit on an apartment.

Diana's Jeep pulled in and parked several rows over from her. Erin hopped out of her truck and tried to brush the seatbelt wrinkles out of her shirt. She had changed into her best slacks. As she was changing she had told herself that she wasn't doing it because she was meeting Diana, but because she wanted to make a good impression on Mrs. Garza. She took a deep breath and started across the parking lot. When she reached them, Diana introduced her. Mrs. Garza looked to be in her mid-to-late fifties. She was dressed in a pale tan linen suit. Her short softly permed hair held a generous amount of gray near the temples. Her eyes were dark and curious like Diana's.

"I love the work you did on the table," Mrs. Garza said, shaking Erin's hand. "Where did you learn to restore furniture?"

"My father taught me. It was sort of a hobby for him."

"Well, if his work is anything like yours then it's an impressive hobby."

Erin thanked her again before she realized they were moving toward the restaurant entrance. She turned to Diana. "If we can get the table, I'll be on my way."

"Nonsense," Mrs. Garza said as she took Erin's arm. "Stay and have dinner with us. It's my treat. Diana has told me how horrible the table looked when you found it at a garage sale. Did you know how valuable it was when you saw it?" She rushed on, not giving Erin a chance to answer or decline the dinner invitation. Before Erin could fully comprehend what was happening, she found herself sitting at a table ordering enchiladas.

While they ate, Mrs. Garza kept the conversation at a slow steady pace.

"Diana, did you tell Erin about our upcoming trip to Mexico City?"

"No. I haven't had a chance to."

"My parents are from there originally," Mrs. Garza explained. "They want to go back to celebrate my father's seventy-fifth birthday."

"That sounds wonderful," Erin said. "When are you going?"

"Not until after school's out," Diana said as she pushed her food around on her plate.

"We're going to fly down on June third and spend a couple of weeks."

"A couple of weeks?" Erin asked. This trip was news to her. "You never mentioned you were going away."

Diana shrugged. "Why should I?" She looked Erin in the eye. "Since when do you care what I do?"

Erin ducked her head and tried to concentrate on her food.

Mrs. Garza glanced from Erin to Diana before quickly changing the subject. She asked Erin a few questions about the steps she took in restoring the table, but mostly they discussed mundane things like the weather and which restaurants they preferred for various dishes. Diana joined the conversation and gradually Erin found herself relaxing and enjoying her food. As soon as the meal was finished, Mrs. Garza called the waiter over and insisted they all order dessert.

"The flan is excellent here," Mrs. Garza said. She leaned toward Erin. "They put too much cinnamon in their empanadas."

"The flan sounds good to me," Erin said.

"Me too," Diana replied.

The waiter nodded and disappeared.

"I allow myself one day a week to eat anything I want," she explained to Erin. "The rest of the time I try to eat healthy, but there is so much delicious food in this town, it's hard."

"Mom, you've weighed the same for as long as I can remember," Diana said.

Erin smiled. "She sounds like my mom. She doesn't have an ounce of fat on her, but she's always watching what she eats."

Mrs. Garza waggled a finger at them. "You're both still young enough you can pack away all those calories without having to pay the consequences. Wait until you're thirty-five or forty and all of that changes. I swear sometimes I gain five pounds from simply reading a menu."

When the desserts arrived the conversation slowed while they ate. Erin savored the richly flavored flan. It was the best she had ever eaten. When the last of the dishes were cleared away, Mrs. Garza and Diana sipped their coffee. Erin chose to stay with her water.

"Erin, Diana tells me you're searching for a second job," Mrs. Garza said without preamble.

At the sudden turn in the conversation, Erin gulped. "Yes,

ma'am, I am." She felt a blush start up her neck. What else had Diana told her mother? Did she know about Ashley?

"I have a dear friend, Mr. Gabe Trevino, who owns a small furniture restoration business." She opened her purse and began to search through it. "I normally contact him whenever I need a piece restored. Oh, here it is." She handed Erin a business card. "When I saw him a couple of weeks ago, he mentioned that he was looking for help. If you're interested you might want to contact him."

Erin took the card and studied it before slipping it into her pocket. "Thank you. I might do that."

Mrs. Garza patted Diana's hand. "As much as I'm enjoying this, I have to go. I have an early meeting with a new client tomorrow and I still have some work I need to finish tonight." She held her hand out. "Erin, I'm so glad to have finally met you. My daughter has talked about you so much, I feel as though I already know you."

Diana blushed. "Mom," she whispered.

Mrs. Garza merely chuckled. "You and Erin run along and get the table while I take care of the check."

Erin thanked her again and followed Diana to the exit. "I like your mom," Erin said as soon as they were outside.

"Thanks. She can be a little hard to say no to sometimes. I hope you didn't mind staying to eat."

"No. I make it a point to never turn down a good meal. Especially free ones."

They walked in silence until they reached the back of the Jeep. The bright lights at the restaurant's entrance dimmed and gave way to the security lights of the parking lot.

"Why are you avoiding me?" Diana asked without warning.

Erin was so taken aback by the question that she faltered. She stared at her for a long moment before replying. "I'm not ready to get involved with anyone."

Diana nodded. "I can understand that, but can't we at least be friends? I meant it when I said I missed talking to you."

Erin shoved her hands into her pockets and used the toe of her shoe to push a pebble around on the pavement. "I miss talking to you too. I guess that sort of scared me."

"Why?"

Erin swallowed. "Because I was starting to like you."

"Is liking me so bad?"

"Yes . . . no . . ." Erin shrugged. "I don't want to get into another mess. I have to get my life straightened out."

Diana remained quiet for a moment before nodding. "I think I understand." She unlocked the back hatch and turned to her. "When you have everything straightened out, will you call me?"

Erin looked at her and didn't move away when Diana leaned in to kiss her. She forgot about everything except for the soft fullness of Diana's lips. When they pulled away, Erin felt as though she had lost something. She grappled with her feelings while Diana removed the table from the Jeep and set it on the pavement. Erin tried to think of a way to express her feelings, but when words failed her she drew Diana to her and kissed her again before grabbing the table and rushing to her truck.

All the way back to the house she cursed her impulsiveness. Why had she kissed Diana? Now Diana would be expecting more from her. Erin shook her head harshly. "I can't give anymore," she said aloud. "I don't want to be in a relationship. I don't want to love anyone. Nothing good ever comes of it."

Mary and Alice were watching television when Erin came in. She stopped long enough to say hello before rushing off to her room. Sleep was long in coming and short in duration.

CHAPTER THIRTY-SIX

Erin drove down the nearly treeless street to her parents' house. *Not exactly treeless*, she reminded herself as she glowered at the small saplings in all the lawns. The three-bedroom, two-and-a-half-bath modern brick home had been among the first to go up in the southwest Austin subdivision. This house held none of the charm or personality of the clapboard home where she and her brothers had grown up in San Antonio. She pulled her truck into the driveway behind her father's old van. Andy's shiny new forest green SUV was parked along the curb. In front of it sat a car with a rental sticker on the back bumper. That would be Tom and Edith. Erin loved her brothers and she liked Andy's wife, Liz, but Tom's wife, Edith, was an entirely different story. She braced herself for the snide comments that were sure to occur whenever she found herself alone with Edith. The two-faced hussy didn't have the guts to say anything in front of Tom or any of the other family members, and Erin had always let her get away with it rather than cause a rift in the family.

As soon as she walked inside there were a few moments of bustling activities and everyone rushed in to say hello and hug her. Even Edith couldn't avoid that. A small dash of evil danced through Erin as Edith leaned forward to give her normal "almost touched you" hug. Rather than accepting the meager offer, Erin grabbed her into an enormous bear hug and planted a loud kiss on her cheek. When Erin stepped away she stared into Edith's eyes, daring her to protest or say something. Clearly flustered, Edith straightened her hundred-dollar blouse before rushing off toward the kitchen on some lame excuse of checking something in the oven. Erin's mom followed, with Liz trailing behind them.

Tom dropped an arm around Erin's shoulder. "We missed you at Christmas, little sister. Mom made a fantastic dinner."

Erin patted his slightly expanding waistline. "Looks like you took care of the leftovers for me. And congratulations on your impending fatherhood."

Tom dropped his arm and mumbled something. Before Erin could pursue it, Andy handed over his three-year-old daughter, Jenny.

"You hold her for a while," he said. "My arm is going to sleep."

"Dang, Andy. What have you been feeding this girl? She's like carrying a bag of cement."

Andy tweaked his daughter's chin. "She's going to be the first female quarterback for the Dallas Cowboys."

"She's already better than the one they have now," their dad called out from his chair in front of the television.

Erin could hear the sounds of a basketball game. She sat in the living room goofing off with her father and brothers for a while before she made her way into the kitchen with the women.

"Something smells good," she said as she untied her mother's apron strings.

"Stop that," her mother said, swatting Erin's hand away. "You never change."

"And you wouldn't have it any other way," Liz said as she retied the strings for her mother-in-law.

"Well, don't go telling her that. She's already spoiled enough," her mom said.

Erin looked over in time to catch Edith's disapproving sniff. Erin ignored her as she sat down at the bar and began to peel the large bowl of potatoes sitting there. She wondered how many times she had done this same thing, sitting in the kitchen with her mom, peeling potatoes. As she worked, she listened to the women talk. She remembered Tom's strange reaction when she congratulated him on the upcoming birth of his first child. Tom and Edith had been trying to have children for almost five years. It was odd that he didn't seem very excited about it.

The basketball game her father had been watching must have ended because all of the guys streamed into the kitchen. Andy put Jenny in a high chair and gave her a handful of toy blocks to play with.

The family gathered around the table, and Erin let the sounds and sights soak into her. She had missed being with them. As she watched her father helping Jenny stack the blocks, she made herself a promise that she would spend more time with them in the future, and never again would she let her dislike for Edith keep her away from her family.

It was after dark before Erin and her father made their way out to his workshop. She had taken the table and lap desk out of her truck earlier and placed them in the shop. The desk was wrapped, but she didn't want her mom to see it until tomorrow. As her father examined the table, she waited nervously for his reaction.

"How bad was it when you found it?" he asked.

"It was filthy but there were no splits or gouges in the wood and thankfully no one had ever painted it."

He nodded.

"What are you going to do with it?"

"I'm thinking about selling it. I could really use the money and I think the offer was decent."

He walked to his worktable where a side chair lay in pieces. "How much did they offer you?" he asked as he began to hand-sand a chair rung.

"She offered four hundred dollars, but I told her I'd have to think about it and let her know Monday. I wanted to talk to you first."

He nodded again. "It was built in the early eighteen hundreds and it was probably made in France."

Erin marveled at her father's knowledge. He had no formal training and although he didn't know the difference in period names, he could look at the way the piece was constructed and from the joints, nails, glue and various other items, determine a fair estimate of when the item was built.

"If I were you, I'd ask six hundred for it."

Erin felt her eyes widen. "Really, Pop?" She rarely called him Pop anymore, but the figure had shocked her. She had expected him to tell her it was worth less than the four hundred dollars offered.

He motioned for her to grab a rag and made a motion in the general direction of the cleaning fluid. "How are you doing with that other stuff?"

She pulled on an old pair of latex gloves before dampening the rag in the cleaning solution. This was when she and her father talked.

"Better. I'm still staying with those friends I was telling you about. They'll let me stay there until I can get a place."

"It's good you have such special friends." He switched to a finer grained sandpaper. "What about this woman Ashley?"

"I haven't heard anything else from her. I guess her parents took her back to Arizona."

"You okay with that?"

"The relationship was a mistake from the start," she admitted. "A big mistake."

"We've all made them at some point. What happened to your friend?" He stopped and thought for a moment. "Diana?"

"It's her mother who wants to buy the table." Erin didn't really want to discuss Diana, so she shifted the subject slightly and told him about the possibility of a second job.

He started sanding a chair leg. "You're already working a lot of hours. You need to take care of yourself." He cleared his throat softly. "Erin, you know your mom and I have helped both of your brothers financially. When they got married we gave them enough money to make a sizeable down payment on a house. We never offered it to you because you never seemed to want it. We didn't want you to feel like we were pushing you to do more."

"I wanted to make it on my own," she said. When they were growing up, she had known they weren't rich, but there always seemed to be enough money to pay for whatever they needed.

"I can understand that and I respect it. Your mom and I aren't wealthy but we're doing all right. I managed to save some as you kids were growing up, and you don't know this, but I never spent any of the money I made at this." He pointed to the chair pieces in front of him.

"No. I didn't know." Over the years, her father had restored and sold a lot of furniture.

"You always liked the old house in San Antonio, didn't you?"

The sudden switch in conversation caught her off guard. "Yeah. I did."

"How would you feel about owning it?"

She frowned. "I can't afford to buy a house. I can't even pay the deposit on an apartment." She bit her tongue, embarrassed by the admission.

He let the statement go by without comment. "Your mom and I never sold the old place. You always seemed to care for it a lot more than either of the boys. We intended to give it to you someday as sort of a wedding present or whatever you call it."

She stared at him, wondering if she had heard correctly. "You still own the house on Mulberry? But I drove by it not long ago and someone's living there."

"Renters. We didn't want the place to sit empty. We thought

221

about giving it to you right away but you seemed to be struggling so with your finances and you were always too proud to ask for anything. We decided it would be more of a burden than a help." He put the chair leg he was working on aside before pulling a stool from beneath the table. "I had this talk with Tom and Andy before they got married, so I may as well just tell you, too. Like I said before, we're not rich, but your mom and I have always done okay. Over the years, we've set aside more than enough to last us for whatever time we have left."

"Dad!"

He held up his hand. "I didn't say we were planning on kicking the bucket tomorrow, so don't have a calf."

Erin couldn't stop the shudder that ran down her spine. She thought of her parents as still being young. They were only in their early sixties, but the thought of losing either of them was more than she could stand to think about.

"When each of you kids was born we started a savings plan for you. Originally we thought it would be used for college." He shrugged.

Erin wondered if her parents were disappointed that none of their children had gone to college.

He started talking again before she could ask. "Your account isn't huge but it's worth about sixty thousand now."

Erin dropped the chair rung she was cleaning. "Dollars?"

He gave her an amused looked. "Yes, Erin. Dollars."

She tried to get her mind around the number. It was too large for her to imagine. She had been struggling for over a month to save less than two thousand dollars and he was telling her she had an account worth sixty thousand.

It was almost as if he was reading her mind. "It's your money to do with as you will. I know you'll manage it well." He shook his head. "You're a lot like me. You were always a lot smarter with your money than Tom and Andy were. Sometimes I think you might be a little too frugal. I'd like to see you take enough of the money to get yourself back on your feet at least."

She tried to concentrate but her brain was firing information faster than she could process it. She could live at the old Mulberry house again. In her mind, she saw her father's old workshop and imagined making it her own. She shook her head. It had to be a dream. Any moment now the alarm would sound and she would wake up. Her father was speaking again. She tried to focus on what he was saying.

" . . . the renters at least thirty-day notice."

"I'm sorry. What did you say?"

"I said that if you're interested in moving back to the old house, we'll have to give the renters notice. I told them when they moved in that I didn't know how long they could stay, and I promised I'd give them at least thirty days to find another place." He looked at her. "They're nice people and have always paid on time. So if they have problems in finding another place, I know you'll work with them." He walked over to a file cabinet and unlocked it. After flipping through a few folders he pulled two out and gave them to her. "Here's the information on the house. Your mom kept a record of all the rent collected and what the taxes and insurance amounted to. Everything was kept in a separate account. We'll need to have the deed changed over into your name, but that won't amount to much. The other file is on the account I was talking about. If you have any questions about anything we can talk about it before you go back." He ruffled Erin's hair as he had when she was a kid. "It's not a lot, but it should help."

Erin threw her arms around him and buried her face in his chest so he wouldn't see her tears.

He hugged her. "You're getting more like your mother everyday. That woman always did cry at the drop of a hat."

Erin laughed suddenly and pulled away. He handed her his handkerchief. "Does she still cry over television commercials?"

"Lord, yes. You should have seen her last week watching one of those Hallmark movies. She cried through every commercial that came on." He put an arm around her shoulder. "We should probably get back inside. Your mom made a chocolate cake and if your brothers get to if before we do, there won't be enough left to feed a mouse."

Erin tucked the file folders beneath her arm. As they walked back to the house, Erin found herself wondering what Diana would think of the old place.

CHAPTER THIRTY-SEVEN

After coming in from the workshop Erin slipped the folders her father had given her into her bag to look over later. Since she was sleeping on the sofa, she didn't have the luxury of sneaking off to her room to look them over. She finally managed to put them out of her mind long enough to enjoy being with her family.

It was after eleven before everyone decided to call it a night. As soon as she was alone, Erin grabbed the folders and snuck off to the kitchen where she could turn on the light and spread the papers out on the table. Before opening the folders, she went to the refrigerator to get herself something to drink. It took her a moment to find the carton of orange juice hidden in the back. With her glass in hand, she opened the folder on the house first and blinked. The renters were paying seven hundred and fifty dollars a month. "They could have bought a house for that much a month," she muttered. As she looked over the papers she found where her mother had made copies of each of the checks, along with documentation for all repairs and expenses incurred on the house. She frowned when she opened the check register and discovered her name was on the account. When she saw the balance, her chin nearly hit the table. She leaned closer to the register and looked at the numbers again, unable to believe what she was seeing. The account held almost twenty-eight thousand dollars. Her hands trembled as she closed the folder and opened the second one. All those years of keeping the books for her husband's plumbing business had given her mother a firm handle on accounting. She flipped through the unfamiliar pages. They appeared to be quarterly statements from an investment firm. The bottom line was the current account balance of sixty-two thousand, one-hundred and eighty-three dollars and twenty-seven cents. Erin read the numbers several times. In a matter of minutes, she had gone from worrying about how much money she would be spending on gas for the trip to Austin to having over eighty thousand dollars.

Suddenly she closed the folders. This was wrong. This wasn't her money. It belonged to her parents and they had worked hard for it. They should be using the money to take trips to exotic islands and whatever it was they wanted to do. Grabbing the folders she raced out of the kitchen and down the hallway to her parents' bedroom. She had to give it back to them now. She knocked and her mother swung the door open.

Her father was sitting on the foot of the bed looking at his watch. "Twenty-four minutes." He sighed as he handed her mother a twenty-dollar bill.

"What's going on?" Erin asked.

Her mother folded the money and slipped it into her pocket. "Your father and I had a wager on how long it would take you to bring the files back. He bet fifteen minutes. I bet twenty." She patted her husband's shoulder. "I knew you'd take time to get a glass of juice first. That's why I hid the carton on the back of the shelf."

"That was cheating," he protested.

"Excuse me," Erin said, a little miffed that they were so sure of

226

her actions. She held out the folders to her father. "This is too much. You guys should be using this and enjoying yourselves. You worked hard."

Her father patted the bed beside him. Her mother sat on the other side of her. "Erin, your mother and I are simple people. We don't need fancy clothes or cars to make us happy and we don't need to travel all over the world. The truth is, we're both a lot happier at home than we are anywhere else."

"But you worked so hard for this," she protested as she held up the folders. "You should be using it for things that make you happy."

Her mother took the folders and placed them in Erin's lap. "We are doing what makes us happy. Don't you see that? If we can make life easier for you, then we're happy."

"What about Andy and Tom?"

"We've already turned their accounts over to them," her mother assured her.

Erin shook her head in frustration. "Dad, I know plumbers charge a fortune, but how could you have possibly saved this much—" She stopped. "I'm sorry. I didn't mean to seem ungrateful."

"You were always the practical one," her mother said as she opened the investment folder. "When you were born we opened this account with five thousand dollars, just as we did with each of the boys. Every year we would try to add a thousand dollars to each account. In lean years there was less and in better years more. When your grandparents died and we sold off the farms we each took our share and split it among the three accounts. That's how it grew to where it is now."

Erin still felt guilty. "All of my life you've taught me the importance of earning what I have. I haven't done anything to earn this."

Her mother took Erin's hand and squeezed it. "This isn't about your earning the right to receive it. It's about us earning the right to give it. To be able to give you this is why we worked so hard all those years."

Erin finally understood. She hugged each of her parents. "I love you both."

"Good, then go away so I can sleep," her father said as he rubbed a hand over his face.

Erin smiled when she saw the glint of a tear. "Dad, I do believe you're having a Hallmark moment."

He shooed her away.

The following morning, Erin woke to the sound of her parents puttering around in the kitchen. As she lay there listening to the comforting sounds her thoughts turned to Diana. Erin couldn't deny the fact that she had strong feelings for her, but she had made the mistake of thinking she was in love with Ashley and that had ended in disaster. She wondered if she would be one of those people who seemed destined to always be alone. Would anyone ever love her the way her parents loved each other? To drive away the thoughts she got dressed and raced out to the workshop to get the lap desk she had restored for her mother. She wanted to give it to her before everyone else was up.

Her parents were at the table drinking coffee when she came through the back door.

"I thought I heard someone moving around out there," her dad said as he got up and poured a glass of juice for her.

She had told him about the desk but since it was wrapped he hadn't yet seen it. "Mom, this is for you. I wanted to give it to you before everyone else got up." She watched her mother's face as she opened the package.

"Erin, it's beautiful." Her mother set the desk on the table and hugged her.

"She restored it herself," her father piped in as he carefully examined her work.

"What's going on?" They looked up to find Tom and Edith standing at the kitchen doorway.

"Look at this beautiful lap desk Erin gave me."

Edith stared at it, clearly unimpressed. "Tom, go get the present we *bought* your mother."

Tom shook his head. "We'll give it to her later. She's busy with Erin's gift now."

Edith turned sharply and stalked off. Tom looked after her and sighed.

Erin's father got up to get Tom a cup of coffee. "Still drink it black?" he asked.

Tom nodded and came over to examine the desk. "Dang, little sister. You're really good. You're getting almost as good as Dad."

A glow of pride warmed her. She didn't think she was anywhere nearly as good as her father, but it was nice that Tom thought so.

"You two should open an antiques business together," Tom said. "In Chicago, people go ape over anything that's sold as an antique." He took the coffee from his father and sat down across from Erin. "I went into a shop and they had those old Lego blocks that we played with as kids and they wanted a small fortune for them. I just wish I'd had the foresight to keep mine." He thought for a moment. "I don't know whatever happened to them."

Their father made a small snorting sound. "I do. Your sister here flushed them down the commode. It took me most of a full day to clear the line out."

Edith burst back into the kitchen with a small box. "Here you go, Mother Fox. Tom picked it out himself."

"Edith," Tom started but quickly stopped at the glare from his wife.

They all waited as she opened the gift. Inside was a flashy cocktail ring that was completely unlike anything her mother would ever wear. She knew there was no way Tom had picked out this particular gift.

"Try it on," Edith urged.

Erin watched as her mother slipped it on her finger and quickly closed her hand to hide the fact that it was too large. When she glanced at Tom he was staring into his coffee cup, but the muscles in his jaws were clenched tightly. It was then that Erin realized that things were not as they should be between her oldest brother and his wife.

229

CHAPTER THIRTY-EIGHT

On the drive back to San Antonio, Erin did a lot of thinking and planning. When she had it all thought out, she realized that her parents had given her everything she'd ever need to build a successful life. It would be up to her to do the work needed to bring it all about.

Later that night, Erin sat in the living room with Mary and Alice and told them about her weekend. When she mentioned the accounts her parents had set up for her they both shared her excitement.

"Does this mean you're going to adopt me?" Mary asked.

"No, but it means I'll be out of your hair soon."

"Oh, you've been no trouble at all," Alice protested. "We hardly ever see you."

"I saw more of you before you moved in," Mary agreed. "At least now you won't have to work so much overtime."

"Well, I have to give the renters at least thirty days' notice.

Mom and Dad are coming back to San Antonio on Thursday and we'll have the deed transferred over into my name then."

"How does it feel to be a property owner?"

Erin took a deep breath and slowly released it. "Sort of scary, actually. If anything breaks, I can't call the building manager and have it taken care of. I'll have to do it myself."

"I told you that someday you'd regret not coming over to help me with my home-improvement projects," Mary said. "Just think of all the knowledge you could have accumulated by now."

"To say nothing of all the bruised knuckles, sore knees and strained muscles," Alice added.

Erin chuckled. "I'm tired. I think I'll turn in early." She bid them good night and started to her room. As she walked through the kitchen, she took the cordless phone and dialed Diana's number as she went on to her room.

"I didn't expect to hear from you," Diana said.

"I've been thinking about you," Erin admitted.

Diana didn't respond.

Erin summoned her courage. "My parents are coming in to town Thursday. They'll be here until Sunday morning. I was wondering if maybe you'd like to have dinner with us on Friday night."

"Meeting the parents? That's a big jump from 'I don't want to get involved.'"

Erin's hands shook. "I still mean that. At least, sort of." When Diana didn't say anything she tried to explain. "A lot happened this weekend. And for the first time, I sort of know what I want out of life." She stopped. Maybe she was moving too quickly.

"I'm listening."

"It started with your mom telling me about the friend of hers with the furniture restoration shop. The idea was sort of planted, I guess. Then when I went home, my parents surprised me." She quickly told Diana about the house and how her parents had given it and the past two years of rental income to her.

"Erin, that's wonderful. You'll have your own place."

"I loved that house. It was more than just growing up there. My dad's workshop was fantastic. I know it'll take me a while to get it stocked back to the same level he always kept it at. He had everything we needed to restore the furniture—tools, reference books, stacks of scrap lumber and every tint of stain you could imagine, but I have time. I'm young and I'm not afraid of hard work. Your mom liked my work and I think I could eventually build up a big enough clientele that I'd be able to do restoration work full time."

"That's a wonderful idea," Diana said. "It sounds like you have your life planned out."

"Not completely," Erin said. "I think I have a good financial plan for my future, but . . . um . . . there are some things that I hope will always be a work in progress."

"What's that?"

Erin's knees began to shake so hard she had to sit down. "My relationship with you. I'd like to get to know you better, but I don't want to rush into it." She wiped sweat off of her forehead. "What I mean is that I want to be sure this time. I respect your friendship and I'd never want to do anything to jeopardize that."

"I think I understand. I suppose I should be glad that you don't want to rush into anything."

"I really like you and I think . . . I want to do this right."

"I really like you too, Erin. How long do you think we should date before announcing the wedding?"

Erin blinked in astonishment.

"Don't panic. I was joking."

Erin wiped the sweat from her face again and tried to steady her voice. "I knew that."

For the first time in weeks, Erin slept soundly through the night. She woke up the following morning filled with energy. Even going to work didn't seem so horrendous. She surprised Sonia by reducing her overtime to the mandatory one hour per day. As she keyed in the data, her fingers seemed to fly effortlessly over the keyboard. On her lunch break, she called Gabe Trevino about the furniture restoration position and was only slightly disappointed that he had already filled it. Thanks to her parents, she was no longer as desperate for money. Time was going to become her most valuable asset.

By the end of the day, she was tired, but rather than the usual dragging exhaustion, today it was a more satisfying feeling. She knew she had improved her stats. She was almost home before she began to get nervous. Today was when she had promised to call Mrs. Garza back about the table. She hoped she wouldn't be too upset about her declining the offer of the sale. Her father had always been reasonable in his prices, and if he said the table was worth six hundred dollars, then you could bet it was.

After a quick hello to Alice, Erin went into the kitchen and called Mrs. Garza. When she informed her that she couldn't sell the table for four hundred she was surprised that Mrs. Garza didn't simply thank her and hang up.

"My client really liked the table. How much would you sell it for?"

"I'd have to ask six hundred," Erin replied confidently.

"When could you deliver it?"

"I could bring it now or any evening after six."

"Bring it tomorrow evening. I usually work until at least eight on Tuesdays."

Erin jotted down the address and promised to have the table there the following day.

"You're looking awfully proud of yourself," Alice said as she came into the kitchen.

"I just sold my first piece of furniture," Erin said, waving the paper that she had written on.

"Congratulations."

"In fact, I feel like celebrating. Let's go out to dinner. My treat," Erin said.

"Are you sure?"

"I'm positive." She took Alice by the arms and danced her around the room.

"Hey, what's going on in here?" Mary asked as she came in to see what all the excitement was about.

"Alice and I are dancing a jig," Erin explained as they swung around the room.

"What's got into you? Sonia mentioned that you were a keying fiend today."

Alice grabbed her head. "Oh, I have to stop. I'm not used to all this youthful exuberance."

"Excuse me?" Mary protested. "Are you saying I'm old?" She grabbed Alice and began to dance her around the floor.

When they returned from dinner there was a message from Erin's father informing her that he had made an appointment with a title company for Friday morning at nine o'clock. She was to let him know as soon as possible if it she couldn't be there. Erin approached Sonia early Tuesday morning and explained that her parents were coming into town and she'd like to spend some time with them. Because Erin had been working so much overtime, Sonia broke the no-unscheduled-vacation policy and allowed her to take Friday off.

The week flew by for Erin. She delivered the table to Mrs. Garza and received her check for six hundred dollars. But more importantly, Mrs. Garza told her she would be interested in seeing any other antique furniture that Erin was interested in selling.

Every night after dinner, Erin called Diana. They talked about their day and eventually Erin began to learn the names of the kids in Diana's class.

On Friday morning, Erin was to meet her parents for breakfast near their hotel. She was so excited she could barely concentrate on driving. It seemed impossible that in a few hours she would be the sole owner of the Mulberry house.

"So who is this woman who will be joining us for dinner tonight?" her mom asked after the waitress had taken their orders.

Erin took a moment to fiddle with her napkin. "Her name is Diana Garza. She lived across the hall from me when I was at the apartment."

"I take it she's someone special," her father said. "Since you've never introduced us to anyone you've dated before."

"Maybe. I'm not sure yet. I know I enjoy talking to her and we like to do a lot of the same things. But we've agreed to take things slow." Erin realized that it probably didn't seem like things were moving slow if she was already introducing her to them. Suddenly she began to fret. What if they didn't like Diana or she didn't like them? By the time Erin's food arrived she was so worried about dinner that she had forgotten about the closing.

It was her mother who finally reached over and squeezed her hand. "Will you stop fretting and eat? Everything will be fine."

Erin wasn't sure whether she was talking about the house or dinner, but she nodded anyway and tried to eat.

The closing went so smoothly that Erin had to laugh about how nervous she had been. After she signed a stack of papers the house finally belonged to her. "I can't believe that I'm really going to live in the old house," she marveled as they left the title company.

"Are you sure you won't be lonesome in that big house all alone?" her mother asked.

The house had three bedrooms but Erin felt certain she'd never be lonesome there. "No. I don't think so. I'll probably spend most of my free time in the shop."

"Before you start buying things for the workshop, come on up and we'll go through my shop. I may have some duplicate stuff you can have," her father said. "I know I have a couple of sanders."

Every year her father received at least one woodworking tool for his birthday and every holiday. She had started giving him gift certificates. It was easier than him having to return things.

Erin's father pulled a newspaper out of his hip pocket. "All right," she said rubbing her hands together. "Are we going to spend the rest of the day hitting garage sales?"

He looked at her and smiled. "I thought we might catch a few. Your mom wants a table to put in the hallway. Why don't you leave your truck here and come with us in the van?"

"If we don't find anything, maybe we should try some of the thrift stores," Erin suggested.

"Good idea," her mother agreed as they all headed to the van.

They spent the day shopping. They didn't find a table that her mother liked, but Erin bought a sewing rocker and two Hitchcock chairs that needed to be recaned. Her father bought a small chest that looked as though it had at least eight or ten coats of paint on it.

As they unloaded her treasures into her truck she agreed to meet them at the TipTop Café at seven. Her father loved the home-style cooking served there. They had eaten there several times over the years.

Erin called Diana as soon as she got home to let her know she would be picking her up at six thirty. They talked for a few minutes before Erin grabbed a quick shower.

CHAPTER THIRTY-NINE

Erin whistled a soft tune as she drove over to pick Diana up. There was a strange moment of déjà vu when she pulled into the parking lot and parked in her old spot. She took her time in climbing the stairs but was still hit with a flood of memories when she stepped out of the stairwell and started down the hallway. The memory of coming home from the coast on that horrible afternoon and finding that practically everything she owned had been destroyed made a shiver crawl down her spine. She had never heard anything else from Ashley. According to Mary, Jess had resigned from the police department and moved to Arizona. Erin held no grudges. She wished them both the best. Pushing the memories away she tucked her shirt in a little better before ringing Diana's doorbell.

The door was answered so quickly that Erin was caught a little off-guard. She smiled brightly when she saw how beautiful Diana looked. Erin tried not to stare at the shapely legs beneath a crisp white sundress. Diana's feet were encased in a pair of white, delicate-looking, open-backed shoes that Erin would have been terrified to try to walk in. "Wow! You look like you just stepped out of some fashion magazine."

Diana twirled to show off her outfit. "Well, I had to look my best. After all, I'll only get one chance to make a good first impression on my girlfriend's parents."

Erin felt her face blushing, but she liked the thought of being Diana's girlfriend. She tried to cover her feelings by offering Diana her arm. "We should probably get going." Diana had done something different with her hair. It looked curlier. "You're wearing your hair different."

Diana looked at her and smiled. "I told you I'm trying to impress your parents."

"They'll love you as much as—" Erin stopped short as she realized what she had almost said.

"Do you think they're as nervous about meeting me as I am them?"

Erin wondered if Diana had missed her slip-up or if she was giving her an out. "I honestly don't think I've ever seen my parents look nervous," she said after giving it some thought. "I've seen them scared, like the time when my brother Andy got hit with a bat during a Little League game. It knocked him out cold and both of them were on the field even before the coach could get to him. I think they're more curious than nervous."

"What did they think of your previous girlfriends?"

Erin shrugged slightly. "You're the first one they've ever met."

Diana did a double-take. "Really?"

"Yeah."

Diana leaned forward and kissed her softly. "I . . . really like you, Erin Fox."

In reply Erin drew her into her arms and kissed her.

When Diana finally stepped away her face was flushed and there was a look of hunger in her eyes that Erin had never noticed before. "You can't keep that up if you expect me to sit through dinner with your parents."

Erin smiled sheepishly. "Sorry, but you started it."

Diana ran a thumb over Erin's lip. "I got lipstick on you," she murmured as she looked into Erin's eyes.

The sound of the door to the stairwell opening pulled them apart and snapped Erin back into reality. *Go slow*, she reminded herself. *Don't mess this up.*

They were both quiet on the ride over to the restaurant but neither seemed to notice. Erin was too busy chastising herself for getting carried away.

When they arrived at the restaurant her parents were already there. After a brief flurry of introductions, they were seated.

"What's good here?" Diana asked.

"Everything," Erin's father replied. "But my favorite is the ham steak."

"The baked fish and the fried chicken are both wonderful," her mom said.

"My favorite dishes are either the pork chops or the barbecued chicken," Erin said.

"It doesn't sound like I can go wrong with anything on the menu."

Erin's mother leaned forward and whispered, "Don't order the peach cobbler. They use too much cinnamon."

"You and my mother would get along perfectly," Diana said and laughed.

"Erin mentioned you teach school," her dad said.

"Yes, second grade."

"How much longer before school lets out?" her mother asked.

Diana glanced at Erin. "Next Thursday will be the kids' last day. I have to go in Friday to wrap things up."

Erin felt an unpleasant tightening in her stomach. She had almost forgotten that Diana would soon be leaving for two weeks. She didn't want to think about it and was happy when Diana changed the conversation and asked her parents how they like living in Austin. As her father began telling them about a tour they had taken of the state capitol building, Erin marveled at how comfortable her parents and Diana seemed to be. It was as though they had known one another for years. As she watched them, a sense of peace-

239

fulness descended over her. Everything about the moment felt perfect. Wasn't that a sign that Diana was the woman she was meant to be with? But not long ago she had been certain that Ashley was that woman. How could she know for sure Diana was the one? If she jumped in too quickly and screwed this up, she would lose Diana's friendship. Were a few nights of sex worth that? Erin pushed the question away. For a while anyway she wanted to simply enjoy the moment. She leaned back and allowed herself to relax.

Time flew by as it seemed to do when all was well. Long before Erin was ready for the night to end, her parents pleaded exhaustion and headed back to their hotel.

"I'm stuffed," Diana moaned as they made their way to Erin's truck. "Let's go somewhere and walk."

Erin looked at Diana's shoes doubtfully. "Are you sure you can walk in those?"

"Yes. They're actually very comfortable."

Erin wasn't sure she agreed but shrugged. "We could drive over to the Dalton Center. It's next to that big retirement village so a lot of older people walk there at night when it's cooler. It's well-lit and there are some paved surfaces we could walk on."

"Being around a lot of people isn't quite what I had in mind," Diana said.

Erin froze. Was she ready to take this to the next stage? The kiss had obviously given Diana mixed signals.

"You're probably right," Diana said. "These shoes aren't very practical for tromping through the woods. Let's go to the Dalton Center."

Erin nodded and helped Diana into the truck. As she went around to her side, she tried to decipher the sense of disappointment she had experienced when Diana chose the Dalton Center. Wasn't that what she had wanted? She stopped and pretended to tie her shoe. What did she want from Diana? A twinge of desire shot through her as she recalled the kiss. She stood quickly and cringed as the dampness between her legs made her feelings all too obvious. Taking it slow was going to be a lot harder than she had anticipated.

CHAPTER FORTY

When they reached the Dalton Center they found several people still out and about. They chose the main trail, essentially a sidewalk, and struck out at a comfortable pace.

"When will you be able to move?" Diana asked.

"The tenants have until the fourteenth of June. If they find a place by then, I guess I'll move in that weekend and start fixing the place up."

"I can help you," Diana offered.

"I thought you were going to be in Mexico City."

"We're flying back on the seventeenth."

"You'll be tired. Besides, it's not as though I have a lot to move. All I have are my clothes and a few odds and ends."

"If you don't want my help just say so." Diana sounded peeved. "You know, you aren't the only person who has ever had to start over in life."

She watched as a group of four women in jogging suits made

their way down the path. "I know. I'm sorry if I sounded like I was whining."

Diana took a deep breath. "You weren't. I'm just . . . frustrated."

"By me?"

Diana gave her an annoyed look. "Yes, by you and me and Ashley and everyone who's ever hurt you . . . oh . . ." She stomped her foot. "I don't want to leave for two weeks, but I want to go to Mexico City with my parents. I want to spend more time with you, but I don't want to push you and scare you off." She turned to Erin and gazed at her. "I want you to be happy."

Erin led her off the path to a bench and sat down. "I am happy."

"You don't seem like you are."

Erin knew she couldn't explain all the emotions racing around inside her. She didn't understand most of them herself. She leaned back and stared up at the faint pattern of stars. The subtle aroma of roses reached her and reminded her of the endless nights she had spent lying on her grandmother's front lawn searching the sky for shooting stars. "My grandmother used to have an enormous flower bed," she said. "Every spring these tiny flowers would bloom. I don't even know what they were. The blossoms were sort of reddish-yellow and no bigger than a dime. When I was six or seven I decided I wanted to pick them and take a bouquet to my teacher, Mrs. Hamilton."

"Courting the girls even then, huh?"

Erin chuckled. "My grandmother told me not to pick them because the flowers would die. Of course, I didn't listen. I found an old coffee can and put some water in it. I picked several of the flowers and put the stems in water, but by the time I had enough for a bouquet, the first ones I picked were dying. So I threw them away and picked some more and I kept doing this until I had picked all the flowers. When I realized I had killed all of the pretty flowers, I started crying and my grandmother found me. I just knew she was going to bust my butt, but she sat me down, dried my tears and told me not to worry about it because the flowers would grow back soon." She rubbed a hand over her head and sat forward. "I've never had a relationship that lasted. Heck, I'm not sure if what I've had even qualifies as a relationship."

"Erin—"

"No. Let me finish. I think you and I might be able to have something special, but I'm afraid of messing it up."

Diana took her hand. "I'm not a flower that's going to die the minute you pick it. I've only been in one relationship and it didn't last as I had thought it would, but I'm not going to let it stop me from ever loving someone else." She turned slightly toward Erin. "I know you're scared, but don't push me away. I'm willing to give you the time you need."

Erin studied the ground in front of her. "I'm going to miss you."

Diana squeezed her hand and leaned into her shoulder. "I certainly hope so."

Erin looked up and smiled. "Come on. I need to walk some more. Mom was right. That peach cobbler had too much cinnamon in it."

When Erin drove Diana home later that evening, her resolve to not take the relationship to the next level wavered when she kissed Diana good night. It was Diana who broke away first.

As Erin climbed back into her truck she was greeted by the tantalizing smell of Diana's perfume. She toyed with the idea of going back up to the apartment. What would it be like to make love to Diana? She closed her eyes and breathed in the scent of the perfume. How much longer should she wait? How much longer *could* she wait?

The next two weeks flew by. Erin and Diana spent as much time together as they could manage. They usually met somewhere halfway between each of their places. Erin quickly discovered that it was easier for her to keep her hands to herself if they were in a public place. On the Friday before the Garzas were leaving for Mexico, Erin and Diana planned to have dinner. Due to the early flight time, Diana intended to spend the night with her parents and asked if Erin would drop her off there after dinner.

Everything changed when South Texas Communications experienced a system failure a little after four on Friday and dumped the entire afternoon's data. Sonia's full team was assigned mandatory overtime. Erin begged Sonia to let her leave for a couple of hours, but the request was refused. All Erin had time to do was make a quick call. She almost cried when Diana's answering machine kicked in. Erin quickly explained and told her she would call if it wasn't too late when she got off. After hanging up, Erin returned to her desk to find that the computers were down. She almost danced a jig until Sonia informed them that the techs had promised to have the system back up and running within the hour. Erin dropped into her chair. There was no way she would be able to get away in time to see Diana.

"Can you believe this crap?" Mary said as she came up to Erin's desk. "The idiots lost four hours of work. They're supposed to run a save every two hours. I'd sure like to know why they didn't." She looked at Erin and stopped ranting. "Hey," she patted Erin's shoulder. "Cheer up. We'll be out of here by ten at the latest. You'll still be able to spend some time with Diana."

"She's spending the night with her parents. It'll be too late for me to go over there banging on their door."

Mary sighed as she turned to go back to her desk. As she walked away, Erin heard her mutter, "I hate this place."

It was almost six before the computers were back up. Erin keyed like a fiend for an hour and a half when the system crashed again. Groans and shouts of anger and frustration rippled through the room.

"Oh, bloody hell," Mary screamed from her area. "Can't they find someone down there who knows their ass from a hole in the ground?"

Sonia gave Mary a warning look before getting on the phone.

Erin could hear the anger in Sonia's voice as she chewed out the tech staff. Without asking permission to leave, she went to try

Diana again. She clutched the phone to her ear when Diana answered.

"I was in the shower the first time you called," she explained. "Are you off?"

"No. The systems are down again." She closed her eyes and pictured Diana standing beside her. "I'm not going to be able to meet you for dinner. I don't know what time we're going to get out of here. I'm sorry I won't be able to drive you over to your folks."

"Don't worry about it. I can drive myself. I just wanted to spend as much time with you as I could."

Erin glanced at her watch. She didn't want Sonia to come looking for her. "I have to go. Have a safe trip and—" Tears blurred her vision. She swallowed the lump that was suddenly blocking her throat. "Have a good time."

"I'll miss you," Diana said.

"Good night." Erin hung up before she made a complete fool of herself. She wiped her eyes quickly and went back to work.

The systems failed two more times before upper management finally gave up and sent everyone home with the stipulation that they would all be back the next morning by seven. It was only a little after ten but Erin was so exhausted she barely had the energy to drive home. Alice had dinner waiting for them, but neither Mary nor Erin ate much before calling it a night.

Erin tossed and turned for what seemed like hours before she finally drifted into a fretful sleep.

CHAPTER FORTY-ONE

Erin and Mary stepped out into the mid-June afternoon sun. The heat danced off the sidewalk in seductive waves.

"Ugh," Mary growled. "I swear as soon as Alice and I retire, we're moving to the coldest state in the Union."

"You can't do that. I'd miss you too much," Erin said, slipping her sunglasses on. "Besides, you hate cold weather almost as much as you hate the heat."

"Why can't it be seventy degrees year-round?"

"Because if it was, you wouldn't have anything to complain about."

Mary waved her off. "Bull. I could think of something."

They chose the longer but shaded path to the parking lot.

"You lucky devil. I can't believe you have two full weeks off." Mary shook her head. "I still don't know how you managed that."

"Sonia likes me because she can depend on me when she needs someone to work overtime." Erin had cut back on her overtime hours but still worked whenever Sonia needed help.

"You're such an ass-kisser." Mary bumped Erin's shoulder to show she was teasing.

"Only when it's a pretty ass," Erin replied.

"Speaking of which, what time is Diana's plane due in tomorrow?"

"Mary! That was horrible."

"Why? She does have a nice tush."

"What are you doing looking?"

"I'm married, not dead. Besides, a little eye candy is good for the soul."

"You'd better not let Alice hear you."

"Why not? She reaps the benefits."

Erin rolled her eyes. "Okay, now I've heard too much." They had reached her truck. She unlocked the door and opened it, hoping it would cool off some before she had to get inside. "Her flight is supposed to be in at a little after six tomorrow night."

"Are you going to the airport to meet her?"

Erin couldn't stop the smile that teased her lips. "Yeah, I thought I would."

Mary leaned against the bed of the truck. "How many times have you talked to her since she left?"

"A few. She used her mother's cell phone."

"It seems to me like the phone has been ringing a lot in the past couple of weeks."

"I'm out of your hair now." The tenant had found an apartment and moved out. Erin had moved her few belongings in the night before.

"You weren't any trouble. We kind of like having you around. But to be honest, it will be sort of nice to not have to get dressed every time I want to raid the fridge in the middle of the night."

"I can't tell you how much I appreciate everything you guys have done for me. Especially not running around the house naked!"

Mary chuckled then asked, "Are you sure you don't want me to come over and help you paint this weekend?"

Erin was planning on repainting all the rooms. "No. I don't know what time I'm going to get started and I may go ahead and start stripping the woodwork in the living room."

"Yeah," Mary said. "I'm sure you'll get a lot done after you pick Diana up from the airport."

"Get away from my truck. I need to get home," Erin teased.

Mary was still laughing as she walked away.

As soon as Erin got home, she changed into an old pair of shorts and a T-shirt and began to remove the baseboards in the living room. After taking them all off, she took them outside and placed them over some makeshift sawhorses. After brushing them with a liberal coat of paint stripper, she went back inside to start spreading out drop cloths. There were hardwood floors throughout the house and she wanted to be extra careful in protecting them while she was painting. She intended to paint the living room sea-foam green and stain the woodwork to match the floors. As she painted, she thought about Diana and how much she had missed her. They had been able to talk on the phone a few times but it wasn't the same. Erin couldn't wait to surprise Diana at the airport the next day.

She stopped painting long enough to scrape the first application of stripper off the woodwork and to eat a quick peanut butter and jelly sandwich. Due to the years of paint buildup, she had to apply a second coat of stripper. She found it ironic that as badly as her father hated paint on furniture, he had been very liberal with it inside his house. She worked late into the night and managed to get most of the living room painted before crawling into the sleeping bag she had borrowed from Mary and Alice. She hadn't yet bought a box spring and mattress for her bed. As she drifted off to sleep she smiled at the thought of Diana being home soon.

The next morning Erin walked through her house and made a list of everything it needed. Afterward she drove to a nearby restaurant and ordered breakfast. As she ate, she prioritized the items on her list. Basically she needed almost everything. The few items that had survived Ashley's rampage were still stored at Mary and Alice's. She had decided to leave them there until she finished painting. Otherwise they would be in her way. She added a new mattress and box springs as her number one priority and then a new refrigerator and a stove. As she moved down the long list, she began to feel overwhelmed. It would take forever to buy all this stuff. She had set aside seven thousand dollars from the rental income her parents had given her to replace the windows and the old heating unit with newer, more efficient ones. Looking at the list, she realized she might have to dip into it again for furniture.

When her food arrived, she put the list away. There was plenty of time to worry about all that stuff later. For the next two weeks, she would concentrate on getting the rooms repainted and the woodwork stripped and stained. If there was time, she would start restoring the hardwood floors.

After breakfast, Erin went home and started working. She planned to work until four and then get ready to leave for the airport by five. She wanted to make sure she was there when Diana's plane arrived.

She whistled as she worked, dividing her time between painting the walls and stripping the wood. It was a little after two when the doorbell rang. She wiped her paint-speckled hands on an old towel as she went to the door. When she opened it she couldn't believe her eyes. "Diana?"

"I took an earlier flight. I thought I'd stop by to see how the house is coming along."

Still dazed, Erin stepped back enough to let her in.

"I've missed you so much," she managed to blurt out before drawing Diana into her arms and kissing her. As the kiss deepened Erin was consumed by desire. She forced herself to pull away. "I'm covered with paint," she apologized.

Diana shook her head. "Don't even start with the excuses. I've waited long enough." She grabbed Erin's hand. "Where's the bathroom?"

"Over there."

Diana tugged Erin along behind her. As soon as they were in the bathroom, Diana turned the water on and didn't hesitate before pulling her shirt off over her head.

Erin could only stare as Diana stepped out of her clothes.

"Are you planning on joining me?" Diana asked as she got into the shower.

Erin shed her clothes in a frenzy and hopped into the shower, pulling the glass door closed behind her.

Diana grabbed the soap and began to scrub Erin's hands. When all evidence of the paint was gone, she pulled Erin into her arms. "No more excuses. It's time for you to show me exactly how good you are with those hands."

When their naked bodies touched for the first time, a shock of pleasure raced through Erin. She turned her head to kiss Diana and began to sputter as the water struck her full in the face. She gasped. In the process she managed to snort water into her nasal passages. The pain nearly blinded her. She covered her face and fell against the wall in a coughing heap. Mortified, all she could do was cough and gasp for air. She heard Diana turn the water off and throw open the shower door. *That was a wonderful start*, she thought as she struggled to regain her composure.

"Here, blow your nose. It'll help."

She opened her eyes to find Diana handing her a large wad of toilet paper.

"I'm such a dunce," she moaned. *Why can't I just vanish now?*

"Come on, take this."

Despite the agony she was feeling, she could only look at the paper. Diana finally pushed it into her hands.

"I can't do this with you watching."

Diana planted her fists on her naked hips. "Oh, please, Erin, do you honestly think I don't know you blow your nose occasionally. I'm a teacher. I've wiped my share of noses."

"Well, not mine."

Diana rolled her eyes before grabbing a towel and leaving the bathroom. She closed the door behind her.

Erin blew her nose and nearly cried out with relief. As she wrapped herself in a towel, her humiliation grew. She wondered if she could stay in the bathroom until Diana gave up and went home. The pile of clothes on the floor assured her that Diana wouldn't be leaving. A quick glance in the mirror at her wet hair and red nose did nothing to help her self-assurance. She slowly opened the door, expecting Diana to be waiting outside. When she didn't see her she tiptoed into the hallway and glanced toward the empty living room.

"I'm in here." Diana called from the bedroom.

Erin couldn't keep from smiling when she found Diana tucked inside the sleeping bag.

"Are you feeling better?" Diana asked.

"Yeah. If I don't die from embarrassment, I think I'll be okay."

Diana scooted over and patted the sleeping bag. "Why don't you come over here and join me?"

"With my luck, the zipper is probably stuck," Erin said as she tossed her towel aside and knelt down.

"You don't have to worry about that. I didn't zip it," Diana murmured as she reached for Erin's hand and pulled her down beside her.

Their kisses grew longer and Erin let herself become lost in the sensations created by Diana's hands and lips. As the intensity of her desire grew, her body began to rock and match the rhythm of her lover's body, until at last she cried out in pleasure.

CHAPTER FORTY-TWO
SIX MONTHS LATER

Erin stood in the doorway and watched Diana, who standing by the Christmas tree. Erin still couldn't believe it was possible for her to be so happy. During the past six months, she had finished the renovations on her home. She and Diana had scoured countless flea markets, antiques stores and garage sales to find the perfect pieces of furniture to complement each room. She had restored the pieces that needed help and lovingly waxed and polished those that hadn't. Diana's skill in choosing accessories had provided the final touches needed to bring it all together.

Diana turned and smiled at her. "How long have you been standing there? I thought you were still asleep."

"I just woke up and missed you. It's still early—come back to bed."

Diana scurried across the room. "That sounds like a good idea.

It's a little cold. I was going to serve you coffee in bed, but I got distracted by the tree. It's so beautiful."

They had met for dinner the previous evening and in a spontaneous burst of mid-December Christmas spirit, Erin bought a tree. After taking it back to the house, they spent several hours putting it up and decorating it.

Once they were snuggled together beneath warm blankets, Erin kissed Diana's forehead. "There's something I've wanted to talk to you about."

"You have my complete attention," Diana said as she slipped her hand beneath Erin's pajama top.

Erin flinched as the cold hand touched her skin.

"Oh, sorry. That wasn't the effect I was hoping for." Diana giggled.

"I thought I had your complete attention."

Diana folded her hands and placed them beneath her cheek. "Okay, I'll be good. Now, what did you want to talk about?"

With Diana watching her so intently, Erin was suddenly nervous about what she was about to suggest. She fluffed her pillow and finally propped herself up against the headboard. "Well, I've been thinking, and well, it's just that . . . it seems to me that . . ." She glanced at the woman she loved and tried to find the words to express what she was feeling.

Diana reached out and took her hand. "What's wrong?"

She looked into Diana's eyes and knew that she had made the right decision. She hoped Diana would agree. "Nothing's wrong," she assured her. "In fact, things have never been better." She took a deep breath. "I would like for you to move in here. Permanently."

Diana sat up.

"After all," Erin continued. "Your lease will be up soon and you already spend a lot of time here." A small twinge of nervousness attacked. She fidgeted with the blanket. "I just thought maybe we should make it official."

Diana smiled before leaning over to kiss her. "I was beginning to wonder if you were ever going to get around to asking me."

"I thought you'd want to wait because of your lease."

Diana kissed her again. "Sometimes you think too much."

"Does that mean you'll move in with me?"

"Erin, I sleep here at least five nights a week. Half of my clothes are already in your closet. I know your neighbors better than you do. I play cards with Mrs. Lowe across the street, and Mr. Lowe is going to show me how to plant a garden come spring. Sweetheart, you're the only person who hasn't realized I already live here."

"I want you here the other two nights, as well."

"There's nowhere else I'd rather be."

"I love you so much," Erin whispered as she pulled Diana to her and kissed her.

Publications from
BELLA BOOKS, INC.
The best in contemporary lesbian fiction

P.O. Box 10543, Tallahassee, FL 32302
Phone: 800-729-4992
www.bellabooks.com

OUT OF THE FIRE by Beth Moore. Author Ann Covington feels at the top of the world when told her book is being made into a movie. Then in walks Casey Duncan the actress who is playing the lead in her movie. Will Casey turn Ann's world upside down?
1-59493-088-0 $13.95

STAKE THROUGH THE HEART: NEW EXPLOITS OF TWILIGHT LESBIANS by Karin Kallmaker, Julia Watts, Barbara Johnson and Therese Szymanski. The playful quartet that penned the acclaimed *Once Upon A Dyke* are dimming the lights for journeys into worlds of breathless seduction.
1-59493-071-6 $15.95

THE HOUSE ON SANDSTONE by KG MacGregor. Carly Griffin returns home to Leland and finds that her old high school friend Justice is awakening more than just old memories.
1-59493-076-7 $13.95

WILD NIGHTS: MOSTLY TRUE STORIES OF WOMEN LOVING WOMEN edited by Therese Szymanski. 264 pp. 23 new stories from today's hottest erotic writers are sure to give you your wildest night ever!
1-59493-069-4 $15.95

COYOTE SKY by Gerri Hill. 248 pp. Sheriff Lee Foxx is trying to cope with the realization that she has fallen in love for the first time. And fallen for author Kate Winters, who is technically unavailable. Will Lee fight to keep Kate in Coyote?
1-59493-065-1 $13.95

VOICES OF THE HEART by Frankie J. Jones. 264 pp. A series of events force Erin to swear off love as she tries to break away from the woman of her dreams. Will Erin ever find the key to her future happiness?
1-59493-068-6 $13.95

SHELTER FROM THE STORM by Peggy J. Herring. 296 pp. A story about family and getting reacquainted with one's past that shows that sometimes you don't appreciate what you have until you almost lose it.
1-59493-064-3 $13.95

WRITING MY LOVE by Claire McNab. 192 pp. Romance writer Vonny Smith believes she will be able to woo her editor Diana through her writing . . .
1-59493-063-5 $13.95

PAID IN FULL by Ann Roberts. 200 pp. Ari Adams will need to choose between the debts of the past and the promise of a happy future.
1-59493-059-7 $13.95

ROMANCING THE ZONE by Kenna White. 272 pp. Liz's world begins to crumble when a secret from her past returns to Ashton . . .
1-59493-060-0 $13.95

SIGN ON THE LINE by Jaime Clevenger. 204 pp. Alexis Getty, a flirtatious delivery driver is committed to finding the rightful owner of a mysterious package.

           1-59493-052-X $13.95

END OF WATCH by Clare Baxter. 256 pp. LAPD Lieutenant L.A Franco Frank follows the lone clue down the unlit steps of memory to a final, unthinkable resolution.

           1-59493-064-4 $13.95

BEHIND THE PINE CURTAIN by Gerri Hill. 280pp. Jacqueline returns home after her father's death and comes face-to-face with her first crush.   1-59493-057-0 $13.95

PIPELINE by Brenda Adcock. 240pp. Joanna faces a lost love returning and pulling her into a seamy underground corporation that kills for money.   1-59493-062-7 $13.95

18TH & CASTRO by Karin Kallmaker. 200pp. First-time couplings and couples who know how to mix lust and love make 18th & Castro the hottest address in the city by the bay.

1-59493-066-X $13.95

JUST THIS ONCE by KG MacGregor. 200pp. Mindful of the obligations back home that she must honor, Wynne Connelly struggles to resist the fascination and allure that a particular woman she meets on her business trip represents.   1-59493-087-2 $13.95

ANTICIPATION by Terri Breneman. 240pp. Two women struggle to remain professional as they work together to find a serial killer.   1-59493-055-4 $13.95

OBSESSION by Jackie Calhoun. 240pp. Lindsey's life is turned upside down when Sarah comes into the family nursery in search of perennials.   1-59493-058-9 $13.95

BENEATH THE WILLOW by Kenna White. 240pp. A torch that still burns brightly even after twenty-five years threatens to consume two childhood friends.

           1-59493-053-8 $13.95

SISTER LOST, SISTER FOUND by Jeanne G'fellers. 224pp. The highly anticipated sequel to No Sister of Mine.   1-59493-056-2 $13.95

THE WEEKEND VISITOR by Jessica Thomas. 240 pp. In this latest Alex Peres mystery, Alex is asked to investigate an assault on a local woman but finds that her client may have more secrets than she lets on.   1-59493-054-6 $13.95

THE KILLING ROOM by Gerri Hill. 392 pp. How can two women forget and go their separate ways?   1-59493-050-3 $12.95

PASSIONATE KISSES by Megan Carter. 240 pp. Will two old friends run from love?

           1-59493-051-1 $12.95

ALWAYS AND FOREVER by Lyn Denison. 224 pp. The girl next door turns Shannon's world upside down.   1-59493-049-X $12.95

BACK TALK by Saxon Bennett. 200 pp. Can a talk show host find love after heartbreak?

           1-59493-028-7 $12.95

THE PERFECT VALENTINE: EROTIC LESBIAN VALENTINE STORIES edited by Barbara Johnson and Therese Szymanski—from Bella After Dark. 328 pp. Stories from the hottest writers around.   1-59493-061-9 $14.95

MURDER AT RANDOM by Claire McNab. 200 pp. The Sixth Denise Cleever Thriller. Denise realizes the fate of thousands is in her hands.   1-59493-047-3 $12.95

THE TIDES OF PASSION by Diana Tremain Braund. 240 pp. Will Susan be able to hold it all together and find the one woman who touches her soul?   1-59493-048-1 $12.95

JUST LIKE THAT by Karin Kallmaker. 240 pp. Disliking each other—and everything they

stand for—even before they meet, Toni and Syrah find feelings can change, just like that.
1-59493-025-2 $12.95

WHEN FIRST WE PRACTICE by Therese Szymanski. 200 pp. Brett and Allie are once again caught in the middle of murder and intrigue.   1-59493-045-7 $12.95

REUNION by Jane Frances. 240 pp. Cathy Braithwaite seems to have it all: good looks, money and a thriving accounting practice . . .   1-59493-046-5 $12.95

BELL, BOOK & DYKE: NEW EXPLOITS OF MAGICAL LESBIANS by Kallmaker, Watts, Johnson and Szymanski. 360 pp. Reluctant witches, tempting spells and skyclad beauties—delve into the mysteries of love, lust and power in this quartet of novellas.
                                                                1-59493-023-6 $14.95

ARTIST'S DREAM by Gerri Hill. 320 pp. When Cassie meets Luke Winston, she can no longer deny her attraction to women . . .   1-59493-042-2 $12.95

NO EVIDENCE by Nancy Sanra. 240 pp. Private Investigator Tally McGinnis once again returns to the horror-filled world of a serial killer.   1-59493-043-04 $12.95

WHEN LOVE FINDS A HOME by Megan Carter. 280 pp. What will it take for Anna and Rona to find their way back to each other again?   1-59493-041-4 $12.95

MEMORIES TO DIE FOR by Adrian Gold. 240 pp. Rachel attempts to avoid her attraction to the charms of Anna Sigurdson . . .   1-59493-038-4 $12.95

SILENT HEART by Claire McNab. 280 pp. Exotic lesbian romance.

                                                                1-59493-044-9 $12.95

MIDNIGHT RAIN by Peggy J. Herring. 240 pp. Bridget McBee is determined to find the woman who saved her life.   1-59493-021-X $12.95

THE MISSING PAGE A Brenda Strange Mystery by Patty G. Henderson. 240 pp. Brenda investigates her client's murder . . .   1-59493-004-X $12.95

WHISPERS ON THE WIND by Frankie J. Jones. 240 pp. Dixon thinks she and her best friend, Elizabeth Colter, would make the perfect couple . . .   1-59493-037-6 $12.95

CALL OF THE DARK: EROTIC LESBIAN TALES OF THE SUPERNATURAL edited by Therese Szymanski—from Bella After Dark. 320 pp.   1-59493-040-6 $14.95

A TIME TO CAST AWAY A Helen Black Mystery by Pat Welch. 240 pp. Helen stops by Alice's apartment—only to find the woman dead . . .   1-59493-036-8 $12.95

DESERT OF THE HEART by Jane Rule. 224 pp. The book that launched the most popular lesbian movie of all time is back.   1-1-59493-035-X $12.95

THE NEXT WORLD by Ursula Steck. 240 pp. Anna's friend Mido is threatened and eventually disappears . . .   1-59493-024-4 $12.95

CALL SHOTGUN by Jaime Clevenger. 240 pp. Kelly gets pulled back into the world of private investigation . . .   1-59493-016-3 $12.95

52 PICKUP by Bonnie J. Morris and E.B. Casey. 240 pp. 52 hot, romantic tales—one for every Saturday night of the year.   1-59493-026-0 $12.95

GOLD FEVER by Lyn Denison. 240 pp. Kate's first love, Ashley, returns to their home town, where Kate now lives . . .   1-1-59493-039-2 $12.95

RISKY INVESTMENT by Beth Moore. 240 pp. Lynn's best friend and roommate needs her to pretend Chris is his fiancé. But nothing is ever easy.   1-59493-019-8 $12.95

HUNTER'S WAY by Gerri Hill. 240 pp. Homicide detective Tori Hunter is forced to team up with the hot-tempered Samantha Kennedy.   1-59493-018-X $12.95

CAR POOL by Karin Kallmaker. 240 pp. Soft shoulders, merging traffic and slippery when wet . . . Anthea and Shay find love in the car pool.   1-59493-013-9 $12.95

NO SISTER OF MINE by Jeanne G'Fellers. 240 pp. Telepathic women fight to coexist with a patriarchal society that wishes their eradication.   ISBN 1-59493-017-1 $12.95

ON THE WINGS OF LOVE by Megan Carter. 240 pp. Stacie's reporting career is on the rocks. She has to interview bestselling author Cheryl, or else! ISBN 1-59493-027-9 $12.95

WICKED GOOD TIME by Diana Tremain Braund. 224 pp. Does Christina need Miki as a protector . . . or want her as a lover?   ISBN 1-59493-031-7 $12.95

THOSE WHO WAIT by Peggy J. Herring. 240 pp. Two brilliant sisters—in love with the same woman!   ISBN 1-59493-032-5 $12.95

ABBY'S PASSION by Jackie Calhoun. 240 pp. Abby's bipolar sister helps turn her world upside down, so she must decide what's most important.   ISBN 1-59493-014-7 $12.95

PICTURE PERFECT by Jane Vollbrecht. 240 pp. Kate is reintroduced to Casey, the daughter of an old friend. Can they withstand Kate's career? ISBN 1-59493-015-5 $12.95

PAPERBACK ROMANCE by Karin Kallmaker. 240 pp. Carolyn falls for tall, dark and . . . female . . . in this classic lesbian romance.   ISBN 1-59493-033-3 $12.95

DAWN OF CHANGE by Gerri Hill. 240 pp. Susan ran away to find peace in remote Kings Canyon—then she met Shawn . . .   ISBN 1-59493-011-2 $12.95

DOWN THE RABBIT HOLE by Lynne Jamneck. 240 pp. Is a killer holding a grudge against FBI Agent Samantha Skellar?   ISBN 1-59493-012-0 $12.95

SEASONS OF THE HEART by Jackie Calhoun. 240 pp. Overwhelmed, Sara saw only one way out—leaving . . .   ISBN 1-59493-030-9 $12.95

TURNING THE TABLES by Jessica Thomas. 240 pp. The 2nd Alex Peres Mystery. *From ghosties and ghoulies and long leggity beasties* . . .   ISBN 1-59493-009-0 $12.95

FOR EVERY SEASON by Frankie Jones. 240 pp. Andi, who is investigating a 65-year-old murder, meets Janice, a charming district attorney . . .   ISBN 1-59493-010-4 $12.95

LOVE ON THE LINE by Laura DeHart Young. 240 pp. Kay leaves a younger woman behind to go on a mission to Alaska . . . will she regret it? ISBN 1-59493-008-2 $12.95

UNDER THE SOUTHERN CROSS by Claire McNab. 200 pp. Lee, an American travel agent, goes down under and meets Australian Alex, and the sparks fly under the Southern Cross.   ISBN 1-59493-029-5 $12.95

SUGAR by Karin Kallmaker. 240 pp. Three women want sugar from Sugar, who can't make up her mind.   ISBN 1-59493-001-5 $12.95

FALL GUY by Claire McNab. 200 pp. 16th Detective Inspector Carol Ashton Mystery.
                    ISBN 1-59493-000-7 $12.95

ONE SUMMER NIGHT by Gerri Hill. 232 pp. Johanna swore to never fall in love again— but then she met the charming Kelly . . .   ISBN 1-59493-007-4 $12.95

TALK OF THE TOWN TOO by Saxon Bennett. 181 pp. Second in the series about wild and fun loving friends.   ISBN 1-931513-77-5 $12.95